What Kind of Man Would I Be?

What Kind of Man Would I Be?

Blake Karrington

www.urbanbooks.net

Urban Books, LLC
300 Farmingdale Road, NY-Route 109
Farmingdale, NY 11735

What Kind of Man Would I Be?

ISBN 13: 978-1-60162-121-4
ISBN 10: 1-60162-121-3

First Mass Market Printing March 2019
First Trade Paperback Printing May 2018
Printed in the United States of America

10 9 8 7 6 5 4 3 2 1

This is a work of fiction. Any references or similarities to actual events, real people, living or dead, or to real locales are intended to give the novel a sense of reality. Any similarity in other names, characters, places, and incidents is entirely coincidental.

Distributed by Kensington Publishing Corp.
Submit Orders to:
Customer Service
400 Hahn Road
Westminster, MD 21157-4627
Phone: 1-800-733-3000
Fax: 1-800-659-2436

Chapter 1

Ant stood in the living room by the window, watching as Janelle, his girlfriend, hustled to pack her two daughters in the car, getting ready to drop them off at school before going to work. It had become a normal routine for her, a routine Ant knew all too well and one that he made sure to capitalize off of. He watched intently as Janelle waved to him as she slid into the car and strapped on her seat belt and pulled out of the driveway in a haste. Unbeknownst to her, Ant wasn't checking to make sure she was safe. He was checking to make sure the coast was clear for him to partake in his extracurricular activities.

"Has she left yet?" Carly asked in a seductive voice, walking up to him and wrapping her arms around his waist.

"Yeah," Ant replied, after seeing Janelle pull off headed down the street.

Carly was Janelle's older sister, and just like Ant, Carly wasn't shit. Carly was always busy chasing men or trying to keep up with the Joneses, and after falling behind on her rent and being evicted out of her own damn apartment, it was her sister, Janelle, who opened her doors, extending her love to her by giving her a place to stay.

Janelle was a family-oriented woman, and she would do anything for the love of her family. So, to her, it was a no-brainer to open her home to her sister, Carly. She thought that by allowing her to stay with her and Ant, it would give Carly the time she needed to get back on her feet and save some money to get her a place of her own. That was three months ago, and Carly was nowhere near having enough cash to put down on a new spot. Truth be told, she wasn't in a hurry to get out and do anything on her own. After all, Carly had the perfect situation going, and most importantly, it was all on her sister's dime.

While living with her sister, Carly had taken it upon herself to not only make herself at home, but also to indulge in the forbidden: Janelle's boyfriend. Every chance she got, she made sure to bounce on Ant's tool as if it were a pogo stick. Did she feel bad about fucking her sister's man?

Hell no. Carly was entitled, and what Carly wanted she knew how to get.

"You know she gon' kill both of us if she ever finds out about this shit," Carly said, kissing the center of Ant's back while her kitty purred and dripped for Ant's touch. As she stroked Ant's back with kisses and slowly began to caress his body, Ant turned to face Carly who was standing at an even five feet five, with mocha-chocolate blemish-free skin, and with the exception of her red six-inch stilettos, naked as the day she was born.

"She's not gonna find out," he responded, taking in her full appearance as his third leg began to rise for the occasion. "And did you get that depo shot like I told you to?" Ant asked, eyeballing Carly suspiciously, not wanting to be trapped in this love triangle that he couldn't seem to get himself out of.

"Boy, I'm ten steps ahead of you. Cum in this pussy all you want. Bend me in every position possible, and let's play which hole feels the best." She growled while reaching down and grabbing a handful of his dick through his sweatpants, massaging it as she kissed and licked his chest. Ant backed her up against the living room wall and started kissing her and taking a handful of her small B-cup breasts into his mouth. He gently bit down on her erect nipples, sending tingling sensations to her already-moist center, making her become even wetter. She wanted the dick, and Ant was more than willing to give it to her.

"You want this dick?" Ant asked to confirm what he already knew.

Carly nodded her head frantically, and he proceeded to glide his right hand down the length of her body, cupping her pussy in his large hand; then he slid his two middle fingers into her wet, pink soft spot, and started finger-fucking her. Carly moaned as she moved her hips back and forth, trying to catch his rhythm. Ant started moving his fingers in a circular motion as he toyed with her clit with his thumb, making sure to press up against her G-spot several times in the process. Carly's body trembled and then tensed up. She let out a loud moan, as she gripped his shoulder and came all over his fingers. She grabbed his hand and brought it up to her mouth.

"Mmm," she moaned as she tasted her own juices, turning Ant on even more. He knew he was about to fuck the shit out of her, but she had no idea of the amount of trouble she had just gotten herself into.

This was the shit Ant loved about Carly. She was super nasty and a real freak, unlike her sister Janelle, who was too damn conservative when it came down to fucking. Janelle would only allow Ant to fuck her two ways: missionary and doggie style.

Carly continued sucking his fingers until there wasn't anything left. Finally, she reached in and pulled his sweats down past his knees. Ant lifted her right leg up and wrapped it around his waist then pushed his long, stiff, thick ten-inch member into her dripping wet center.

"Oh shit." Carly grimaced, feeling his shaft stretching her pussy open.

Ant picked her left leg up and wrapped it around him as he thrust deeper inside of her, causing her to grip his chest, scratching so hard she almost drew blood.

That only made Ant want to go harder. He grabbed her legs, placing them on his shoulders as he grabbed her by the wrists and pinned her arms against the wall. Ant began drilling in her pussy as if his tool were a power drill. He sped up his pace, plowing inside her so deep and hard that her body was bouncing against the wall, causing Carly to shout out. She grimaced with every stroke, but Ant could tell that she was enjoying the pleasure that he was giving her. He fucked her against the wall for what seemed like hours. Her legs started feeling weak, and her body started jerking uncontrollably. Her eyes rolled in her head, and Ant knew that she was about to cum.

A few more strokes later, Carly exploded on his long, thick dick. He thrust in her one last time before releasing his load of kids inside her, but he was nowhere finished doing damage to her middle. Janelle would be at work for at least nine hours, giving him all day to fuck Carly with no worries about being caught. This was just the life he always wanted, but in the back of his mind, he knew that Janelle had his heart. He needed to figure out a way to make this love triangle work for all parties involved. For now, the only thing that was on his mind was trying to figure out how to bust several nuts before the love of his life returned home.

Dorrian sat in the strip mall parking lot waiting for Los to come out of his condo that sat on top of a bunch of small retail stores and a few office buildings. It had been about a month since Los's license had been suspended for falling behind on his child support payments, and Dorrian had been picking him up and taking him to work every morning. It wasn't a big deal to Dorrian though, because Los's barbershop was only a few blocks away from his club. That was his initial reason, but now, looking out for his boy had come with a bonus.

"There she goes," Dorrian mumbled to himself as a woman emerged from the side of the building and started walking down the sidewalk of the strip mall.

She was right on time as usual. Seeing her walking down the strip mall every morning was the highlight of Dorrian's day. She was gorgeous, so much so that Dorrian was somewhat intimidated by her. She was short and curvy, with big, bright, beautiful eyes, which he could see from a distance. His eyes scanned her body from head to toe, taking in her features. What he loved the most about this woman was her natural look. She wore no makeup, and her natural cinnamon locks hung well beyond her shoulders to the center of her back. Her skin was smooth and blemish free, and it had a natural glow about it. To Dorrian, she was flawless, which was shocking to him because he never realized how much he was attracted to the earthy type. Beautiful females poured into his club every weekend, and he had bad-ass strippers flying in from all over the country, but never in his life had he seen someone as genuinely beautiful as this woman. No fake nails, hair, eyelashes, or scanty clothing; she was simply her. The way she walked, the way she smiled when her coworkers made a joke. This woman was truly amazing, and Dorrian had fallen for her and hadn't even met her yet.

"Come on, nigga. Open the damn door," Los said, knocking on the passenger side window, snapping Dorrian out of his trance.

"Damn, brah, you know how to fuck up a wet dream," Dorrian joked once Los got into the car. "Ay, what's that building over there anyway?" Dorrian pointed, looking at his future soul mate walking through the double doors.

"Oh, that's a dental office. Why? I know you ain't looking at ol' girl. You know I already fucked shawty a few weeks back. She's a straight freak," Los said with a straight face. He almost took the life out of Dorrian with that comment. Not knowing how to control his feelings that instantly displayed on his face, Dorrian was trying to find the right words to say until Los burst into laughter saying, "Naw, nigga, I'm just fuckin' wit' you." Los laughed, putting his boy out of his misery.

"Nigga, you better stop playin'. I'm trying to fuck around and make shawty wifey soon," Dorrian stated as he stared with amazement.

"What? Not you, playboy. I know you ain't talking about turnin' in ya playa card. Not wit' all those bitches you got walkin' around ya club damn near naked," Los spoke.

"Fuck that, homeboy. I'm about to be thirty-nine in a couple of months. I can't keep running around here with all these young girls every night."

"Shit, I can. Pass a nigga some of those hoes, brah."

All Dorrian could do was laugh at Los, who, for whatever reason, seemed like he never wanted to truly grow up. He still thought that life was only about getting money and sticking his dick in as many bitches as he could. Dorrian had finally passed that stage and was ready to make some necessary changes to ensure that loneliness wouldn't stare him in the eyes during his second stage of life on this earth. He wanted to be able to have a woman in his world he could call his wife, and if God was willing, he even wanted to have a few kids; and ol' girl was definitely wifey material. So, unlike Los who was about to turn thirty-five with three kids and no thought of settling down, Dorrian was ready to make that leap, and he needed to make his move soon.

Ant jumped up out of Carly's bed with his dick stuck to his leg from the fuck session they had. He darted toward his bedroom after hearing his phone ring. He knew, more than likely, it was Janelle calling to see if he'd left the house yet. The woman seemed to even be worse than his mama.

"Yo," he answered, taking the phone with him into the bathroom as he stood over the toilet to relieve his bladder.

"Don't forget to take the trash out with you before you go," Janelle said as she parked the car at her job. "And where is my sister?" she asked, rattling off question after question and barking demands.

"I don't know. I'm trying to piss so I can get up and get the fuck outta here," he said, aiming his piss directly in the toilet so she could hear it. "She might be in her room. Do you want me to go and check?"

He spoke as if he was in a rush and didn't have that kind of time, so Janelle declined. Instead, she stayed on the phone and sweated Ant about going out and getting a job today. He wanted a woman, not another mother, and he sighed in irritation as Janelle continued her rant.

He had been lying up in her bed long enough without contributing to the bills. The effect of being in prison for the last five years should have worn off by now, and it was time to show and prove all the things he had promised during his bid. He claimed that he was trying to be her future husband and stepfather to her two little girls. Ant had sworn that he had all this love for Janelle, but Janelle was done with all the false promises. He was going to have to put up or get his ass put out if he did not start to bring some real money to the table. Janelle was about her business, and she needed a man who held the same drive and determination as herself. It was one thing to be down for family, but it was another thing to be down for a nigga who ain't trying to better himself, and Janelle wasn't a fool by any stretch of the word. She was simply a woman in love, but her love had limits.

"Ant, I'm not fuckin' playin' wit' yo' ass. Get out there and find a job. There's so much you can do. I need a partner, not another kid," Janelle snapped before hanging up on him.

When Ant hung up the phone and reached to turn the shower on, Carly was standing in the doorway, shaking her head with a smile on her face. She heard Janelle's last comment and knew Ant wasn't going to do anything except fuck her all morning and through the afternoon. He gave Janelle the same game every day, and every day she went for it.

"You better stop playin' my sister. You know her ass is too smart for the dumb shit." Carly giggled, walking up and kissing the center of Ant's chest.

"I know you ain't talkin'. You just as bad as me. Yo' ass lying up on her too. Not to mention, you getting this dick that's supposed to be hers," he said, throwing his arms over her shoulder. "You ain't shit." He laughed as he kissed Carly's lips and then her neck.

"I guess we ain't shit together, but my pussy and your dick seem to complement each other well," Carly responded as she allowed her body to melt in his arms as he sucked on her neck.

He lifted Carly up and took her into the shower with him. Neither one of them truly knew or cared about the validity of the statements they were making. Their fucking around had begun a month and some weeks back, and even before then, Carly had been giving Ant hints about wanting him to herself. She never thought about how much this would hurt her sister, who took her in when she had nowhere else to go. She would walk around with just her bra on when Janelle was not around, or make sure she took her bath with the bathroom door open, knowing full well he was watching. Ant wasn't a dummy. He knew she wanted him to fuck her. So, when the opportunity presented itself one day, he decided to join her in the shower. Carly didn't protest, and Ant had never regretted it or looked back. In his mind, there wasn't anything better than pussy but new pussy, and Carly had that tight wet-wet that niggas loved.

Carly didn't care about fooling around with her sister's man. As a matter of fact, since their affair began, she had never thought about the consequences of what they were doing. Ant was good for her. He had a big dick and knew how to use it perfectly well, more than most men she had been with. She felt that, in a way, she was doing her little sister a huge favor. She knew her little sis was a terrible lover. Her baby daddy had called her names and made jokes about her sex game. Carly felt it was best that she keep Ant happy to keep him in the house. The way she saw it, it was either Ant screwed her or another woman. Carly thought that it was best kept in the family since she knew how important family was to Janelle.

Janelle had always got everyone's attention, and she always had all the hot men. Carly thought that Janelle had always had it all and that her life was going according to plan. In Carly's eyes, Janelle was living a perfect life, free of drama and chaos, but not anymore. Even if she had no idea what was going on, Carly was getting back at her. Besides, Ant should have really been her man in the first place.

She remembered the first day she saw him. It was at a barbecue over at their cousin's. Ant came in looking fine as hell. The mere sight of him made her legs go weak. He was a walking chocolate bar, and she would have loved for him to melt in her mouth, but as soon as she was about to make her move, Janelle had come from nowhere and pushed up on him. The little bitch was always like that, taking things that did not belong to her, even as far back as when they were little, and Carly couldn't stand her ass. Now it seemed as if the tables had turned and she had the man, and there was nothing that Janelle could do about it.

Falicia and Rhonda, the girls Los hired to be the eye candy in the shop, were waiting out front of the barbershop for Los to get there to open the shop. As soon as Los stepped out of Dorrian's car, they immediately started cursing him out. Just recently, Los started letting Rhonda braid hair in the back to increase business. Other than that, their jobs were limited to them washing and drying hair and flirting with the male customers who came in the shop to get their hair cut.

"Next time you late, yo' ass is getting docked," Falicia joked as she cut her eyes at Los.

"What? You can't dock me. I own this mutha-fucka," he said, raising his fist for some dap from Dorrian.

"Well we gon' deduct some of this pussy from you then," Rhonda cut in, walking over and opening the blinds. "How about that?"

Los started laughing as he walked over and slapped Rhonda on the ass. "Shit, I own that pussy, too." Los laughed, throwing his fist up for another dap with Dorrian.

Los was sexing both Falicia and Rhonda, and on several occasions, he had both of them at the same time. Just some of the perks he got for being the owner of the shop. Both girls were young and not looking for much in life except good times and nights out on the town. Two things that Los were more than willing to give them. He had the nightlife hookup because of his and Dorrian's relationship. And for Falicia and Rhonda, free drinks and VIP were all they desired. The employment at the shop was just icing on the cake.

"Well, well, well, look what the cat dragged in," Los said when Roshon walked into the shop right behind them.

"What's good wit' ya, brah?" Dorrian greeted him, getting up from the chair to give Roshon a dap and thug hug.

"Hey, Roshon," both Falicia and Rhonda said in sync, waving their fingers and batting their lashes hard at him.

Roshon was Dorrian and Los's childhood friend, and one of the brothers who had made it out of the hood a long time ago but came through regularly to show love. After graduating college with a master's degree in business, then going back to school to get a degree in economics, Roshon became a successful stockbroker/financial manager. He was always good with numbers, and it wasn't long before Global Enterprise snatched him up. Though he was making good money, he never turned his back on his friends and on the streets where he had grown up. That was why everybody who knew him loved him: he could always be counted on at any time.

"I'ma drop li'l man off to you later on in the week so you can tighten him up," he told Los. "I need you to hit me off today though. It's gonna be a busy week for me."

"Fo' sho. Fo' sho. But look, you know Doe gon' have the spot jumping this weekend."

"Shit, nigga, I got da spot jumpin' every weekend," Dorrian cut in. "I got the photo shoot for the Red Zone energy drink and then it's gonna be a crazy after-party."

"No doubt, homie. You know ya boy comin' through, so hold my VIP spot down," Roshon said, giving him dap.

"A'ight, brah, you know I got you," Dorrian guaranteed.

When it came to throwing parties, Dorrian was the man. Club 1838 had the best strippers, best drinks, and the best DJ in town. With a surprise guest coming through regularly, VIP specials popping off all night, and certified models hosting every weekend, there wasn't a place in the city everybody who was somebody wanted to be except Dorrian's spot.

"A'ight, niggas, I got shit to do. I'll get up with y'all a li'l later," Dorrian said as he dapped up Roshon and Los then left the shop.

For some reason, Dorrian couldn't get the female from the dental office off his mind, and he needed to find out why, so as soon as he left the barbershop, he decided to stop waiting on some cosmic miracle to happen, and he took matters in his own hands. There was more to this woman then what the eye could see, and Dorrian was determined to find out what it was that made him so attracted to her. Normally, he didn't maintain a fascination with females for an extended period of time. Sometimes, whatever relationship he had would be damn near over before he became fascinated with a woman, but this chick had been in his head from the first time he saw her.

Dorrian pulled into a parking space outside of the dental office and sat in his car staring at his phone contemplating whether to call the office. After a couple minutes of thinking, Dorrian decided to make the call. He pushed the call button, and the phone instantly began to ring.

"Charlotte Dental," a female voice answered.

This has to be her, Dorrian thought, almost choking up at the elegant sound of her sexy voice. Her voice was the perfect match to the woman he had fantasized about every day since the first day he saw her. He was lost in his own thoughts and couldn't find the right words to say.

"Hello, Charlotte Dental?" the female repeated after not getting a response.

"Hi, how are you? I was interested in getting my teeth cleaned," he blurted out, and secretly he kicked himself for the excitement in his tone.

Fuck it, I just said the first thing that came to mind, he thought as he waited for the sexy-sounding woman to check the schedule for an available date.

"Well, we have an opening next week. Say Monday the twenty-first around noon?" the female asked.

"I was hoping you had something available today. Next week is not a good week for me," Dorrian answered, wanting to see her sooner.

The woman paused for a moment, and Dorrian could hear her flicking around on the computer keyboard. "I'm sorry, sir, but the earliest I can get you in to see the dentist this week is on Friday, and that will be in the evening, around 5 o'clock," she informed him.

Dorrian pondered the date and time of the appointment, then thought that it worked perfectly fine. He had a photo shoot on Friday in the late evening, and having a set of pearly white teeth would do him justice. He agreed to the appointment, and after giving her his information as requested, he ended the call and immediately began thinking about what he was going to say to his future lady once they were face-to-face. He didn't have the slightest clue, but what he did know was that on Friday at five o'clock in the evening, he was going to be at his appointment and wasn't leaving without shorty's number.

Chapter 2

The phone flashing and vibrating on the nightstand next to the bed jolted Janelle out of her sleep. She could hear the shower water running in the bathroom, and she knew that Ant wasn't coming out anytime soon. She thought that this was the perfect time to look through his phone to see what the hell he'd been up to. Sitting erect in bed, she wiped the sleep from her eyes and focused on the task at hand. Her woman's intuition was at an all-time high, and she wanted to find out just what Ant was up to.

Normally, she didn't feel the need to check her man's phone, but Ant had been doing shit lately that had led her to believe that he wasn't being completely faithful to her. Plus, she'd caught him in several lies over the past few weeks.

Janelle slid out of the bed, walked up to the bathroom door, and peeked in, just to make sure that Ant was nowhere near done showering. When she saw that he was just covering his body with soap, she knew that she had enough time to snoop around. Tiptoeing back to the bed and grabbing his phone, she prayed that his password was the same. *Bingo,* she thought as she put in his mom's birthday, and her access was granted.

"Let's see what this nigga been up to," Janelle mumbled to herself as she prepared herself for the worst. What Ant didn't know was that Janelle knew him all too well and knew something was going on with him, and no matter how hard he tried to hide it, she could see right through him.

The screen of the phone had gone dark, but as soon as she picked it up, it lit up again. Ant stayed on his phone far too long, and at times he would smirk, smile, text, and update his social media status with new pictures and fresh comments. He and his phone were like one, and for Ant not to have it with him was like him not being able to breathe. Several times in the recent past when Janelle reached for the phone, Ant would yell and become enraged, indicating to her that he had something to hide. She was going to find out what it was.

"Yeah, you slippin' this morning," Janelle said as she began going through his phone.

Janelle was a strong woman, but even though she felt in her heart that her man was up to no good, it didn't make it any better for her to see the deceit staring her in the face. Upon opening his messages, Janelle felt her heart shattering into a million pieces. The many conversations with close friends began to play in her mind on repeat. *When you go looking for shit, you'll find it,* she thought as she stared with her mouth agape at a message glaring back at her:

Hey, daddy, my little box is still quivering from the injection you gave her the other night. She's gonna need another dose of that real soon. Oh, and I made reservations for us at Myrtle Beach this weekend. Damn, I'm horny just thinking about it. XOXO Pam

Seeing this message only confirmed Janelle's reservations. Janelle gritted her teeth as she read the end of the message repeatedly. Ant had lied and told her that he needed the car to go out of town to visit one of his ill relatives, but according to this message, the bastard was going to use her car to pick up another woman, take her out of town, and fuck her. Ant had never taken her out of town. How could he when he had no job or money? So, if she had to guess, Ant was going to use her money to treat this chick. The blood running through Janelle's body began to boil over as if she were physically capable of boiling an egg with her blood. She began seeing red and wanted some answers.

"The nerve of him," Janelle mumbled under her breath. And to think that she was actually going to allow this nigga to use her car and leave her stuck in the house for the weekend.

Janelle's eyes began to fill up with tears, and the hurt quickly turned into anger. Just then, the bathroom door opened, and Ant emerged from the steamed-filled bathroom wrapping a towel around his waist. He took one look at Janelle sitting on the edge of the bed, with his phone in her hand and the look of murder in her eyes, and he knew that she was pissed and drama was gonna be on and popping. Before Janelle could start in on Ant, he picked a fight with her, trying to deflect what he already knew. He knew he was caught, and he relied on his charm and fucked-up ways to try to turn the tables around to make Janelle feel sorry about going through his phone.

"What are you doin' fucking with my phone!" Ant snapped as he tied the towel around his waist, trying to play it cool.

"I'm ya girl, and I pay the bill on this bitch, so I can do whatever the fuck I want when it comes to this phone. If yo' ass wasn't being so goddamn sneaky, you wouldn't have to worry about me goin' through ya shit."

"Ain't nobody being sneaky. That's yo' ass being insecure."

"Oh, I'm being insecure. Well, tell that to that bitch Pam who just texted you talking about y'all goin' to some fuckin' Myrtle Beach this weekend," Janelle snapped, throwing the phone at him.

He tried to catch the phone before it could hit him or the wall, but she threw it too far to the right, so it ended up hitting the wall and smashing into several pieces. Ant rushed over to where the phone landed and tried to retrieve the broken pieces of the phone from the ground, but by the time he could reach the phone, Janelle had hopped off the bed and was raining punches on him.

"You not gon' treat me like this, Ant," Janelle cried between punches and tears. "I do too fuckin' much for you to do me this way. Who da fuck is Pam?" she screamed.

Ant attempted to grab her hands to restrain her, but she managed to swing out with a hard right punch, landing right in his mouth and splitting his lip.

"Yo, what the fuck?" Ant yelled, looking at Janelle with anger in his eyes and a trail of blood trickling down the corner of his mouth.

Janelle froze for a second, not knowing if or when he was going to retaliate. Ant wiped the blood from the corner of his mouth.

"Yo, you busted my lip. The fuck wrong with you?" he questioned, breathing heavily as if he was about to jump on Janelle; but Janelle was too angry to worry about what he might do to her. She stormed over to the dresser. She was on autopilot, and it was time for her to completely show her ass.

"You worried 'bout a busted lip when you need to be worried "bout a job. Tell that bitch you broke. Tell that bitch that I'm footing the bills over at this muthafucka. You think I'm a fucking fool? Nigga, you think this is a joke? I held yo' trifling ass down, and you give me your ass to kiss. Me! Me!" Janelle said, pointing to herself for emphasis.

Janelle continued her rant while snatching his things from the dresser drawer. Knowing that Ant probably wasn't going to leave without a police escort, Janelle simply reached on the dresser and snatched the ceramic vase, tossing it at Ant's head before running out of the bedroom.

Just like the phone, the vase barely missed him. Ant had had enough. He raced out of the bedroom after Janelle, chasing her into the living room. She picked up a candle holder and flung it at him. He tried to duck again but was hit in the side of his head below his ear.

"Ahh, bitch, you got me fucked up if you think I won't beat your ass!" Ant screamed just as Janelle's six-year-old daughter, Kalani, came running out of her bedroom.

"Mommy?" she cried out, getting Janelle's attention.

"Go back to your room, Kalani!" Janelle screamed.

Ant paused for a moment as he stared at little Kalani's terrified face. He had grown up watching his mother's countless boyfriends whoop her ass on a regular basis, and as mad as Janelle had him, he still couldn't bring himself to hit her in front of her child. So instead of putting his hands on her and putting her child in the same situation he grew up in, he walked away and went back to the bathroom, locking the door behind him. He was hoping that separation would give Janelle a chance to calm down and him some time to think of a good lie for the situation. But Janelle was on some other shit this morning. As soon as Ant sat on the bench beside the door to think, Janelle had run up the stairs and was banging and kicking on the door.

"Open this damn door! I'm not done with yo' ass!" she shouted through the door.

"Yo, chill the fuck out, Janelle! You going to break down the damn door!" Ant yelled.

"It's my motherfucking door to break, nigga!" she screamed while still banging and kicking.

He had never seen Janelle go crazy like this. He had a feeling that this might be the thing that made her ass kick him to the curb, and his mother had told him before he got out of prison that her place wasn't an option for him. Ant shook his head as he pinched the bridge of his nose, trying to suppress his anger. He leaned his head against the wall and let out a frustrated sigh. He needed to think of something and fast because he had no money and no place to go. Thinking about all of the lies that he told Pam, he knew he couldn't ask her for anything, so it was time he faced this music.

"Roshon, there's a sheriff deputy here to see you," Daisy, Roshon's assistant, said through the speakerphone.

Roshon's stomach flipped hearing this. He had no clue what a sheriff deputy would want with him, and truth be told, he wasn't eager to find out. Slowly, he got up from his chair and walked over to the office door, opening it to see Daisy walking with the officer down the hall toward him. The worried look on her face caused Roshon's anxiety to heighten, and for a split second, he was thinking about making a run for it. One of the first lessons he learned growing up in the hood was you see the popo, you run like hell, no questions asked.

"Mr. Reynolds?" the officer asked with a deep voice.

For some reason, Roshon was sure that the officer was there to take him to jail, even though he hadn't done anything except been born a black male in America. He glanced over at the exit door just in case he had to make a mad dash for it, before answering the officer.

"Yes, that's me," he replied, figuring out an escape route in his head.

"You have been served, sir," the officer said, handing him the white envelope. "Try to have a good day," he said with a quick head nod before turning on his heels and heading out the door.

Daisy placed her hand over her chest and let out a sigh of relief. Roshon chuckled to himself as he shook his head at the realization of how silly it would have been had he run for nothing.

"Oh my God. I didn't know if something had happened to Roshon Jr. or what," Daisy said, resting up against the wall still clutching her imaginary pearls.

The worried look on her face had slowly faded away as she looked at the serious expression

Roshon had while reading the contents of the envelope. His whole face turned red as he clenched his left fist. Roshon could feel the veins in his temples starting to swell, and it took several deep breaths in order for him to feel some sort of calm.

"Roshon, are you okay?" Daisy asked, placing her hand on his shoulder.

"Uh, yeah, Daisy, I'm good. Just gotta handle a few things. Thanks for bringing him down here discretely."

"Of course, but are you sure you're okay?" she asked again.

"Yeah, I'm sure." He smiled, patting Daisy's hand before turning around and going back into his office.

He closed the door and walked over to his desk, fighting the urge to sling everything onto the floor. "This bitch!" he snapped, looking down at the summons. "You gotta be fucking kidding me," he said. His phone started buzzing, and he glanced down at it. "This ho done lost her mind," he mumbled, seeing Brandi's number flashing on the screen.

Brandi was his ex-fiancée and the mother of his son, Roshon Jr. She had three other children, all by different men, and had been in and out of relationships on a quest to find a good man.

Brandi was one of those females who believed that having a baby would make a man stay with her. You would think that after having four illegitimate kids, she would have figured out that she was wrong.

"What do you want, Brandi?" Roshon answered the phone with anger and irritation seeping from his tone.

"Hey, boo. Whatcha doin'?" she asked in a chipper voice as if she weren't the reason he'd just been served.

"Stop fuckin' playin' games with me," Roshon barked. "What do you want?"

Not only was Brandi bold, but she was crazy as hell. "Can I borrow some money? Me and Roshon Jr. need some stuff. He needs shoes, and I'm tryin' to get my hair done," Brandi said seriously.

Roshon chuckled out of anger. He was two seconds away from cursing Brandi all the way out, but he realized that he had more important things to do than sit there going back and forth, arguing with her over some dumb shit. In about thirty minutes, he had a meeting with a huge account, and he needed to be at the top of his game. He had crunched all the numbers and come up with the perfect proposal. He was sure that he could land the account. If he brokered this deal, he was going to make a cool six-figure bonus, which he so desperately wanted right now.

"Brandi, look, I ain't got time for yo' games. I got shit to do." Getting this bonus would make him a king in the office and possibly lead to yet another promotion. He needed to stay focused and not let Brandi's bullshit get to him.

"Games? Nigga, this ain't no game. My—"

Roshon cut her off. "Good-bye, Brandi," he said, then hung up the phone without so much as allowing her to speak another word.

Just to be sure there were no more interruptions by her or anyone else, Roshon turned his phone off completely, threw the summons in his drawer, and told Daisy to hold all his calls. He was on his grind, chasing that bag so, as of right now, the whole world was on hold.

"Hey, li'l man, you ready?" Los asked, placing the smooth wood across the barber chair. Roshon Jr. nodded his head excitedly as he started to climb into the barber seat. Los grabbed him, trying to lift him to the chair, but Roshon Jr. protested.

"I got it, Uncle Los," he said, climbing up the seat on his own. For Roshon Jr. to do things on his own, he wanted to show his uncle he was indeed a big boy, and Los simply smiled at his independence.

"Oh, I forgot you a big boy now. I'ma call you Big RJ from now on," Los said, giving RJ some dap. "So, you gon' stay wit' ya pops this weekend?"

"No, sir. Not this weekend," RJ answered, his head hanging low. "I have to wait another whole week. He said that he's gonna take me golfing and then to the new aquarium."

RJ's face lit up when he told his uncle Los his and his father's plans. He really loved spending time with his dad and hanging out doing father-and-son activities. Roshon always made sure that the time he spent with RJ was fun, as well as educational. Roshon grew up in the hood and had to take full initiative to learn anything outside of the streets. He didn't want his son growing up without experiencing the joys of life, and he made sure that every opportunity spent together was also a learning opportunity. It was indeed Roshon's mission to make sure that his son was successful and not a statistic. "Ya pops ain't never ask me to go play golf. You think I can come along wit' you guys?"

"You can come, but I'm not getting your balls or carrying ya golf clubs," RJ replied, looking up at his uncle with a serious face.

Los smiled and rubbed the top of his head. RJ was a good kid, and this whole custody issue with Brandi was bullshit. Roshon was a great dad and spent all of his free time with RJ. Now, because of Brandi's foolish antics in the courtroom, he only got to see his son every other weekend.

"Li'l man, I thought you was a big boy now. Look at all those muscles. You mean to tell me that you can't carry my golf clubs?" Los joked, grabbing RJ's arms and making him flex his muscles.

Everyone in the shop burst into laughter watching RJ making his tough guy face and growling. Suddenly, the whole barbershop got quiet, and Los looked up to see what made everyone grow silent. Standing in the doorway with her arms folded and a scowl on her face was Keera, his worst nightmare. Los let out a frustrated sigh as he shook his head, already knowing that her ass was about to do the most, and he hated being in any type of drama.

"You sorry muthafucka. I know you seen my text and heard ya phone ring when I was calling yo' dog ass," Keera said as she flipped on him.

Los tried to position himself just in case she decided to tee off on him, which she was known for doing. Keera was crazy for real. Not just any kind of crazy. Keera was state-certified crazy and was ordered by the court to take psych meds or else be admitted to a mental hospital. Add Los's mind games in the mix, and Keera's ass was a complete psycho.

People didn't understand why he was dealing with her, and at times, Los didn't know either. Maybe it was true what they said about crazy women: they had the best sex. Or maybe he might just be a little crazy himself for fucking with her off and on over the past few years.

"Keera, don't come in here with all that loud rah-rah shit. I'm working, and I'm busy, and I know you see my nephew right here. G'on with that shit."

"Nigga, stop lying. Yo' ass ain't that damn busy that you couldn't answer the damn phone!" she shouted, storming over toward him.

Los grabbed her up in his arms before she could start swinging on him. "Baby, chill. You see I got customers in here. Calm the hell down. You know I wanna see you and shit, but a nigga been hella busy. I ain't lying."

Despite her battered mental state, Keera was a gem, and damn fine in any man's eyes. Comparing her to a celebrity, she looked like Teyana Taylor, but a tad cuter with a thicker body, and she was very comfortable in her sexuality. Keera was a freak and stayed wanting to fuck. She had that come-back pussy, too. You know: that shit that's so good that no matter what her crazy ass does, a nigga always wants to come back for more. Hell, the only time she acted like she was sane was when a nigga was digging in her guts. That was the main reason why Los couldn't leave her alone.

"Nigga, you ain't shit. You could have been a man about it if all you wanted was some pussy, wit' yo' thirsty ass."

"Yo, watch ya mouth around the kid, man," Los checked her as if she herself were a child.

She was in striking range, and Los knew it. Everybody in the shop was looking back and forth between Keera and Los as if they were watching a tennis match trying to see who was going to score. Los was already tired of the drama, plus he didn't like nosey-ass people being all up in his business. Even though in the barbershop it was like everyone was family, still Los didn't like his business in the streets. Keera's ways always kept the shop circulating his business, and she always acted as if she didn't give a damn.

"Oh, so I have to watch my mouth when you didn't have a problem screaming and cussing while I was putting this on you? 'Oh, baby, get this nut outta this dick. This big muthafucka got yo' name on it. Take this dick, ma. Fuck, this is some good pussy. You crazy, big-booty, tight, wet pussy–having bitch. A nigga not going no-damn-where. I'm swimming in this shit. Don't give my shit away.'"

Keera went on and on talking about their rendezvous in the bedroom. Snickers could be heard throughout the shop, and RJ covered his ears because thoughts of his parents arguing began flooding his mind as Keera carried on as if she didn't have a care in the world.

"Yo, Keera, don't be coming in my place of business with that dumb shit. That's sex talk. That's what the fuck we niggas say. Now take yo' ass home, and I'll call yo' ass when I get ready," Los added, turning around and putting the clippers back up to RJ's head as if he was simply blowing Keera off.

That was the wrong response, as Keera's blood began to boil.

"What, you bitch-ass nigga? What you mean you gon' call me when you get ready, and what the fuck does that mean that was just sex talk? Nigga, you busted all up in this pussy, raw. So, it's just sex talk, huh? Is that what you niggas say while you tapping ass?" Keera addressed the shop as she reached over Los, grabbing a container of blue disinfectant off the counter.

"What the fuck are you doing?" Los questioned as he rushed toward her and tried to take the disinfectant out of her hands.

Keera had a tight grip on the bottle, and Los found himself struggling to get the bottle from her. In the mix of them wrestling over the bottle, it slipped out of her hand and went crashing onto the floor. The solution splashed everywhere. RJ started screaming at the top of his lungs as he started holding his eyes, crying, and bouncing all around the chair.

"Oh shit!" Los shouted, realizing that the solution went into RJ's eyes.

Keera was oblivious to RJ's screams and continued storming around the shop, ranting and shouting all types of obscenities as she started knocking stuff over. Rhonda rushed over to RJ, snatched him up, and carried him over to the shampoo sink so she could wash his eyes out.

Los was pissed the hell off and had had enough of Keera's foolishness. He stomped over to her, grabbed her by her thin throat, and slammed her up against the wall.

"Bitch, you done lost ya fuckin' mind. I should break ya fuckin' neck!" he yelled as Keera continued swinging and screaming.

"Let me go, nigga. Get ya fuckin' hands off me!" she yelled. In an instant, Keera switched her whole attitude. "Los, why you make me do this? You know I love you. I . . . I just want us to be together," she whined as tears filled her eyes.

Los looked at her like she was crazy. Her bipolar ass started to calm down, and now she wanted to start crying and shit. Los wanted to bash her skull in for what she had done. If anything happened to RJ behind this mess, Roshon would have a field day kicking his ass, and that was a fade he would have to catch because he should have had better control of the situation.

"You know what, Keera? I ain't even entertaining yo' dumb ass. Get the fuck outta my shit, now. I'll come through later and deal with yo' ass."

That's all Keera wanted to hear, and with no more confrontation or hesitation, Keera turned around and started walking to her car, smiling.

As she approached her car, she remembered her initial reason for coming to the shop in the first place. She needed to talk with Los. It seemed like every time she tried to talk to him about the way he was treating his son, the baby they had made and the one he refused to claim, he always avoided the subject. It hurt her to see the way Los treated Roshon Jr. He genuinely loved him. Every time she saw him with Roshon Jr., it drove her crazy. Why couldn't he love li'l William the way that he loved RJ? He pampered RJ but refused to be a father to his own son. Sometimes she wanted to hurt Los so bad for hurting her and for not loving their child. How was it so easy for him to lie up and fuck her whenever he wanted, but not be a father to his own child? Better question was why couldn't she leave him alone knowing that he wouldn't claim or take care of the child they'd created?

A few minutes had passed, and Ant was sure Janelle had to be out of energy. She had been cussing, crying, kicking, and banging on the door for a good fifteen minutes, and he figured that once she had exhausted herself, then maybe he could talk his way out of the situation. He slowly opened the door and peeked out to see where Janelle was at. She was nowhere in sight. He slowly tiptoed out of the room, looking around, wondering if he should throw on some clothes and get the hell out of there to give her more time to come to her senses.

Once he heard the kitchen cabinet slam shut, he decided that getting dressed would be the best option. He grabbed a pair of boxers and a pair of basketball shorts and slid them on. Then he grabbed a T-shirt and some socks and put them on as well. He stepped into his Nike Slides then headed downstairs so that he could try to have a conversation with Janelle, in hopes that he could smooth things over with her. When he got downstairs, Janelle was in the kitchen making Kalani a bowl of cereal.

He walked over to her and placed his arms around her waist. "Baby, can we talk now, like adults? I know you still pissed off, and you have every right to be, but on some real shit, you know that's some bullshit. That trick Pam is just a ho. I ain't smashing her. I was just fucking with her mind, trying to get some money out of her. You know it's been hard for a nigga trying to get a job so that I can contribute. All I want to do is to pull my weight around here. I don't feel like a man with you taking care of me. That bitch Pam ain't got nothing on you. The bitch is fucking old. You know how I feel about you. I love you, baby, on everything," Ant explained, then kissed the back of her neck.

"Don't you put your fucking hands on me!" Janelle screamed, pushing him away with so much force that he stumbled back. "You are a lying motherfucker, Ant, and I refuse to let you keep treating me like this! You think I am fucking dumb, huh? You think I'm stupid not to see that you playing the fuck outta me? You know this shit just keep happening and—"

Janelle was cut off by three loud booms at the front door. “Police! Open up!”

Before Janelle or Ant could respond, Kalani ran to the door, turned the two deadbolts, and unlocked the door. Two police officers entered the apartment with their hands on their guns. A third entered with a Taser extended.

“Get your hands up!” the first officer yelled. Ant did as he was instructed while another of the cops patted him down. Ant looked at him like he was crazy considering that he hadn’t done anything, but Ant knew he was on papers, so he didn’t say anything. He also knew he couldn’t afford another charge on his record, so he started getting his story ready before the police asked questions.

“Ma’am, sir, what is going on here? We received a domestic disturbance call,” the muscular black officer spoke, looking down at Kalani, then at Janelle and Ant.

Ant thought that he was fucked. Janelle was still angry with him, and one thing he’d learned was when a woman was mad, she was liable to do anything, and in situations like this, the police usually took the woman’s side, so he had to get his story out before Janelle or his ass might be back in jail.

"Man, I don't know what's going on. She attacked me when I got out of the shower," Ant said, looking at Janelle, who was standing there with a shocked look on her face. Ant didn't really want to throw her under the bus, but he figured that it would be best for the situation. The police would more than likely assess the situation then go about their business.

"I have no idea what the fuck got into her." Ant felt the tender spot on the back of his head, then pulled his hands down to see the blood on the tips of his fingers.

"We need a medic at 1212 Piedmont Circle," the officer said in his radio. "All right, I need for both of you to take a seat. Hinton, take the little girl to her room," the officer instructed.

"Hey, we need to talk to your mommy and daddy. Can you show me your room?" Officer Hinton asked as she bent down to Kalani.

"Yeah, I'll show you. My sister is sleeping in there. And he is not my daddy. He's mommy's boyfriend. His name is Ant," Kalani said while taking Officer Hinton's hand and leading her down the hall.

The white officer, Officer Johnson, closed the door to the apartment and looked into the kitchen. Janelle wanted to ask him what the fuck he was looking for but she bit her tongue.

"So, sir, you are saying she attacked you?" the black officer, Officer Jacobs, asked as he took out his notepad.

"Yeah. Look at me, man," Ant said. He closed his eyes and groaned in pain, exaggerating how truly hurt he was.

"Ma'am, are you injured or hurt?"

Janelle shook her head as she glared at Ant, who she knew was acting. Officer Jacobs sighed. He could see Ant's busted lip and the injury to the back of his head. He hated calls like this. In his mind, Janelle was being the typical black female resorting to punching and throwing shit instead of talking out whatever the issue was. Here she was with this dude in this government apartment, acting like fucking animals, with kids down the hall.

Johnson came out of the kitchen with a dish towel and handed it to Ant to place on his head.

"Sir, do you want to press charges?" Officer Jacobs asked. Ant looked at Janelle. He exhaled and was silent for a moment.

"Nigga, I know your punk ass ain't even thinking about—"

"Ma'am!" Officer Jacobs said. "Be quiet and have a seat!"

"Nah, I don't want to press charges, man."

"Are you sure?"

"Yeah, man," Ant said.

"And what is your full name, sir?"

"Antwan Peterson," Ant said, looking at Janelle.

"Okay, Mr. Peterson, is this your primary residence?

"Yes, sir."

"Well you know, due to the fact that you have been injured and that you do not want to press charges, you or she will need to leave the premises for at least forty-eight hours," Jacobs informed him.

Antwan sighed. The adrenaline rush from fighting with Janelle was wearing off, and the pain was now hitting him. "I can't do that, sir. I don't have anywhere else to go. All my family is in another state," Ant lied.

Officer Jacobs turned to Janelle, who had taken out her cigarettes.

"Miss . . ."

"Henderson," Janelle stated.

"Miss Henderson, do you have family you can go stay with?"

"Stay with? Why? I'm not leaving here. This is my fucking house."

"Look, watch your mouth. We can't leave you both here, and Mr. Peterson has nowhere to go. So I'm going to ask you again, do you have any family you could go stay with?"

"And I'm going to tell you again, this is my motherfucking house!" Janelle screamed even louder. She was so damn furious at the bullshit the cops were suggesting that she actually leave her home for Ant's ass. What the hell kinda fuckery was this? Wasn't it the woman who was supposed to be protected?

Officer Jacobs had grown tired of Janelle's attitude and was now not offering options but rather telling her how it was going to be. Ant could see the cop's anger, so he stayed quiet.

"All right, well, this is what is going to happen. Due to this being an assault, and we can see the injuries, we don't need Mr. Peterson to press charges, but we will if you continue this way. So, you can either leave and go stay with family, or I can arrest you now, and you can sit downtown while it's figured out."

"Is he serious?" Janelle asked Officer Johnson.

"Yeah, unfortunately, because Mr. Peterson only has this place as an option for residency, and you have another option. Yes, you are going to have to leave. We can't leave both of you here," Johnson responded as medics entered the apartment.

"Can you get the pictures?" Johnson asked the second female officer who had just entered the house.

Ant just stood there shaking his head. The apartment was now filled with police and medics like it was some major murder case. *All this because of a fucking text.*

"Ms. Henderson, Officer Mackins will wait while you pack your things."

"This shit is crazy. You gotta be fucking kidding me! I gotta take me and my children out of my own fucking home?" Janelle asked, fighting back tears.

"No, ma'am. You have another choice, and that's going to jail," Officer Johnson said, placing his hands on his hips near the handcuffs.

Janelle looked over at Ant, who was now being attended to by one of the EMTs. She felt her blood pressure rise so high that she swore she could hear her blood rushing through her veins. She wanted to beat the shit out of him until he passed out. All of this was because he could not keep his fucking dick to himself.

"Ma'am," Officer Mackins said, pointing to the hallway. Janelle walked to the closet in the hallway and grabbed two large overnight bags. She walked down the hall in a daze. Her mind just could not process what was actually happening.

With the cop watching her, Janelle picked out stuff she knew would last her and her girls for a few days. She was so fucking pissed at Ant, but she could not let it show in front of the cops. It was bad enough she had to leave her house, but to be thrown in jail wasn't an option, especially with her having two kids. She could see that the cops didn't like her and were taking sides with Ant's stupid ass.

"Men," she muttered angrily. For now, she would be on her best behavior, but she was going to certainly make him pay. Ant caused all this drama, and now she was forfeiting her home and going off to stay with her coworker. She would have tried staying with her mom, but after taking Carly in, she didn't want to leave drama only to find herself in more drama.

"He can believe this shit isn't over," Janelle spoke through gritted teeth and a flared nose.

"Come on, miss, we have to hurry up," the cop snapped.

She threw her a glare and carried her sleeping daughter while she gave one of the bags to the other officer. Kalani walked next to Janelle. "Mommy, where are we going?" Kalani asked.

"To go stay with TT Phaedra for a few days. Come on," Janelle said, tugging her daughter's hand. She shot Ant one final look, one filled with anger and vengeance. He should enjoy his victory for now because it was not going to last long.

Ant nodded at the cops in appreciation who told him to take some aspirin, and if the crazy lady returned to give them a call.

Alone in the house, he thanked his lucky stars that he had not done shit to her. He would have been the one leaving the house or spending the night in jail.

He returned to the room and frowned as he saw the pieces of his phone. "Damn," he cursed. How was he going to pay to get that shit repaired? He doubted it could be. He had not one dime to buy a new one. All thanks to that whore Pam. Why the fuck, of all days, did she pick this morning to send him a message about shit they already talked about? She was definitely going to pay for this.

He heard the front door open. He hoped Janelle wasn't back because he was going to be forced to call the cops on her ass. He stopped when he saw Carly. She had stayed at her girlfriend's place the night before and now had returned.

"What the hell happened here? That old woman next door said the popo was just here. Niggas broke in or something?" she asked, looking around for anything missing.

"Nah, your sister was tripping, and someone called the police on her crazy ass. She was throwing shit, going off on the cops and everything.

Fucked a nigga up, too. I'm glad I didn't touch her, or they would have been carrying my ass to jail. Instead, they told her to get the fuck out and go cool off or they were taking her to jail."

Carly's eyes widened as she looked over Ant's face and saw his injuries. "Oh no, she didn't. Why she do this shit to you?" Carly snapped, showing her true feelings for Ant, and Ant was loving it. He had her right where he wanted her, and if he couldn't use Janelle, he damn sure was going to use Carly.

"Calm down," Ant said, somewhat amused. He wondered what it would have been like to see two sisters fighting over him. Had the police not sent Janelle on her way, Ant was sure that shit would have gone left had Janelle still been in the house.

"My poor baby," Carly crooned, hugging him. "Come on, you need some rest."

She led him to one of the chairs, went to the kitchen, and returned with a cold drink and told him to tell her what had happened. Ant started from the beginning, yet made sure to leave out the details of the message he had gotten from Pam. He was sure if he told Carly, there was going to be another fight tonight. Not only did he not have the strength for it, but he was sure the police would not be so understanding the next time around.

Ant gave Carly his version of the truth, which had about 10 percent of the truth in the lies he told.

Carly shook her head and clutched her invisible pearls. "You know the girl got a temper. I'm just glad it's not over us. The bitch would have killed you and would have been looking for my ass. She will be all right. She ain't going to do nothing but go to Phaedra's house. That bitch stays trying to get her to stay with her. She might want to taste that kitty, but Janelle's non-sex-appeal-having ass wouldn't know how to ride a tongue if her pussy slipped and fell onto one." Carly cackled.

She patted Ant's face and looked lovingly into his eyes. "All you need is some aspirin and rest," she said, rubbing gently down his face and then biting her lip as she only had visions of making him feel better.

He grinned, catching all of her innuendos, and sexily replied, "What, my baby a nurse now?" Not understanding that he was playing her like the fool she was, Carly fell right into Ant's trap after hearing him call her his girl.

"Yeah, a dirty nurse who wants you to fuck her rough, hard, and bad. I'm ready to take daddy in my mouth. You know I've been working on my throat exercises," Carly said, stroking his dick through his pants. He smiled and lifted her up, making her squeal. If there was one good thing that was going to come out of this, it was going to be having Carly all to himself without hiding it. Ant was going to make the best of a fucked-up situation, all while playing Carly for every dime he knew she possibly had. He knew this was about to be epic. He loved angry, nasty sex, and Carly was about to perform in her best show ever.

Los looked in his rearview mirror at RJ sleeping peacefully in the back seat. It was a smart move on Roshon's part to list Los as a person who could take RJ for medical care in his parents' absence. Los was grateful when the doctor told him that RJ's eyes were going to be fine. He said that his eyes would be irritated for a couple of days before they were back to normal. The one thing Los did regret was calling Brandi and telling her what happened. She had flipped out, calling him all kinds of names, and swearing Roshon was going to pay for it. Los could understand her being upset about her son's safety, but truth be told, Los knew she really didn't give a damn about RJ. She put up the front just so she could gas Roshon out of some money. As far as Los was concerned, Brandi was community property, and of all four of her baby daddies, Roshon was the only one worth something. As a result of this, she tried to take advantage of it daily. He wondered what the hell his buddy had ever seen in such a bitch, but then, Roshon was a calm guy who saw the good in everyone.

"Wassup, brah, I'm downstairs," Los told Roshon when he pulled up to his office building.

"A'ight. I saw you on the camera. I'm walking out to the elevator now," Roshon told him as he left his office.

It took Roshon a couple of minutes, but he eventually walked through the two large double doors. "Damn, brah, what happened?" Roshon asked, walking up and giving Los dap. He opened the back door to find RJ asleep with Los's aviator glasses on.

"Maaan, you know da chick Keera came through the shop on some bullshit, mad 'cause I ain't been calling her. She got to cussing and knocking shit over. Bitch had the nerve to be mad because I haven't been calling her back," Los explained.

Roshon knew Keera all too well, but he also knew there was more to the story than what Los was telling him. "Yo, did you ever find out if that kid is yours?" Roshon asked, knowing Keera's anger and aggression came from somewhere.

"Didn't take no test, but I know that ugly-ass baby ain't mine. The bitch is looking for a come up."

"Yeah, well, you gotta get ya bitches under control. We can't have—"

"Nah, man. That's my bad, bro," Los said, cutting him off. "You know I would never do nothing to hurt RJ. That's my li'l man too," he said as he lifted RJ up and walked him over to Roshon's black 750.

Roshon didn't want to hear no excuses when it came to his son. "I keep telling you and Doe to stop stickin' y'all dicks in the first chick who opens her legs to you. Shit like this always gonna happen, especially since y'all are businessmen with a lot to offer. You know after thirty, chicks start getting desperate to find a nigga to take care of them. You gotta be smarter than that."

Roshon had love for his boys, and he didn't want to see them go through some of the things he had been through. By all means, Roshon wasn't against monogamous relationships. His main thing was making sure whoever a nigga was giving his heart to was the right one.

Even he'd fallen victim to making some bad choices: choices that had him in the predicament he was in right now. But at least he had learned some hardcore lessons and was not going to mess around with a woman until he was sure she wasn't as crazy as Brandi was.

Roshon strapped RJ into the car, securing his seat belt, and gave Los a sympathetic look. "Man, on some real nigga shit, I appreciate you for looking out for my li'l dude, but this shit could have gone in a whole other direction, and I'm not sure I would be this calm. Take care of that problem that you have, and make sure this type of shit don't happen again, or you and I will have a real fucking problem."

Roshon, never being one to explain what was understood, simply nodded toward Los and slid in his ride and pulled off, leaving Los with his thoughts.

Los got back in his car with a lot on his brain. He knew that Keera was crazy, but he also knew that there was something about her that kept drawing him toward her. It was inexplicable, but he didn't want it to end.

He picked up the phone and called her number. Keera picked up on the third ring.

"Keera, I'm on my way. I don't want any shit outta you. We need to talk. I have some shit to say to you."

Without giving her a chance to respond, Los killed the line and brought his engine to life. He pulled away and headed to Keera's. It was going to be one hell of a night, but Los was in it for the long haul.

Chapter 3

Dorrian checked his e-mails while he sat in the lobby of the dental office. He had received an e-mail confirming the photo shoot that he had later that evening with Red Zone Drinks at his club. Not only was he sitting in the dental office, waiting for the opportunity to meet the woman he couldn't seem to get off his mind, but he wanted to make sure his smile was white and bright for the photo shoot.

Aside from being a businessman, Dorrian was your typical pretty boy: always dressed to impress no matter the occasion. He stood six feet two, weighing 240 pounds with an athletic build. His mom was Dominican, and his pops was a light brown African American. He had nice wavy hair that he kept in a low-faded Caesar-style cut. He had worn a goatee for years, and he had just recently started to allow the full beard to grow out. His complexion was one that most women would envy no matter their race. His skin was a nice dark tan mixed with red tones.

"Mr. Hoyle, you can come back now," the petite, curvy, caramel dental assistant said, coming out into the lobby.

She looks even better up close, Dorrian thought as he happily followed the assistant into the back room. As they were walking down the corridor, he couldn't help but notice the cute little hump she had for an ass and the way her long locks draped down her back and stopped right at the small of her back. He could imagine how she would look bent over while he was hitting her from the back. Her long locks were just the right length for him to tug on. Even though her uniform was loose fitting, he could still make out her hourglass figure. She was bad, and she walked with her head held high as if she was full of confidence. The scent of her Tom Ford White Patchouli perfume radiated from her body and invaded Dorrian's nostrils, making him want to pull her close to him so he could get a good whiff and take in her scent.

"Dr. Miller will be with you shortly, so let's get you ready," she said as she placed his chart on the counter and started skimming through it. "I see from your chart that you're here for a cleaning," she continued, placing the paper bib around his neck and being as professional as she possibly could. Dorrian was indeed checking her out, but little did he know, he'd taken her breath away the moment he smiled and said hello.

"Yeah, I got a photo shoot tonight, so I gotta have my pearly whites up to par," Dorrian replied with a slight chuckle.

"I think you already have a beautiful smile," the woman responded, flashing a beautiful smile of her own.

Dorrian picked up on her flirtatious tone almost instantly, and he wasn't about to let that slide by him. This was the opportunity that he had been waiting for, and he didn't waste any time jumping on that and spitting a little bit of game.

"Well, you know, I need them to look perfect. Flawless in every way, just like you," he said, scanning over all of her sexiness. "If you don't mind me asking, what is your name?" Dorrian asked in a soft, pleasant tone.

"My name is Arlene, but people just call me Lene for short." She blushed, trying not to stare at his handsome face.

As she began to prepare the solution, Dorrian's cell phone went off. Since the doctor had not arrived yet, Arlene gave him the okay to answer it. "Yeah, what's good wit' you, Los?" he answered.

"Yeah, you love dis dick, don't you? You crazy bitch, throw it back." The loud voice could be heard clear as day out of nowhere.

Dorrian pulled the phone away from his ear and looked at it sideways with his face twisted up. A female voice could be heard in the background moaning and talking back.

"Yes, I love daddy dick!" the female voice yelled out. "Give it to me."

"Yo' ass gon' stop acting crazy?" the male voice spoke.

Dorrian couldn't help but laugh recognizing Los's voice. He was in the middle of pounding some female out. This was something that he, Los, and sometimes Ant would do when they were fucking a new chick. They would call each other so that the other could listen in on how they were laying pipe to the female of the hour. It was so loud and clear, Dorrian could hear the headboard knocking. He adjusted his growing erection, hearing the sound of gushy pussy and soft moans escaping the woman's lips. Dorrian wished that he was close by so Los could tag him in on the action. He was in need of a good session and wanted to take part in what sounded like SummerSlam 2017.

"Yes, daddy, I'ma stop acting crazy. I'm sorry, baby. Oh, my God, I love dis dick. You better fuck this wet pussy, daddy. Give it to me. I'm ready to bust, daddy, I'm ready to bust! Oooohhh shit. Ooohhhh right there. Get it out, get it out! Take this nut. I need to bust!"

The female screamed as Los continued pounding. Arlene shook her head, trying her best not to laugh. Dorrian yelled into the phone a couple of times, acting like it had to be a mistake, and then he finally hung up. Dorrian was a bit of a freak, and if it weren't for Arlene standing right there, he probably would have listened to the whole session. He was hoping like hell that there would be a round two so he could listen and get himself off later. It was something that he did with his boys, and when pussy was involved, it was never fun unless the homies could have some.

"Sorry about that," he apologized. "But listen, I don't know what time you get off—"

"Please don't," Arlene stopped him before he could shoot his shot.

"Damn, maybe I should have asked you before I answered my phone. You shot my ass down with the quickness, and I didn't even ask the full damn question," Dorrian stated with his hand over his heart as if he was hurt by her letting him down. He was indeed hurt, but he wasn't even close to giving up on her.

"Nah, trust me, it has nothing to do with ya crazy friend." Arlene chuckled. "I just don't date patients. This is my job, you know, and before you make me go against my rules, I would rather you not ask me."

Arlene was indeed attracted to Dorrian, but she didn't want to disrespect her boss or maybe even lose her job with something that might not be worth it. She thought it'd be best to shoot down the idea rather than getting her feelings hurt in the long run. After all, Dorrian did appear to be a ladies' man.

"Nah, I understand, and trust me, I wouldn't put you in any position you wouldn't want to be in." He smiled before continuing. "Maybe in another lifetime," Dorrian surrendered in a humble fashion, knowing deep down, after seeing her up close, he was not going to let go of her. He was going to do everything to make sure she was his woman. Now just wasn't the time to give her the full-court press, but Dorrian was sure that that time would come.

Arlene felt bad about rejecting Dorrian, and she wanted to explain the situation to him a little bit more, but before she could utter a word, Dr. Miller walked into the room.

They both were thinking, *maybe another day, another time. If it's meant to be, it will happen*. Arlene professionally assisted the dentist as she allowed her mind to take her places that she never thought it would go.

***

Roshon sat on the toilet, watching RJ play with his toys in the bathtub. Since the incident at the barbershop, Roshon had convinced Brandi to let RJ stay with him for a few days to keep an eye on him. Although his eyes were getting better, it was still a struggle trying to put the eye drops in his eyes. RJ would whine, kick, and try to grab Roshon's hands to stop him from putting the drops in his eyes. Roshon checked the time on his watch and saw that it was a little past RJ's bedtime.

"A'ight, li'l man, let the water out," Roshon said, getting up from the toilet and grabbing a towel from the cabinet.

"Awww, just five more minutes, Dad," RJ whined, splashing the water around.

"Nope. Come on. You gotta get ready for bed. Plus, it's time for you to have ya eye drops," Roshon told him, as he poured water from a bucket over RJ's head to get the soap bubbles off of him.

It was times like this Roshon had to admit that being a dad was cool. When he looked at RJ, he felt a sense of pride that he'd created such a beautiful being. RJ had Roshon's blood running through his veins, and he looked just like him only in a smaller package. To say that Roshon loved his son was an understatement. He adored his li'l man and would do anything for him without question.

"Okay, you got ten minutes to brush your teeth and put your pajamas on. You can watch one episode of *SpongeBob* and then it's bedtime," Roshon said before softly pushing RJ's head then walking off.

Roshon descended the stairs to the kitchen where he found a nice cold Corona in the fridge. He started to walk toward his office when his cell phone started to vibrate in his back pocket. The hairs on the back of his neck stood up, and that could only mean one thing. "Yeah," he answered, not even looking at the screen.

"I know you ain't answering ya phone with no attitude," Brandi spat.

"RJ is getting ready for bed. I will have him at ya house in the morning," Roshon said as he took a seat at his desk.

"Nigga, he been over there longer than what he should've been already. I'm coming to get my son," she snapped with an attitude.

"Look, I'm trying to be nice to you. You know you aren't even supposed to come to my house after that check situation," Roshon reminded her.

About a year ago, Brandi had stolen some checks out of his checkbook while he was upstairs getting RJ ready to go home. She had initially tried to deny it, but surveillance tapes had her in the bank cashing the checks she had written to herself and signing Roshon's name. Roshon had to convince the bank not to prosecute by saying that he had forgotten about writing them.

Roshon clenched his teeth and opened and closed his hand, flexing it, and trying to keep calm. The last thing he wanted to do was get into a shouting match with Brandi in front of his son. If Brandi was on her way, it wasn't out of concern for RJ's well-being. Roshon knew her all too well, and nine times out of ten, she needed a babysitter.

"Brandi, whatever plans you got for tonight, they will not include my son watching your other children. Let's not forget he's a child himself."

"Damn, nigga, you act like he ain't my son too. And they not just my other children. They're RJ's brothers and sister."

"Like I said, don't come over here, 'cause you're not getting him. As a matter of fact, I'll call you when I'm ready to bring him home."

"What! You can't do that. I will call the cops on you. It's yo' fault why he got hurt in the first place. Yo' trifling-ass friends and those dirty fucking hoes almost blinded my boy. What do you think the judge would say about that, huh?"

Brandi blasted. "So, like I said, open the fuckin' door when I get there!" she screamed then hung up.

Roshon slammed his hand on the desk as he took in a deep breath, trying his hardest to remain calm. Brandi was really tap-dancing on his last nerve, and he didn't want to explode. He regretted ever lying with her and having a child. However, he didn't regret his son.

"Dumb bitch," he mumbled, taking a swig of the Corona.

Brandi's attitude seemed to be getting worse by the day. At first, he thought that he was tripping, but the more he dealt with her, the more he saw it. Roshon was mostly a laid-back, calm dude, and always tried to negotiate with Brandi, but Brandi seemed to take the fact that he was lenient with her for granted. Truth be told, she simply didn't give a fuck.

The sound of the house alarm chiming signaling that someone came in the door caught Roshon's attention. He slammed his beer down on the desk, then shot to the living room to see who came in the door. Mrs. Johnson, RJ's nanny, was hauling groceries to the kitchen. She had been a friend of his mom's and was also like a mother to him. She was kicking seventy but was still as strong as a horse, with a firm hand and an attitude.

"Are you gonna help me or just stand there?" Mrs. Johnson asked, walking past him. "I got something else for RJ's eyes," she continued.

"Yeah, they are still really red, and he hates the drops."

Mrs. Johnson laughed thinking about the fight little RJ had been putting up. "You don't have to worry about RJ. I'll take good care of him," Mrs. Johnson assured him as she put the food away. "Mrs. J got him now."

The front doorbell rang, getting Roshon's attention. As he got closer to the door, he could hear Brandi yelling at her other kids. Roshon really didn't feel like dealing with Brandi, but he knew he had to or else he would end up having to physically do something to her, which he knew he was not capable of.

"You gon' let us in or what?" Brandi sassed.

Roshon opened the door. He looked down at the infant in the stroller along with her four-year-old and two-year-old holding on to the side of it. Brandi snarled then pushed her way through the door. "And I ain't got no money, so you gon' have to pay for the cab," she said, barging into the house as if she owned it.

Roshon shook his head then walked outside to pay the cab driver. "Don't leave, but you can keep the meter running," Roshon said, passing the cabbie fifty dollars.

The cabbie nodded then put his earbuds in. By the time Roshon got back in the house, Brandi had all her kids out on the living room floor with their toys. Mrs. Johnson stood there with a blank look on her face, holding the diaper bag.

"Brandi, what are you doing?" Roshon asked, walking over and picking up a couple of the toys she laid out.

"I came to see my son," she responded. "Can I do that? Do you have a problem with me spending time with my son, the one I carried, the one I was in labor with for thirty-two hours trying to squeeze something the size of a watermelon out of something the size of a lemon? You got a problem with that?"

"Yeah, I get that, but why is you unpacking yo' kids? You only got a few minutes then he's going to bed. He needs to rest. Plus, I told the cab to stay put," Roshon said, taking the diaper bag from Mrs. Johnson and placing it on the stroller.

Roshon stood, hovering over Brandi and her children, making them feel uncomfortable. He looked at Brandi and then at his watch.

"Look, I'm hurrying, okay? Damn, you act like us being here is a problem. I'm letting RJ stay, so the least you can do is let us chill for a minute. You act like his siblings can't mingle for a minute. Fuck the cab, you can afford it. We just wanna chill for a minute."

"Like I told you, RJ needs his rest, and I got shit to do. So, go ahead and see ya son so you can leave," Roshon said, pointing to the steps.

Brandi looked over at the steps, stood, and smoothed her clothes out before ascending the stairs. Roshon sighed and forced a fake smile on for the other kids sitting on the floor. Their little eyes locked on to Roshon as he walked off toward the kitchen.

A short moment later, Brandi came down the steps and went to the stroller. "I left RJ's favorite blanket in the cab. I promised him that I would bring it, and you'll never get him to go to sleep without it," Brandi said, heading for the door.

Roshon walked back into the living room, and the children were still in the same place Brandi left them. The infant was lying there playing with his feet while the other two continued staring at him like they were afraid of what Roshon might do to them. RJ running downstairs sort of eased the tension in the room. The little girl, who was the two-year-old, leaned over and whispered in RJ's ear.

"Daddy, can Olivia have something to eat?" RJ asked.

Roshon looked at Mrs. Johnson, who smiled then took the two bigger children into the kitchen. The infant was on the floor cooing, and right when Roshon was about to pick him up, he paused and realized Brandi wasn't back yet. When he ran over and opened the front door, the cab was gone.

"You gotta be fuckin' kidding me. Her trifling ass left!" Roshon snapped, running back to his office to get his phone.

He quickly dialed Brandi's number, but the phone rang once then went to voicemail. A quick redial got him the same results. Roshon couldn't believe the stunt that Brandi just pulled. He began sweating, and he needed to calm down quickly. Taking in a deep breath, he calmly decided to dial her number again, hoping for different results. He dialed her number again. This time she answered.

"What? Why the fuck are you calling me, nigga?" she asked.

"Stop playin' and come get ya fuckin' kids Brandi," Roshon barked.

"Damn, nigga. I let you keep RJ a week before you were supposed to have him. The least you can do is watch my kids while I take care of something. Shit, you got a fuckin' nanny there for crying out loud. Let RJ and his siblings enjoy that shit. I got shit to do, just like you. Nigga, I'll be back when I get back."

Roshon pulled the phone away from his ear as the things she was saying had his blood pressure shooting through the roof.

"Brandi, come get your kids or I swear you'll be picking them up from the police station with a nice visit from DCFS. I'm not their dad, and I refuse to allow you to burden me with your issues. Call their daddy. You got ten minutes and not a second longer!" Roshon yelled with spit flying out of his mouth with every word he spoke.

"I fuckin' hate yo' black ass. I'm coming back. I just need to get RJ's blanket. It's not gonna kill you to watch them for—"

"Ten minutes, Brandi!" Roshon yelled then hung up the phone.

He threw his phone on the table, angry and fed up with Brandi's foolishness. She had become the biggest mistake of his life, and he was definitely paying the ultimate price for messing with her. What made things worse was that Roshon knew she had loads of potential but failed to use any of it. She was under the impression that she was entitled to a luxurious life and adoration from her man, and in return, all she had to bring to the table was some good sex and a bunch of kids. She had the game messed up, and if she thought for one second she was going to play Roshon and pimp his pockets, she had another thing coming. Tonight, Roshon was going to act like an ass, and if Brandi hated him now, she was going to wish that he was dead by tomorrow morning.

Los lay in bed trying to figure out a way to leave without making Keera feel some type of way. After all, him just hitting it and running was the sole reason she acted so crazy in the first place. He hardly ever spent time with her outside of the bedroom, and the one or two times he did take her out, it was because he had needed her to do something for him that was so serious he had to butter her up first.

"Pass the weed, nigga," Keera said, lifting her head from his chest.

Los took another deep pull before passing it off to her. He was mad as hell that his phone wasn't ringing. He was looking for any excuse to roll out. Tonight was Dorrian's photo shoot at the club, but it was also a big party being thrown by him to promote Red Zone. Anybody and everybody who was somebody in Charlotte was going to show out, and Los had to have his face in the place.

"Listen, I gotta get ready to go," Los said then looked over at Keera for her reaction.

Her face got tight, and with the blunt still in her hand, she took a long, deep pull of the weed, making sure the tip of the blunt was red hot. Knowing that she was about to do something stupid like burn his chest, Los cleaned up his statement real quick. "But I'm coming back to spend the night with you, so I'ma need that extra key," he spoke.

Keera's expression became brighter almost instantly at the thought of Los spending the night since he hadn't done that in quite some time. It was last minute, but that was the best Los could come up with to avoid being burnt or having to fight with her. "Yeah, that's wassup, boo. And maybe in the morning you can take ya son out for a change. You spending time with him is well overdue," Keera added while she had him against the ropes.

I don't know why this crazy bitch keeps saying that's my son, Los thought as he looked to the ceiling. He'd been ducking a DNA test for a minute now, and Keera had been slipping as well in bringing the topic back up. Eventually, Los was going to have to get the test done. But at this point in his life, it simply wasn't a good time.

Club 1838 was jam-packed for the party, and surprisingly, it was only 10:00 p.m. Normally, the club didn't start jumping until midnight, but tonight it was going down. Dorrian had models from Straight Stuntin' as hosts, along with a few local rap artists hitting the stage.

"Damn, what's good, brah?" Los greeted him when he walked up on Dorrian, who was in VIP checking out his photos from earlier.

"What up, playboy?" he returned, showing Los some love.

Ant walked into the VIP with his hands raised, giving Dorrian dap with a thug hug. "Damn, boy, you gon' show out tonight," Ant said, looking around the club.

"Where da hell is the bottles?" Ant spoke, looking around and enjoying the atmosphere. For him, it was good to be able to hit the club with his guys and free his mind of the bullshit that was running freely in his life.

"Nigga, what the fuck happened to yo' damn head, and where in the hell is my cousin Janelle?" Dorrian asked Ant, and now all eyes were on him.

"Nigga, mind yo' business. Shit is always an adventure and stay getting kind of wild with us. I'm the king of the jungle. Call a nigga Mufasa in this bitch. Now where the bottle at? We here to turn the fuck up, not get in my fucking business." Ant deflected the conversation, not really trying to get into the saturation with his boy over his cousin. Ant knew he was living foul, and if it came down to it, he didn't want to have to box with his homie over his girl.

Truth being told, Ant couldn't look Dorrian in the face, knowing that he was fucking Carly too. The thing with Carly was that she was starting to crowd his space, and even though he needed her for her bread, he wasn't about to be tied down to her, so when he got the call to come out tonight and celebrate, he hopped at the chance to turn up with his guys.

"Nigga, where da hell is the bread?" Dorrian playfully shot back. "Don't get it fucked up, I still got a business to run, brah." Dorrian laughed, turning to give Los some dap on that one.

"By the way, did either of you fools see Roshon yet? He told me he was coming through tonight."

"Yeah, I talked to him earlier today. He told me he was going to put li'l man to bed before he came out," Los said.

"Oh, speaking of li'l man, what's up with yo' crazy-ass broads hurtin' my godson?" Dorrian asked.

"Your godson? Nigga, first of all, that's my godson, and second, I already took care of that," Los spoke.

"Yeah, I bet you did. I heard how you took care of that." Dorrian chuckled, referring to the phone call he got at the dentist's office. "Don't make me send Misha at that ass. You know she'll beat the crazy out of Keera."

"Yeah, whatever. But let's get dis shit poppin'. I don't know about Ant, but I got money," Los said, pulling out a wad of money. All it took was a wave of the hand from Dorrian, and a naked body-painted waitress shimmied over to the VIP.

Los and Ant both sized the waitress up realizing that she didn't have any clothes on, and the only thing that was covering her nudity was a thin layer of body paint. They both looked over at Dorrian and gave him the thumbs-up, knowing that tonight was going to be one of those nights.

Ant looked around at his boys who were turning up, and he wished that for a second he was able to live the life they were living. He was tired of being the broke friend, and after tonight he knew that things were going to change for the better. He was going to change his circumstances by any means necessary.

"Dorrian, you seen that nigga Roshon yet?" Ant asked with a piping hot new plan brewing in his mind.

Roshon turned down the dogwood-lined street of Covecreek Drive, looking in his rearview mirror at Brandi's kids who were fast asleep. He was furious about Brandi not coming back to get them, and if it weren't for Mrs. Johnson pleading for the young children, Roshon would have dropped them off at the police station. Instead, he did the next best thing, which was take them to Brandi's parents' house. They weren't child protective services or the police station, but once they got in contact with her, she was going to get the third degree.

"Nana," the little boy who was awake said, pointing to the large brick house.

"Yeah, Nana," Roshon replied as he pulled into the driveway.

Roshon disliked having to bother Brandi's parents with this nonsense, but he had shit to do, and these weren't his kids, and he didn't feel responsible. It was a shame that Brandi was a piece of shit when her parents were good people and shouldn't have to readjust their life for the continued mishaps of their daughter. By now, they had become used to it and dealt with it as it came. It was obvious by the unsurprised look Mrs. Covington had on her face when she opened the door.

"Where is she? Or, should I ask, what type of trouble has she gotten herself into?" were the first words that came out of Brandi's mom's mouth.

"I don't know, ma'am, and I really don't care. I don't know what's going on wit' ya daughter, but she came by my house to see RJ and then said she was going to step outside for a second. She ended up jumping in a cab and leaving," Roshon explained, passing her the diaper bags while ushering her kids in the house with their grandparents. "I'm really sorry. I didn't mean to say it like that, and I certainly don't mean to be bothering you, but I didn't know nowhere else to take them."

"No, it's okay, and I hate that you have to endure this from that child of mine. I will have a nice talk with her personally about this. She lay down and had these kids, and now is the time for her to step up and raise them. Thank you, Roshon. I surely wished that things would have worked out differently with you two. You are a standup type of man," Mrs. Covington complimented him. Roshon felt that he'd already offended Mrs. Covington by saying that he didn't know or care about her daughter, so he simply smiled and backpedaled toward his car.

As Roshon was leaving the house, a little voice spoke out. "Bye-bye, Mr. Roshon," the little girl said before taking refuge behind her grandmother's leg. Roshon managed to crack a smile, and he waved to her before he got into his car. He didn't even get a chance to start the automobile when his phone began to vibrate in the center console. At first, he thought it was Brandi, but when he looked at the screen, Los's name and number flashed.

"What it do, Los?" Roshon answered. As soon as Roshon heard the club music in the background, he remembered Dorrian's party tonight. Messing around with Brandi had his mind somewhere else.

"Aw, man, homie, we waitin' on you!" Los yelled over the music.

After what he'd just been through, Roshon really didn't feel like doing any clubbing. His main focus was getting back to RJ, who was a little hurt about his siblings having to leave.

"Yeah, well I'm probably not coming out tonight. A lot is goin' on right now," Roshon said as he started his engine.

"Wanna holla at me about it?" Los offered.

Los was his boy, and he always kept it one hundred with him. Roshon let out a deep sigh, and although he knew his boys were partying, he wanted to get this weight off his shoulders.

"Dis bitch left her mafucking kids at my house then took off. Chick pulled a crazy stunt, homie."

"Damn, brah. So what you do? Don't tell me you hurt the kids? That's not even yo' style. What the fuck you do, nigga?" Los asked with concern.

"Shit, what in da hell you think I did? I wouldn't do shit stupid like that. After all, they are my son's siblings, and I could never look him in his eyes and tell him that I did something to harm his siblings, or his horrible-ass mom for that matter. I did the next best thing for the kids. I'm pulling out of her mom's house now. I was about to—"

Los cut him off in laughter, imagining all those kids in the back seat of his BMW.

"Come on, homie, that shit ain't funny."

"Shit. First ya baby mom tried to turn you into her own personal daycare center, and then you had to convert the 750 into a soccer mom minivan in order to travel across town. Shit, if that ain't funny then tell me what is," Los joked, trying to cheer up his friend. It was kind of working, too.

"Ah, nigga, you funny as shit," Roshon said, chuckling a little bit about the whole situation. "But look, I gotta get back to RJ. Tell Doe I said to call me when he gets free."

"A'ight, homie, one," Los said then hung up the phone.

Roshon pulled out of Mr. and Mrs. Covington's driveway and headed home to be with his son for the night. It was bad enough his mom wasn't a good parent, and he would be damned if his son didn't have a great role model in his life. The club life could wait, but when it came to being a man, that started the moment the doctors told him, "Congratulations, it's a boy."

Chapter 4

Dorrian was in his office in the club going through the records when his phone rang. He looked down at the screen and didn't recognize the number. He wasn't about to answer it, but then he thought that it might be a business call, so he answered it.

"This is Dorrian," he answered, making sure he was speaking professionally. If Dorrian wasn't good at being anything else, he was good at being a businessman, and he took pride in the way he got things done.

"Wassup, big cousin, this Janelle. How are you?"

"Hey, cuzzo, I'm good. You haven't called me in so long I didn't recognize the number. Please don't tell me we got a funeral to go to. You know that's the only time folks call is for a funeral or some damn money," Dorrian half joked, laughing while resting the phone between his ear and shoulder while still going through his records.

"No, not nobody in our family, but I swear if you don't get ya boy Ant out of my house, I'm gonna kill him." The tone in Janelle's voice indicated that whatever was on her mind was something serious, and Dorrian felt the need to give Janelle his full attention. He set his papers on his desk while now holding his phone in one hand to his ear, and placing his free hand up to his chin.

Janelle broke down the whole situation about what happened between her, Ant, and the cops. Dorrian couldn't believe what he was hearing. Janelle was mad as hell, and staying with a coworker only added insult to injury.

"Damn, cuz, that's fucked up. I wish I'd known. I would have hollered at his ass the other night," Dorrian said in disbelief as he shook his head.

He couldn't grasp how Janelle had to be the one who had to leave when it was her own house.

"Some crazy law in Mecklenburg County. It's called the Cool Down Law, or some shit like that. My girl is a paralegal, and she tried to explain it to me, but I wasn't trying to hear that shit, especially after he was portrayed by the cops as the victim. This shit is crazy," Janelle vented.

"Oh, that nigga is playin' the victim, huh? He was just up in the club with me, chilling hard. I asked the fucker what happened to his damn head and he was acting like shit popping over there in the bedroom. I didn't wanna hear that shit, so we shut down that convo real quick. But, cuzzo, on some real shit, I told you when you first started fucking with him, Ant is my boy, and I got mad love for him, but he ain't shit when it comes to being in a relationship."

"Nah, cousin. I understand all of that, and I ain't trying to put you in the middle of your friend and family, but I need this nigga up out my house so me and my kids can go back home. You the only one he going to listen to," Janelle added.

"But didn't you say that you only had to be gone forty-eight hours? You know I'll come scoop you and walk you back in. Now if he on some clown shit, I'm passing out red noses," Dorrian added, and Janelle knew he was serious.

"Cuzzo, I doubt if he on bullshit like that. He need to be scared of Carly. Shit! I need to call her ass before she starts thinking the worst. Fuck my life! This is some real fucked-up shit," Janelle seethed.

"What's going on?"

Janelle told Dorrian about Carly staying with her and Ant. Dorrian didn't want to be the one to put it out there in the universe that Carly might not be the most trustworthy when it came to men, but Dorrian loved his family and had to spit that true knowledge.

"Nelle, look, cuzzo, you know I love you, and I think it's commendable that you took Carly in, but you know that's why auntie put her ass out, sleeping around with unc and shit."

"Dorrian, don't start that shit. That nigga not my damn daddy, and he damn sure not your uncle. I'll be damned if I allow a nigga to lie up on me and not welcome my own damn blood with open arms."

Dorrian figured this conversation just hit a brick wall, so he did what any other family member would have done: exited stage left.

"A'ight, cuzzo." Dorrian sighed. "I'ma holla at him later on. Just hang in there, and tell Phaedra I'm ready to knock the dust off her pussy when she ready," Dorrian joked trying to make sure he and Janelle were on good terms when he hung up.

"Whatever, nigga. Phaedra ain't on shit," Janelle replied, and then they both exchanged good-byes. Just as Dorrian was hanging up the phone, someone knocked on his door.

"I gotta remember to holla at that nigga, Ant. His ass on some clown shit," Dorrian spoke to himself, and then he shouted for whoever was knocking on the door to come in. The door opened, and Toto, one of his top hostesses, entered the room.

"Hey, D, the new DJ is downstairs," she said, walking over and taking a seat on the edge of his desk.

"Cool, I'll be down there in a minute. But is Red here? I need to go over this paperwork with him today."

"Not yet. He did call about twenty minutes ago and said that he was on his way. Do you want me to let you know when he gets here?" she said, twirling her gum around her finger.

"Yeah, and let Polo know I'll be down when Red get here. Tell him food and drinks are on the house," Dorrian said then opened his laptop.

As Toto was leaving, Dorrian clicked the bulldog on his screen surveillance cameras. He smiled when he saw Misha coming up the steps. She was also one of his top hostesses, and she was part of the reason why so many males came out to the club. "Come in," Dorrian said before she could knock on the door.

"What, you psychic now?" Misha smiled as she sauntered inside.

"Something like that," he replied, licking his lips. "I tell you one thing: you sure as hell workin' those jeans."

Misha laughed as she took a seat on his desk. Every part of her body was thick to death, and her large, double-D breasts sat upright in their natural form. Misha was five feet nine, 180 pounds with a forty-two-inch ass and she had a set of shiny lips that led to one of the best deep throat dick sucks in the Queen City. She was pushing her limits today, walking up in Dorrian's office looking as good as she was.

"So, what you doin' here?" Dorrian asked, not being able to take his eyes off of her assets.

"Nothing. I thought I would just stop by since I was in the neighborhood. I was hoping I could get a shot of that good-good before I went out of town," she said with a seductive glare.

"Damn, Misha. I wish you would have called first. You know I like to take my time wit' dat ass. I got a few people downstairs waiting on me," Dorrian said, rubbing his bulging dick through his pants.

Misha stood up and walked around to his side of the desk. "I'll tell you what," she said, lowering her halter top below her breasts. "Let me give you something quick to hold you over."

She dropped to her knees right between his legs as he sat in the chair, unbuckling and unzipping his pants, and pulling out his stiff dick in one swift motion. Dorrian closed his eyes and threw his head back as Misha's warm, wet mouth smothered his dick. Dorrian looked down and watched as her head began to bob up and down in slow motion. He reached down and began rubbing and pinching her rock-hard nipples.

"Damn, MiMi," Dorrian said as she sucked his whole dick to the back of her throat. "Shit," he hissed as he grabbed her head and began guiding it up and down.

Without missing a beat, Misha reached down and undid her pants, allowing her fat, juicy ass to flop out of her jeans as she pulled them down.

"You about to make me cum," he said, gripping a handful of her hair. Misha peeled her hair from his fingers, then slid his dick out of her mouth.

"Come in this pussy," she insisted, standing up and taking one leg out of her pants. "Be careful. You know things tend to get messy," she said as she turned around and sat on his rod. "You know how I like it, baby: hard and deep." She moved her hips in a circular motion, adjusting to his size as she held on to the arm of the chair for balance and leverage.

Misha was in the reverse cowgirl position, and once her pussy opened up a little bit, she began bouncing up and down on Dorrian's pole as if she were in a race for the gold. Her pussy was so wet that her juices started slowly rolling down his shaft.

"Yes, fuck me hard," she groaned as she sped up her pace, bouncing so hard on his member that her pussy started making farting noises, making Dorrian even more aroused.

"Damn, baby, she talking to me, ain't she? She like that dick." Dorrian screwed up his face as he watched Misha's ass bounce on his dick. His face was contorted, and his toes were curled, but he was not about to nut that fast. Dorrian held on to both of her ass cheeks as she commenced bouncing up and down on his dick, moaning, and shouting all types of obscenities. He pushed his nut to the back of his head because beating her insides until she squirted her gushy juices all over him was his goal.

She started squeezing and tugging on her nipples. Dorrian was turned up to the max and had to slow her down. He was not about to bust prematurely. He slid his hand down her stomach and eased his dick out of her wetness. He began toying with her pussy with his thick fingers as sexy moans erupted from her lips.

"Ooooh yes, play with that pussy, baby. I love that shit, but I need that big dick back inside me. Fuck me, daddy," she moaned, and Dorrian was happy to meet her request. "Dorrian, oh shit, your big dick feels so good," she whined, throwing her head back against his shoulder. Dorrian loved a good fuck and loved it when his freak of the hour talked shit to him because he loved talking shit back.

"You love this dick, don't you?" Dorrian asked as he nibbled on her ear.

Misha's body started to quiver, and her eyes started rolling in her head.

Dorrian gently shoved her forward until her chest was on his knees, and her hands were palming the ground. He gripped both of her ass cheeks and started lifting her up and down on his rod as he forcefully slammed into her.

"Oh fuck, Dorrian, I'm about to cum." Her voice trembled as she spoke, and her whole body started shivering.

"Yeah, cum on this dick. Make a mess like you always do," Dorrian coached, speeding up his pace.

Dorrian knew that Misha was a squirter, and it wouldn't be too long before he would be covered in her juices.

"Yes, baby, yes," she screamed, rocking her hips back and forth and looking back at Dorrian, who was watching her ass jiggle with every stroke.

"Mmm, uhhhh." She stared Dorrian in his eyes with a look of complete satisfaction as a gush of warm liquid shot out of her, soaking his lap and splashing onto his shirt.

"You always make me messy. You gon' pay for messing up my clothes," Dorrian told her as he lifted her up and bent her over his desk.

Placing one leg up on the desk and pinning her arms behind her back, Dorrian rammed his dick into her slippery, wet center and he started pounding in her like a jackhammer.

"Dorrian, shit, fuck, damn," she rambled on, not knowing what to say.

As she had promised, things were getting messy. Her pussy started making a smacking sound, and a river of her juices was running down their thighs. Misha only wanted a quickie, but when the dick and pussy fit perfectly together, a quickie was never possible.

"Oh shit! I'm about to bust all up in this pussy!" Dorrian grunted as he pushed his dick as hard and as far as it could go, and shot his nut deep inside her uterus.

He collapsed back in the chair, trying to recover from the nut he just had. Misha peeled herself off the desk, dropped to her knees, and started sucking his dick again, tasting all her juices on his shaft.

A knock on the door interrupted their fuck session. With his dick still inside of Misha's mouth, he shouted, "Come back in a minute. I'm busy." And just like that, playtime was over, and it was back to business.

Roshon leaned up against his office desk drinking the last of his Fiji water, grinning from ear to ear so much that it started to hurt his face. Ten minutes ago, he had just closed a major deal of a lifetime. He was the first person in his company to land a multimillion-dollar deal. He was feeling like the man. He wasn't trying to toot his own horn, but he had to be the best broker in his firm. Who else could've landed a $75 million contract with the growth potential of 3 percent annually? His bonus would be in the high six figures, not to mention the other perks of a promotion: quarterly bonuses, a better office, and a better parking space in the company parking garage. These were all the things he had been working for since he started working at Global Star.

"Hell yeah, life is gonna be sweet." He beamed as he looked over the contract again.

A light knock at the door brought Roshon down from his high for a moment. "Come in,"

Roshon said casually as if he didn't just make history.

"Roshon, my million-dollar kid," Mr. Humus greeted him as he entered the office with a tall blonde. "You did a hell of a job," he added, shaking Roshon's hand.

"Yes, I was impressed with the way you handled yourself," the female chimed in, extending her hand for a shake.

Roshon took her hand. "Thank you," he replied, shaking her hand.

"That was quite a performance. I guess I don't have to tell you what this means for our bank accounts." Mr. Humus smiled.

Mr. Humus was a tall, slender white man who wore suspenders, slacks, and cowboy boots with the spurs. He was definitely a Texan, and even though he was usually a straightforward guy, Roshon could see some bullshit coming from a mile away.

"Well, thanks, Mr. Humus. I'm excited about what potential this account holds for us. It's an honor to be managing it!"

"Well, Roshon, that's part of the reason I'm here. This here is Ms. Natalie Simpson. You must have seen her around. She just moved over from Fort Worth."

Roshon looked at her for a moment then turned back to Mr. Humus. Natalie was a white woman in her mid-thirties. She had long, white-blond hair, and a set of breasts on her that set off the rest of her country-thick frame. She looked good, but not good enough for the bullshit that was about to come.

"You see, Roshon, we have those who are hunters and then we have those who prepare and cook the meals," Mr. Humus said as he walked over to the window. "You, my friend, are a hunter. A damn good hunter, I might add."

"Come on, Mr. Humus, shoot it straight," Roshon said, wanting him to cut to the chase.

"Son, what I'm saying is that Ms. Simpson here will be managing the Oya account, and believe me, I know you worked hard for it."

Mr. Humus didn't know the half of it. So much of Roshon's time and efforts went into this. Part of the reason he only got to have RJ every other weekend came from the dedication he had to his job. So, for Mr. Humus to even come at him this way was a complete smack in the face. He didn't even have a good reason for doing it except that he thought Natalie was more equipped for and experienced in the field of managing accounts.

"So, what I'm gonna need from you is to bring Ms. Simpson up to speed with everything, and then I believe a vacation is warranted. Hell, with the bonus you're about to get, I think you'll be able to enjoy yourself royally," Mr. Humus said then sped out of the office before Roshon could even protest.

The air in the room became so thin, Roshon found it hard to breathe. It was as if somebody punched him clean out, knocking the wind right out of him. Landing an account was one thing, but the best part of the job was the managing part. So many other doors were opened for the one who could manage an account, and for one that was this big, it could have really put Roshon where he wanted to be. Surely, if Ms. Simpson weren't still standing in his office Roshon probably would have cried. That's how much this meant to him.

Los didn't know how Keera got him to take a DNA test, but he found himself sitting in the Any Lab Test Now office getting his inner cheek swabbed.

"Don't sit there looking stupid now. This is what you wanted, right?" Keera snapped. "You tryin' to play me like I'm one of these dirty-ass hoes out here. When the test results come back, you better step up and play your part, too," she warned.

The only reason she wasn't acting a whole ass was because she had baby William with her. She felt disrespected even having to go this far in order for Los to accept responsibility for the child he helped create. Keera might have acted crazy, but one thing she knew for sure was who her baby father was. Not only was Los the only man she was with at the time, he was also the only man Keera wanted to be with.

Los knew it, too. He was just in denial and was hoping she had crept off one of those nights he wasn't around. Truth was, Los wasn't ready to be a father to another child, and like a lot of men, that was the only reason he had denied it for so long. He was already behind on child support payments, and unlike his other baby mamas, he was sure that Keera was going to require money and time from him. William had some health issues, and there was no way that Los was ready to commit to something like that. Not only that, but Los clowned baby William every chance he got. He was just hoping that time would make Keera give up. But now the certainty of the matter was that in a couple of days, the test results would be back, and he would know for sure if baby William was in fact his. Until that day came, he was going to be on edge like he was waiting for an HIV test to come back.

"Yeah, nigga, yo' ass gon' pay now," Keera said with a smile after the technician collected, labeled, and sealed the DNA she collected from baby William and Los.

"Keera, g'on with that shit. Now ain't the time for all that extra shit." Los seethed as he snatched up his phone and keys and made a beeline to the door.

"Oh, so that's what you doing now, Los? Is it really like that?"

"Keera, I told you go on with that foolishness."

Keera was struggling, trying to argue with Los and handle baby William. Los looked back at the scene, and rather than arguing with Keera, he stared at her as if he were looking at her for the very first time. He blocked out all the bad memories as his mind started thinking of only happy times that they shared.

"Nigga, why are you looking all fucked up? What's wrong with you? Goofy-ass muthafucka," Keera continued.

Los walked up on Keera, never speaking a word. He assisted her with baby William and then gave her a wink.

Keera was confused, but Los wasn't. In his mind, if baby William was indeed his child, he would have to face the situation just as he faced anything else: head-on.

***

Roshon sat in his office with Natalie going over some of the files for the Oya account. He had an obvious attitude and didn't want to be there. Natalie could feel the vibe and in a sense understood how he felt about having someone come in and ride the coattails of his success. It had happened to her several times in her earlier years, but she also knew that it was going to make Roshon a better broker.

"Roshon, can I have a word with you for a second?" Natalie said, putting the papers she was looking at onto his desk.

Roshon lifted his head from the file he was reading. "Sure, what else can I do for you?" he responded in a sarcastic way.

Natalie smiled. "Look, I don't want you to have any animosity toward me because of this. Personally, I think you're a very brilliant, intelligent man, and if I plan on managing this new account, I'm going to need your help the whole way through," Natalie said in a sincere tone. "I need for you to look at this as a partnership instead of me taking over. I give you my word that you'll do just as much managing this account as I will."

Her words provided a little bit of comfort, but Roshon wouldn't be convinced until she showed him through her actions. Mr. Humus had already lied to Roshon about being able to manage the account if he had landed the Oya deal, so for him to believe what Natalie was talking about had to be done strictly off proof.

"Look, I appreciate the gesture, and I hope that you stand by your word, but in the event that you try to play me—"

Roshon's phone vibrated loudly on the desk and caused him to stop talking. He looked at the screen, and it was RJ calling from the cell phone Roshon had bought for him.

"Hold on, I gotta take this," Roshon told Natalie then got up and walked out of the office. "Wassup, son?" Roshon answered.

"Dad, can you come and get me? I'm at school, and my mom didn't come pick me up," Little RJ said, watching the last of the children leave the school yard with their parents.

"Don't move. I'm on my way," Roshon told RJ. "I want you to stay on the phone with me until I get there. Can you do that? Is your battery charged up enough?" Roshon asked.

"Yes, my battery is charged up, Dad," RJ replied.

Roshon walked back into his office in search of his car keys.

Natalie looked on and saw the concerned look he had on his face. "Is everything all right?" she asked.

As far as Roshon was concerned, he was off the clock at Global and had now checked into his second job as a daddy. The only thing Natalie got out of him was an apology and a good-bye wave as he darted out of the office with smoke steaming from his Gucci loafers.

Roshon had had enough of the bullshit. He was hot as a firecracker as he hustled to the school to pick RJ up. Still on the phone with his son, he spoke, "Daddy is almost there. Are you all right? Did anyone mess with you?"

"I'm fine, Daddy, and if someone say something to me, boom, right in the nuts, just like you taught me. But if it's girl, I can't hit a girl, Daddy."

Roshon smiled knowing that after all of his talks with his son, his words were sticking inside his head. "That's right, son. We don't put our hands on ladies."

"Not until they ask us, right, Daddy?"

Roshon laughed. "Little man, you're something else. Daddy is pulling up now. Do you see me?"

"I see you, Daddy."

Hanging up the phone and killing his engine, Roshon hopped out of the car and opened his arms wide to receive his son. His mind was made up. It was time to go back to court and have the judge review this case. It was time to put some stability in RJ's life, and he wasn't going to get that being let down every other day by his mom.

Roshon didn't want to keep RJ from his mom. He just wanted him to have stability.

Chapter 5

Dorrian knocked hard on the metal storm door then took a step back and waited for Ant to come to the door, which took a minute for him to do. He was too busy fucking Carly and needed to give her time to run into her room before he answered. A few minutes later, Ant came to the door and peeked through the curtain on the window, looking around suspiciously. When he noticed Dorrian, a smile grew on his face.

"Big D, what's good, big brah?" Ant greeted him when he finally opened the door. "Come on in," he said, looking over his shoulder first to make sure Carly was out of sight.

"Shit, nigga, ain't shit new. You know how it is: same shit, different toilet," Dorrian said, stepping in and taking a look around the house, checking to make sure shit was sweet.

Shit, li'l cousin doing good, he thought, seeing how well furnished the place was. He was damn proud of his cousin, even though her asshole of a baby daddy left her and was paying child support whenever the hell he felt like it. Despite the odds, Janelle was doing big things. It was crazy how Dorrian couldn't stand to see a nigga not take care of his kids, but somehow that same judgment didn't fall on his boy Los.

"Can I get you a beer or something?" Ant offered as if he were the one who bought the groceries. The fact of the matter was, he wasn't sure what Carly did to get her bread, but she always came through for his ass and filled the refrigerator up. Ant played on her emotions and pretended to be playing house with her, and like the good little wife she was trying to be, she made sure all of his needs were being met.

"Nah, I'm not gonna stay that long. You know Janelle gave me a call yesterday, telling me about y'all li'l situation. Funny thing is, I saw you at the club, and you failed to mention any of this shit."

"Oh yeah, what she say?" Ant asked like he didn't know already.

"Nothing much except that she wants her house back."

Ant immediately got on the defensive and rose to his feet.

"Ant, on some real shit, nigga, sit yo' ass down. I came over here on some respectful shit because you my boy, but you already know how I get down. You come at me on some fuck type shit, I'ma handle yo' ass."

Ant sat down and paid attention to what Dorrian had to say. He knew the shit he was doing was foul and could have his ass kicking up dirt or swimming in the bottom of the ocean.

"Ant, Janelle told me about that clown-ass move you pulled. You seriously played victim and got her kicked out her shit with her kids?"

"Naw, she did that. I wasn't playing a victim. She was wilding, yo."

"So you mean to tell me that a female got yo' ass so shook that you had the police remove her and her kids and she's taking care of you? Nigga, you don't have shit. How the fuck you gon' come at her like that? The cooling off period is lifted, and she wants yo' ass out her shit. On the strength that you my boy, I'm coming over here to let you know, man to man, that you need to figure shit out and keep it moving."

"Where the fuck I'ma go?"

"Nigga, you a grown-ass man. Figure that shit out, but you getting the fuck up outta here. Now if she come home and y'all make up and shit, that's one thing, but as of today, she want you out."

Ant wasn't going to put up too much of an argument because, for one, Dorrian wasn't no soft-ass dude by a long shot and would more than likely beat his ass if they got into a fight. The second reason was simple: Ant didn't have a pot to piss in and a window to toss it out. Ant put his cards on the table.

"Dorrian, this shit is two types of fucked up, and no matter how you slice the shit, it's just fucked up. I've been trying to do right by Janelle, but her ass been on some other shit lately. Do you think I could squat at your place until I get myself together?"

"Fuck naw. You know my rules about friends and staying with me. You my boy, but the only help I can extend to you is a job, and then you work to get your own. I'll even spot you an advance on your first two checks, but the moment you play the okie dokie, yo' ass is out."

Ant was nodding his head in understanding. He had mad love for Dorrian. Dorrian had always been like a big brother to him and kept spitting knowledge his way. The only thing that Ant hated more than being broke was actually going out and working a real job with people telling him what to do. Dorrian was asking question after question and trying to get Ant to agree to his terms.

"Well, you know that whole nine-to-five thing not for me."

"And, nigga, this crib ain't either, so I'm letting you know now you have twenty-four hours to get yo' shit and leave," Dorrian added with finality.

Ant's mind was going a mile per minute, and he needed to think of something fast. He didn't consider accepting a job from Dorrian an option, but maybe borrowing some money could be an option. He just needed to play on Dorrian's emotions.

"D, you know a nigga fucked up right now. I'm just not the type I see walking in the club being a bouncer or some shit."

"Nigga, who promoted yo' ass to bouncer? You're starting in the kitchen, mopping floors. Soon you'll be on fries after washing lettuce," Dorrian teased while making comments as if he were an extra in the late-eighties' movie *Coming to America*.

"Dorrian, man, on some real shit, can you let me hold something until I figure this shit out? I'll be out by tomorrow, and on God, I'm leaving yo' cousin alone. Her ass ain't shit but trouble."

"Yeah, I told both y'all asses to leave each other alone." Dorrian laughed, pulling off a few hundred-dollar bills and handing them to Ant.

Deep down, Ant knew he had to do right sooner or later. With not having anywhere else to go, he knew that he would have to get a job and make ends meet some kind of way. He just didn't have any intention of doing that at the moment. He was going to find that officer's card and make sure that Janelle didn't bring her ass back home. Now he had money to fuck around with, and it was time to floss for the hoes.

Dorrian stood up and was preparing to leave; then he turned around and spoke. "Ant, nigga, if I have to come over here tomorrow because you on some fuck shit, it won't be pretty," Dorrian warned, and Ant knew he was serious about his threat. Walking to the door, Dorrian stopped again and asked, "Where's Carly? She still staying up in here?"

Ant frowned as if he were annoyed by the question, not wanting to give them away. "Yeah, she still up in here. She got to be somewhere around here. Her ass come and goes as she pleases and never tells me shit. Just gets up and she's out," he lied. "I'll tell her you came around."

"Cool. Stay safe, bro, and don't forget tomorrow is moving day. Do the right thing and keep it the fuck moving. You my homie, and I'll hate to have to put hands on you, but I will," Dorrian said, meaning every word as he left.

Ant sighed when he closed the door behind Dorrian. A wicked smile stretched across his face as he realized he played his boy for his coins and was about to play his boy's cousin even more. Retrieving the card that the officer left him, Ant called the police station and played the role of a battered man. Pleased with his performance, he headed up the stairs to finish digging Carly out. With money in his pocket and the house free and clear of Janelle for a few days, Ant was walking on cloud nine. He had things planned out perfectly in his head.

It was time for him to get the hell up out of that house and show everybody that he had the hustle that it took to be successful. He didn't know what he was going to do, but he knew he was going to try something. *It is my time.*

Carly returned from her room and broke Ant from his critical thinking. "Dorrian was here talking shit, huh?" she asked, shaking her head. "Nigga couldn't just mind his business, but then again, Janelle has always been his favorite cousin. Don't tell me you gonna listen to all that bullshit he kicking? You ain't gonna leave me here all alone, are you?" she asked.

"Girl, bring yo' sexy ass here. You know damn well no man puts fear in my heart. I simply be playing the role, and these cats fall hard for that shit. A few bros and a couple of, 'Nigga, I'm jammed up,' and boom, just like that, help is on the way. Now get yo' ass up there and spread them legs so I can jump off in those guts."

Ant was playing a very dangerous game, and as his luck would have it, the game he was playing was slowly going to come to an end sooner rather than later. One could only hope that it didn't end badly for him.

"I still haven't heard from her, Mrs. Covington," Roshon said into the phone. "RJ's fine though. He's gonna stay with me until Brandi pops back up."

"Roshon, I know you and my daughter have y'all differences, but can you please try to track her down so she can come get these kids? I'm getting too old for this shit," Mrs. Covington said, feeding the infant cradled in her arms.

Roshon sympathized with her, knowing Brandi was on some real bullshit right now. It didn't faze him much because he was already used to the disappointment and didn't expect Brandi to do anything less than what she was doing. Sitting there thinking about it, he was going to use her neglectfulness toward RJ against her in their next court hearing, as well as the situation from when he picked him up from school. He had made up his mind that instead of fighting the increase in child support, he was going to shoot for full custody of his son. He felt like he had everything going in his favor: a great job that came with benefits, a nice house, and an in-house nanny who RJ knew and loved. It sounded fucked up, but Roshon wasn't interested at all in trying to find Brandi, at least not until after the court hearing next Tuesday.

Roshon ended the call with fake promises to do what he could to find Brandi, but he knew deep down, whatever bullshit she got herself into, he wanted no part of it. His only concern was RJ, and it would be up to Mr. and Mrs. Covington to find their no-good-ass daughter.

Roshon walked into the kitchen, and a smile stretched on his face seeing RJ recite his black history facts with his headphones on his ear as if he were a rapper.

When he spotted Roshon, he ran into his arms yelling, "Daddy!"

"Li'l man, what are you in here doing?"

"I'm doing my black history rap. I can't be a fool. I have to stay in school. Follow the plan, be a man, don't sag my pants and learn my history so tomorrow won't be a mystery," he recited almost as perfectly as his dad had stated to him a million times over.

Running his fingers through his son's hair, Roshon instructed RJ to run upstairs and prepare for dinner. Thoughts of RJ possibly staying with him full-time began to flood his mind, and it caused a peaceful look to find its way to his face. "One day at a time, Roshon, one day at a time," he spoke aloud to himself.

Dorrian was driving down the street on his way to Los's shop to pick him up. As he rolled past the crowded bus stop, he caught a glimpse of someone who immediately caught his attention. He stepped on the brakes, causing his car to jerk and the other cars behind him to honk their horns. Dorrian didn't care though. Arlene was standing at the bus stop, and that's something he couldn't have his woman doing. Technically, she was not his woman, but Dorrian was a persistent man, and he knew that, sooner or later, Arlene would give in to him.

Dorrian threw his car in park, turned on his hazards, and hopped out of his car, leaving it parked in the middle of the street. Flashing the drivers of the honking horns the finger, he started across the street to the bus stop where Arlene had her head buried into her iPhone. When she heard the commotion with the traffic, she looked up from her iPhone and saw Dorrian jogging across the street, dodging cars.

"Boy, are you crazy! You almost got hit by that car," Arlene said as he was approaching her.

"Boy? I ain't no boy. I'm a goddamn man, and yeah, you damn right I'm crazy," he replied with a huge grin on his face. "Yo, ma, on some real shit, for the past week, you are all I have been thinking about. Like for real, I can't get yo' pretty ass off my mind. I thought about coming back to Dr. Miller and getting my teeth cleaned again just so I could see you."

"Yeah, so what was you thinking about when I came to mind?" Arlene asked, slightly blushing from his comment.

Cars were still blowing their horns behind Dorrian's truck, but he didn't give a fuck. He was fixated on Arlene and nothing else at that moment. "Our future: that's what I've been thinking about."

"Our future?" she asked with a curious look on her face. "What do you mean our future?"

"Our future: yours and mine, together. How about you let me take you out, and I can tell you all about it?" He smirked, leaning up against the pole.

"Come on, Mr. Hoyle. I told you I don't—"

"Please, call me Dorrian," he interrupted.

"Well, Dorrian, I told you I don't get involved with patients."

"Fuck it then. I will never go back to that dental office again, so you won't have to worry about me being a patient anymore," Dorrian said with a serious face. "Look, shawty, I'm not playing games. I'm honestly feeling you, and I know you probably hear shit like this all the time, but I ain't kicking bullshit. I'm straight up with my shit. I ain't one of those 'love at first sight' niggas and shit, but you, Ms. Arlene, you make me feel things that I've never felt before. Now, I ain't asking for yo' hand in marriage. All I'm asking is that you have dinner or lunch with me one time. If you don't enjoy yourself, then I give you my word I'll never bother you again," Dorrian spoke.

Arlene stood in silence, with her arms folded across her chest and her eyes rolling upward, thinking about giving Dorrian a chance.

"So, you down or what?" he asked, eager to know her answer.

She looked into his eyes and saw a level of sincerity she hadn't seen in a man in a very long time. She didn't know what it was about him that had her attention, but she was willing to go against all her rules and give him a chance, even with all that had happened in her past.

"A'ight, Dorrian, we can go out," she answered, and Dorrian couldn't stop grinning.

"Come on, ma, let me take you to work," Dorrian said, reaching out for her hand.

Arlene giggled, then picked up her purse and took Dorrian's hand as he led her across the street to his truck.

Roshon was fortunate enough to be able to work from home for the next couple of days, given that all he really needed to do was finish bringing Natalie up to speed about the Oya account. By being home, he was able to spend more time with RJ, something he hadn't done in a long time, and for what it was worth, he was enjoying every minute of it.

"So, I guess we can wrap it up for the day," Natalie said, leaning back in her office chair.

"Good, 'cause you workin' the hell out of me," Roshon joked.

Natalie had to admit they did get a lot of work done in the two-hour conference call they had. "So look, seeing as how I know you haven't celebrated yet, how about you let me take you out for a drink?" Natalie offered.

"If I didn't know any better, it sounds like you are trying to take me out on a date." Roshon smiled, leaning forward on his desk.

"If you need to call it that in order for me to get you out of the house, then so be it," she responded.

Natalie knew from experience that in their line of work and by how hard Roshon was working, he didn't get out much. She understood the importance of having to separate your personal life from your job and finding a balance between the two, but she also knew that putting your all into work, and not taking time to let loose and have some fun, could make a person stressed out. This date, or whatever it may be, was something that was long overdue for the both of them. Especially since she was interested in him.

Around the office, Roshon was reserved and kind of laid-back, but when he was doing his presentation for the Oya account, he was a beast, and Natalie wanted the beast in him to come out and claim her as his. However, she wasn't sure if he would be interested in her because she was white. She didn't know if he'd ever dated a white woman but she, on the other hand, loved black men. She'd dated a few, and from what she could tell, despite all the stereotypical bullshit about black men, they knew how to treat a woman and could put it down in the bedroom.

After Ms. Daisy confirmed that he was single, Natalie decided that she would make a move on him. In her eyes, they would be perfect together. They both had kids they adored, and they both had ambition and were a couple of real go-getters who understood that if you wanted something out of life, you had to put in some hard work.

"So, what do you say? Are we celebrating or what?" she asked.

He frowned then nodded. "What do you have in mind?" he asked.

"Dinner and then we get drinks at the bar later on. I will send you the location."

"A'ight, we can do that, but I can't stay too late because I got my son," he said.

She nodded in understanding. "Just a few drinks, and you will be back home, tucked in bed," she teased.

Roshon chuckled. "Yeah, sure, we'll see about that. Talk to you later, Natalie," he said before ending the call.

Natalie was so excited about her date with Roshon that she got up out of her seat, pumped her fist in the air, and then started twerking. For a thick white girl, Natalie had rhythm and twerked like she could be an honorary member of the twerk team.

"Now, let's see what bar we are going to go to," Natalie mumbled as she sat back down in the chair and started surfing the Internet. She was looking for someplace that they could go to that wasn't noisy and crowded. She wanted a quintessential place where they could sit and talk and get to know each other on a more personal level. She wanted to know more about him, and for him to know more about her so that he could look at her as more than just a work colleague.

"Thank God it's Friday," Los said, grabbing his trimmers off the hook. "It's gonna be so many bitches at the club tonight," he continued.

"Yeah, I hear your boy Dorrian is bringing in chicks from Atlanta and Miami," Pablo said, putting his clippers on the mat.

CIAA weekend always had Charlotte turned up every year. Dorrian had sold out of VIP passes the first day he ran the ad on the radio and on his social media. His club was about to be on fire tonight. "Aww, man, speak of the devil," Los said, pointing at Dorrian who had walked right through the front door.

"Ya boy is in the building," Dorrian said with his hands in the air. "Los, I need you to tighten me up real quick. I got something special on the menu before tonight's festivities," he said, walking around the room and giving everybody dap.

"Yo, you finally got a date with ol' girl from the dentist's office?" Los asked.

"Yep. I'm taking her out to lunch later on," Dorrian responded.

"Ay, you know ya boy Roy is mad at you," Ant said, folding the newspaper he was reading and putting it to the side.

"You talkin' 'bout the nigga who owns Charries?" Dorrian shot back. "That nigga betta sit his ass down somewhere. I got shit locked down. The skin game is mine around these parts."

"Yeah, that's right. That nigga just mad 'cause he ain't makin' no money with those crack-head-looking broads he got over there." Los laughed. "Those bitches got bullet wounds and razor scars on their bodies and shit, and half of them can't dance for shit. Hell, when a nigga screams, 'Left cheek, right cheek,' I wanna see that cheek move." Los laughed, air smacking an invisible booty.

All the fellas in the shop agreed with either a nod of the head or a dap of the fist. There was no question as to who had the best strippers in town. Dorrian's club thrived off the beautiful women he had dancing every weekend. He took pride in his selection of females, and on certain nights, he even had a strict weight requirement for his dancers.

"Oh shit, here comes trouble," Ant announced watching as Keera and her girlfriend Pebbles crossed the street.

Los let out a deep, frustrated sigh. Not only did Keera have ghetto-ass Pebbles with her, but she was also carrying baby William. Los didn't feel like dealing with her, especially since, as of yesterday, the DNA test still hadn't come in the mail. He was so ready to get the thought that Keera had of that baby being his out of her mind. She wasn't the first chick to put a baby on him, and he knew she wouldn't be last. Los had put all three of his baby mothers through the same shit, and there wasn't anything wrong physically or mentally with them kids. *What does Keera expect? Does she really think I am about to claim a baby who is mentally fucked up?*

"Well, hello, everyone," Keera said with a cheerful attitude when she walked into the barbershop and nobody spoke.

A few muffled greetings were given back from the people in the shop who knew her. She was in what seemed to be a good mood as she walked over to Los.

"I just wanted to bring your son by before I drop him off to my mom's house for the weekend," Keera said with baby William in her arms. When Keera cleared baby William's face of the blanket, Los gave a frown as he looked down on William's face being contorted and his eyes being a little crossed. He was pissed that Keera had brought this baby out into public around him and now his friends and customers. He needed her and everyone around to know that this wasn't his child, so he searched his mind for the most ignorant and disrespectful words he could find.

"Yo, bitch, didn't I tell you that wasn't my son?" he growled. "I don't make no fucking retarded-ass babies, so stop coming around here with the bullshit," he said as he put the cape over Dorrian to prepare to cut his hair.

Keera's heart sank to her stomach, and she tried her best not to start crying. She was a strong woman, and she had so much love for Los, but she could not hold it in anymore. The past few days had been so much for her, from shouting all the time at Los, to the DNA test, and now this. Although baby William wasn't mentally challenged, and only was in need of an operation to repair his right lung, he still was a special needs child whom she loved unconditionally, and she felt like his father should do the same.

Ever since she had gotten pregnant, Los had been saying one fucked-up thing after another about her and her baby, and she was fed up. Keera wouldn't be surprised if all the pain and drama she went through with Los during her pregnancy was the cause of Williams's condition. In all their years of being together, she had never fucked any other man except for Los. Even though she knew for a fact Los was fucking bitches all around town, she loved him and wouldn't let any other man have what belonged to him.

As Keera stared at Los with hatred in her eyes, she couldn't stop the tears from slowly rolling down her face. Pebbles slowly walked up to Keera and patted her back, trying to stop her from crying. She wiped away her tears. Keera was tired of crying over the ignorant shit that came out of Los's mouth, and she refused to continue to show weakness in front of his heartless ass. She was gonna be strong.

As she swallowed her pride and turned to leave, she decided to give Los one last chance to be a real man. Los recently showed her his heart, and it was tearing her up that he decided to show his ass like this in front of his guys. The man she fell in love with had to be there. She was tired of the same old thing, the back and forth, the crazy fights, and she simply wanted peace and her son's father to claim him, and not just in private but in public.

Taking in a deep breath, Keera cleared her throat and asked, "Will you come over tonight so we can talk?" Her tone was genuine and laced with hurt, but she had to find a way to reach back into Los's heart.

"Keera, let me be clear since you didn't understand me trying to be nice the first time. Fuck you and that baby, and no, it's nothing to talk about!" he screamed and went back to shaping up Dorrian's head. All of the life was taken out of Keera as she turned, with baby William in her hands and Pebbles at her back, and exited the shop.

"Damn, bro, that was some cold shit to say," Dorrian spoke, breaking the silence. He knew Keera could act up, but damn, she didn't deserve that, and the baby definitely did not.

"Yeah, that was fucked up," Ant added.

Everybody in the shop made a comment about his choice of words.

"A'ight, everybody, get back to work," Los demanded, not wanting to hear the people's remarks anymore.

When nobody moved right away, Los looked around the room. "What da fuck is the problem? Get back to work. Ant, you shut yo' broke ass up! You borrow a few hundred dollars from this man, knowing damn well yo' broke ass won't pay it back, yet you wanna judge me. Fuck outta here. You still lying up over there on Janelle? Oh, I forgot, yo' broke ass too busy calling the police to get by with more time. What a fuckin' joke."

Los was clearly hitting below the belt. He wanted to take this situation and turn it around on someone as fast as he could so that he didn't have to worry about taking the heat for the fucked-up shit that left his mouth.

Deep down inside, Los was having a battle within himself, and he figured he'd clown baby William before his boys had a chance to. Knowing Keera and how deep her love for him ran, Los had a feeling that baby William was indeed his, and he was trying his hardest to come up with a way to justify all of the fucked-up shit he'd said.

Seeing that Keera didn't show her ass or act crazy made Los feel like shit. Ever since the day they went to take the DNA test and he showed Keera the attention that she'd been begging for, her attitude had completely changed, and he was loving her for it.

"Yo, Los, that's real fucked up. Kick a brother while he's down? That ain't you, brah. That ain't cool," Dorrian stated looking at Los with disappointment in his eyes.

"Nigga, you want a cut or nah?" Los retorted, still on the defensive.

"No matter what you do or say, you have to eat all of those fucked-up words that you spat toward that child if the DNA test proves him to be yours. Man the fuck up! I'm outta here."

Snatching the cape from around his neck, Dorrian left the shop upset at Los. Los had broken every code possible in the "bro handbook," and Dorrian wasn't about to sit there and condone it.

With nothing left to say, Los snatched up his water bottle and headed toward the back of the shop, embarrassed by his actions.

When Keera arrived back to the car, her legs and hands were still shaking as she buckled William in his car seat. Pebbles was still trying to comfort her and let her know that she didn't need a man's help in raising or loving her child. The words were falling on deaf ears because Keera had made up in her mind that Los was going to do the right thing. After what he did in the shop, and the things he said regarding her and her son, she'd had enough.

She reached into her glove compartment and grabbed her small chrome .380 automatic. Pebbles's eyes grew wide with fear. Before Pebbles could speak, Keera was heading right back into the barbershop with the gun in her hand and Pebbles running after her with her heels slowing her down. She flung open the door and stormed into the salon, waving the gun. The whole mood in the room changed, and a couple of the smarter customers got up and ran out the door.

"Where in the fuck is he!" Keera screamed as tears streamed down her face. She wasn't thinking about baby William being alone, strapped in the car seat. She was only thinking about making Los feel the same amount of pain that her heart was in.

Looking around the shop like a madwoman, Keera walked up to Ant who had his hand in the surrender position.

"Where in the fuck is he?" Keera spoke through gritted teeth.

Before Ant could respond, Los came out of the back with his water bottle in hand. He was like a deer stuck in headlights when he saw the state of mind that Keera was in.

"Keera, you better cool da fuck down," Los warned, dropping the water bottle he had in his hand.

His words went unheard as Keera cocked the chrome .380 automatic back, putting a bullet in the chamber. Without saying a word, she walked up to Los and shot him in the leg, then stepped back slightly just in case he tried to lunge forward. The bullet crashed through his shin bone, shattering it into pieces. He immediately fell to the ground, groaning in pain.

With the gun still in her hand, Keera reached into her back pocket and pulled out a white envelope then tossed it down at his face. It was the paternity test that came in the mail this morning, and just as she thought, there was a 99.99 percent chance that Los was the father of baby William.

"If you ever call our son retarded again, I'ma shoot you in your face next time. You're his freakin' father, you asshole. You got that? You can't deny him no fucking more, so I suggest you get your shit together and own up to your responsibilities. I ain't gonna have this discussion with you anymore. You know me, Los. Don't fucking play with me," she concluded before turning around and walking out of the barbershop as if she hadn't just shot Los.

Los lay on the floor, holding his leg, looking at the left corner of the envelope with the DNA testing office's address on it, and shouting out in pain. His leg was hurting like shit, but he wasn't sure what was hurting more: his ego or his leg. Keera had really put a new twist on her crazy this time around, and Los didn't know what she might do next.

***

Dorrian couldn't believe that he'd just walked out of the shop because Los was tripping. He was halfway to his destination when he got a message from Ant telling him and Roshon to meet him at the hospital because Los was shot. Dorrian's mind raced as he tried to figure out if someone ran up in the shop right after he left. Changing his plans, he took the next exit and was a few minutes away from the hospital. No matter what type of disagreement the guys had, they always found a way to be there for each other when they needed one another.

Roshon couldn't believe what he was hearing as Ant tried to give him the short version of what happened with Los. Roshon pushed his 750 to the limit, trying to get to the hospital, and as soon as he pulled into Carolinas Medical Center, Ant, Falicia, and Dorrian were standing by the emergency entrance.

"Yo, what up? Is he okay?" Roshon asked as he got out of the car. Ant ran down everything that happened, calming Roshon's nerves. He started to make his way into the hospital when his phone rang. He thought about not answering it when he saw that it was Brandi calling, but he remembered giving Mrs. Covington his word that he would contact her if Brandi popped up.

"Yo," Roshon answered, looking up at the hospital.

"Roshon," Brandi called out slightly above a whisper.

Roshon could barely recognize her voice. She sounded high and drunk, or both, which was highly probable. Roshon went straight in on her. "Where da fuck have you been, and why in da hell haven't you picked up your kids from your mama?" he barked.

"Roshon, I'm sorry. Can you please just come and get me? I . . . I promise I'ma get my shit together," she pleaded. "I'ma do the right thing. Just please come pick me up."

Roshon had heard these statements before and knew that they meant nothing once she got what she wanted. The days of playing him were over and had been for a while now.

"I can't do it. I got a lot of shit on my plate right now. Call your mom 'cause she's worried about you," Roshon said then hung up the phone. She wasn't his problem, and as long as RJ was at his house safe and secure, he couldn't care less about what Brandi had going on. For now, all Roshon wanted to do was get into the hospital and check up on his boy Los, which was exactly what he did.

A tear slipped down Brandi's face as Roshon hung up on her. "He ain't coming?" her youngest's father, Joe, asked.

Brandi shook her head as more tears poured from her eyes. She knew Roshon not coming was going to make Joe even more upset than he currently was. They had been doing all they could to get up the cash that Joe owed his plug. He and Brandi had smoked up most of the product, and the money from the little they had sold had been spent. Joe had Brandi up in a weekly motel for the last week selling pussy on backpages.com. Her body was exhausted between all the fucking and the drugs they were doing together. She had convinced him that she could get the money from Roshon, but now that that had fallen through, there was no way he was going to let her stop.

"I told you that simple-ass nigga wasn't going to come through. You should just give me his address so me and my brother can go rob the nigga."

"I told you he not like that. He ain't going to have no cash in his house, because he keeps his money in the bank," Brandi responded, hoping that Joe would leave that conversation alone.

"Well, we both know how much he loves RJ. We ain't got to hurt him for real, just make that square sucker think we would and he will pay. I can have my brother fake kidnap—"

"No, no, no! I told you before I'm not doing that shit," Brandi said with a strong tone, which was unusual for her when speaking to Joe. But when it came to her children, she wasn't scared of shit.

"Well, that's what it is then. You just going to have to suck some more dicks and fuck a few more of these crackers to get this bread up. But we going to get this money, because before a nigga kill me, I will kill somebody else to make sure I'm straight, you feel me?" Joe asked, making sure Brandi understood his threat. Brandi shook her head knowing full well that Joe was capable of doing anything to anybody, including her kids.

"Come on, snap out of it," Joe said, his gold teeth gleaming. "You wanna get high before we go back to this shit?"

Brandi wanted to say no. She wanted to walk away from it all, but she knew she couldn't. Her body was already completely drained, and she wasn't sure how much more she could take. She weakly nodded at Joe who was already preparing the needle to go in her vein. Her eyes closed as she felt the venom slip into her. She hissed in pain at first and then smiled in ecstasy.

Chapter 6

"Yes, daddy, beat dis pussy up. Fuck me up! Beat me, fuck me, choke me!" Carly yelled out while pulling on her hard, sensitive nipples while Ant drilled into her from the back. Skin smacking was the only sound that could be heard echoing from the walls of Janelle's master bedroom.

"Make me cum, daddy," she cooed.

She was tooting her ass up in the air, giving Ant full access to beat and drill inside her welcoming, warm center. Ant loved the angle at which he was pounding. A devilish smile stayed on his face as he watched Carly's pussy devour his manhood like it was nothing. Carly's pussy was soft, tight, deep, and could take one hell of a pounding session. It was shocking to Ant that he lasted this long without busting off.

In one swift motion, Ant went from hitting that pussy from the back to making Carly ride him like a bull.

"Ride this dick, you nasty bitch. You want my cum all in that pussy, don't you?" Ant said, reaching up and grabbing her throat. He loved seeing her sex faces as he beat and choked her. It seemed to always turn her on, allowing her juices to drip like a leaky faucet.

Carly loved rough sex. If she wasn't being choked, smacked, or completely dominated by her partner, she wasn't going to get off.

"Work that pussy for daddy," he said, reaching around and sticking his middle finger in her asshole. "Make it pop. Make it pop."

Carly went crazy. She reached back to spread her ass cheeks apart then commenced bouncing up and down on Ant's rod and his finger that was gliding in and out of her asshole. The clicking sound from her wet box echoed throughout the whole room. She sped up, feeling herself about to cum all over his dick. When he smacked the side of her face and then choked her again, Carly hit her high note.

"I'm cumming, daddy. Yes, I'm cumming, daddy," she screamed out, rocking her hips back and forth.

"Where you want daddy to cum at?" Ant asked, now feeling himself about to burst. "Tell daddy where you want it."

"Cum in my ass, daddy. I wanna feel it in my ass," she whined, reaching back and grabbing the base of his dick.

She took Ant's throbbing, pulsating dick out of her pussy then sat back down on it, taking every inch of it into her ass. Ant grabbed both of her ass cheeks and began slamming her ass up and down on his dick. Within seconds, his thick, creamy cum squirted inside of her. Feeling it, she rubbed her clit at high speed and managed to chase down another orgasm before Ant finally pulled his massive dick out of her. Ant was done, and as Carly flopped down onto the bed beside him, Ant reached over onto the nightstand and laid Janelle's picture face down.

Ant got up from the bed and went to the bathroom to take a piss. Carly spread her legs apart and smiled as she stared at her swollen, red pussy. The best thing that had ever happened was Janelle getting kicked out of the house. *In your face, bitch,* Carly thought happily as she rubbed her tender box, loving how sore her pussy always felt after fucking Ant. Luck was fucking shining on her. And to think she and Ant had been running around hiding for a while. Now they could fuck all they wanted, and anywhere they wanted. Shit, they already fucked in every room in the house, including the kids' room. She patted the bed in delight.

"Yes, bitch. I fucked yo' man in yo' king-sized bed," she boasted, thinking about how she and Ant made use of that big-ass bed. Her eyes went to Janelle's picture. It had not escaped her that Ant had pulled it down. It was all the confirmation she needed that she had taken over her sister's life. She flicked her tongue out. *That's the way shit ought to be,* she thought as she rolled over onto her side, turning away from Janelle's picture.

Even though Janelle had not been there physically, she was glad her sister had, in a sense, watched her fucking her man. She giggled at the thought of it. The bitch had called her yesterday to find out how Ant was doing: "I'm sure he gon' crawl back to me. The nigga got to miss my pussy, sis. He got nothing else, only a matter of pride, and his stupid pride gon' fall," Janelle had said. "I'm sure his broke ass ain't doing good. I called to the station to make sure shit was cool for me to come back home, and they talking 'bout Ant called them saying he think I need a few more days to cool off because he wants peace in his home. What type of shit is that?" she added.

Carly had wanted to tell her that her man had never been better. No, their man. She had won in the end, and it was because of her superior pussy. Ah, the power of a pussy over a man could not be ascertained. Ant came out of the toilet, his dick dangling. *And it is all mine,* she thought, licking her lips.

"Come on," Ant whined. "Got to allow this baby to rest or it's gon' fall off. Now we don't want that, do we?" he teased.

Carly laughed as he joined her in the bed. He closed his eyes and soon he was half asleep. She stared at his body and could feel her pussy getting wet again. *When he wakes up, he is going to treat me to a second round.*

Roshon sat in Picasso's bar waiting for Natalie to join him for lunch. After Los's unfortunate incident yesterday, he had to cancel and reschedule their date. Finally, Natalie pulled into the parking lot in a white 2015 Dodge Ram 2500 SLT with big-boy chrome wheels that matched the chrome trimmings around the truck.

"Oh shit, look at the white girl stuntin'." He chuckled under his breath as she jumped down out of the truck. "Damn, shawty fat as fuck though, for a white girl," he added, looking her up and down as she sashayed across the parking lot.

She was rocking the hell out of a pair of Seven jeans and a white V-neck that hugged her upper body. She had a little fat around the edges, but she wore it well. Her large 38D breasts overshadowed her stomach so her little bump could hardly be seen. This was the first time Roshon had seen Natalie outside of corporate attire, and she was even more attractive and thicker than Roshon first thought.

"Glad you made it," Roshon spoke, getting up from his seat when she walked over to the table.

Natalie extended her arms to give him a hug, which Roshon embraced. She smelled so good, and her scent almost gave Roshon a hard-on.

"What you doin' driving that big truck?" Roshon asked, looking at the 2500 through the window.

"That's my baby. I bought that truck the same year it came out. I remember, driving it for the first time, I was hooked." Natalie giggled as she took a seat. "Besides, I love everything big and meaty," she said in a teasing, seductive tone.

Roshon smirked as he gave her the once-over, taking in her voluptuous, curvaceous figure. Natalie was sexy as fuck. She kind of put him in mind of the plus-size model Ashley Graham, only Natalie's hair was blond.

"I hear you, but you know it's a huge difference between handling big white trucks and handling big black trucks?" Roshon smiled, waving for the waitress to come over.

"Well, I love big black trucks and can handle them very well. Hell, I'm looking forward to test driving one real soon. You know of any in particular that you would recommend?" Natalie asked with a large smile. She was enjoying the verbal sparring.

Roshon leaned closer, giving her his sexiest look. "I'm sure I can point you in the right direction. Shit, maybe one day soon I'll have to take you out for a test run. You look like you can drive a stick very well." He licked his lips as he looked her up and down. "I'll tell you one thing: you also look good outside of your work clothes, I must say."

"Yeah, I definitely can drive a stick. Shit, I can drive anything I put my hands on. The question is, can you handle my driving?" She winked.

Natalie seemed to be a totally different person outside of the office. She seemed more relaxed, and she was quick-witted. Not to mention her whole swagger changed up drastically. Roshon was definitely interested in getting to know her outside of the office. For a white girl from Texas, she seemed to be kind of hip.

"I don't mean to change up the convo or to pry, but is everything okay with your son?" Natalie asked, looking across at Roshon. "You don't have to answer if it's none of my business."

"Nah, nah, it's cool. Yeah, my li'l man is okay. His mom never picked him up from school, so that's why I rushed out of the office like that."

"Yeah, I understand how you feel. My kids mean everything to me also," Natalie said, digging in her bag and grabbing a picture of them.

"Oh, you don't be playing. You was trying to have your own b-ball team," Roshon joked seeing three young white children in the photo.

"Yeah, well, I've been told that I'm a natural breeder. It's hard to pull out once you're in," she responded, hoping to get the conversation back to where it was since she now knew everything was okay with Roshon's son.

That comment made Roshon pick his head back up from the picture to look at Natalie. They had a moment, staring into each other's eyes. "Ya husband let you—"

"Ex-husband," Natalie corrected him before Roshon could finish his sentence. Natalie thought that it was necessary to let him know that she was not taken and was on the market in case he had thoughts about shooting his shot at her.

"Ex, huh?" Roshon questioned as the wheels began spinning in his head.

"Yeah. I was married to a lying, cheating bastard for seven years. Even though his ass couldn't keep his dick in his pants, I still tried to make it work. It took him having a threesome with my best friend and her husband to get me to finally say I was done. I've been divorced and single for three years now."

"Damn, shawty, the nigga was batting for the other team?" Roshon inquired with a serious tone in his voice.

Natalie burst out laughing. "No. At least I don't think so. From what I found out, my husband and my best friend had been fucking around for a while, and she used to have threesomes with her husband all the time. She told her husband that she had a fantasy of fucking two men at once, and he thought that it would be hot to watch another man fuck his wife. I don't know the type of freaky shit they were on, but my husband was my best friend's choice. She wanted to have her cake and eat it, too, and in the end, the bitch got what she deserved. It wasn't so hot to watch another man make your bitch squirt when you could barely make her have an orgasm. That shit fucked up his head, and he ended up leaving her."

"Damn, talk about some fucking karma." Roshon chuckled shaking his head.

"I know, right. They say karma is a bitch. I guess that shit's true." She laughed.

Roshon and Natalie spent the rest of the lunch talking and getting to know each other on a more personal level, and after a few more drinks, Natalie really got loose. She was all over Roshon, tonguing him down and feeling on his manhood. She was obviously feeling Roshon, and he was definitely feeling her too.

Los was in the recovery room, finally coming down off the anesthesia. He had slept through the whole surgery and had been back in his room for at least an hour. From what was told to him, he knew the doctor was able to remove the bullet and piece back together as much of his bone as he could, using metal rods to keep it in place. It was almost a guarantee that he would be walking with a limp for the rest of his life.

"Fuckin' bitch," he spoke out, but his voice was hoarse, so his words came out slightly above a whisper.

"Los, you say something? You woke?" a voice asked, getting Los's attention.

He looked over in the direction of the voice. Keera was sitting there with a sad look on her face as if she weren't the reason he was lying there with his leg elevated twenty-five degrees.

"What the fuck you doing here, Keera?" Los asked. "Don't you think you did enough to me, or did you come to finish the job?"

Keera got up and slowly walked over to his bed and took a seat in the open chair. "Los, don't blame this only on me. It's both of our faults. You the one talking shit about our son and disrespecting me in front of everyone like I'm not the mother of your child. This happened because you wouldn't acknowledge ya son," Keera said, reaching into her bag and pulling out another copy of the paternity test. She leaned over and placed the paper on his stomach, but it was not needed. Los had already read the results.

"What do you want from me, Keera?" he asked, knocking the letter off his stomach. "I'm not ready to be a father again. I got three children already, and I can't keep up with the child support payments on them."

"Whose fault is that? You the one wanna run around here busting nuts in bitches then wanna scream, 'I ain't ready to be a father.' Fuck you, Los! I wasn't ready to be a mother either. This shit wasn't planned, but you know what? I took responsibility for mine. I didn't have a fucking choice. Unlike you, I can't just walk away from my son. I can't throw him a way like you. Like it or not, William is here, and he's your son. He needs his daddy just as much as he needs his mother."

Los wasn't sure if it was the drugs or the trauma of him being shot, but Keera was making a lot of sense. Something was very different about her. She was calmer and more relaxed as opposed to her normal loud and ghetto self. He knew what he had said in the barbershop was fucked up, and he knew that somehow, someway, he had to make things right. Keera had some valid points concerning William. He needed to step up and be a man. He needed to make amends with Keera.

"Look, whenever I get out of here, bring William by my house. Me, you, and him are going to sit down and try to make some sense out of all this," Los told Keera.

"Make sense, Los? There's no making sense. William is your son. What else do I need to prove?"

"I didn't mean it like that, Keera. I get it. He's my son. All I'm saying is that we need to sit down and come up with some type of plan. I want to be in his life. I mean, I don't have much to give, but I'm willing to do what I can."

Hearing Los say that he wanted to be in William's life made Keera smile. Through all of her craziness, that's all she'd been asking for. With tears in her eyes, she grabbed Los's hand.

"That's all I wanted from you, Los. It's a shame that I had to go through all this to get you to at least agree to sit down and do something other than fuck me. I just wanted you to talk to me. William is my life, and I'll do anything to make sure he has whatever he needs."

"Even shoot his father?" Los asked sarcastically.

Keera shrugged her shoulder. "If that's what it took for you to even acknowledge him as your son, then shooting you was well worth it in my eyes."

Los shook his head. "You are one crazy bitch." He chuckled.

"Remember that," she stated, looking at him with raised brows. Los snickered then closed his eyes.

"I'ma go and let you get some rest," Keera said before turning to walk away. She opened the door then turned around. "Los," she called out. He turned his head to face her. "Thanks," she added with a huge smile on her face. Los nodded his head, then Keera walked out of the door, leaving Los alone and wondering how in the hell he was gonna take care of another child.

Dorrian drove his truck slowly down the dark, narrow street looking for the address that Arlene had texted him earlier. It had taken him dozens of phone conversations, hundreds of texts, and some FaceTime chats to get her to agree to let him pick her up from her house. It was basically their first date since he had to cancel lunch with her due to the fact that Los got shot.

Although they had spent countless hours on video chat, talking, flirting, and doing minor sexual shit over the phone and laptop, he had not actually taken her out on a real date. It was all virtual, and the shit was driving him crazy. Don't get it wrong. It was cool watching her or hearing the sexy shit she was doing. That shit heightened his anticipation, but it wasn't the type of shit he was used to.

All the females he ever dealt with couldn't keep their damn panties dry around him. They loved being touched by him just as much as they loved being seen with him. It was some type of status thing. Being seen with him was like letting other bitches know he was with them, which in their minds made them high on his list. Dorrian didn't give a fuck what they thought. He let them think whatever they had to think so he could smash. None of them ever realized that they were just occupying space at the time. He might take them out to his club or a fancy restaurant, but at the end of the night he dicked them down and sent their asses on their merry little way.

Arlene was different though. He had never met any other woman like her. The conversations that they had were stimulating both mentally and sexually, and when they talked about going on a date, she said something that he'd never heard in all his years. Arlene told them that she would like to take him out sometimes and that it was okay for a woman to pay sometimes. She said that she could hold her own, and if her man took care of her, then she would take care of him and all his needs. Dorrian was shocked to hear that come out of a woman's mouth. All the women he'd ever fucked with never offered to pay for a damn double cheeseburger at McDonald's, and they were nothing but a damn dollar. Although Dorrian appreciated her kind gesture, he would never let his woman pay for shit, even if she could hold her own.

Tonight was the first time she agreed to meet him outside of a video chat, and even though he was going over to her house for a little Netflix and chill, Dorrian was eager to see her and find out where tonight would lead them. For most people, "Netflix and chill" was code for tearing up the bedsheets. With Arlene, he had a feeling that she really meant for them to watch Netflix and relax. He was hoping that tonight would be more than sitting on the couch, watching *Luke*

Cage, and having a conversation, but Dorrian was cool either way. He really enjoyed conversing with Arlene.

Dorrian turned on his high beams to make sure he was pulling into the proper driveway. The street wasn't very well lit, and only a few of the homes had numbers on the outside.

"A'ight, here we go: 5220-B," Dorrian mumbled to himself.

He reached into the center console and pulled out his travel-size bottle of Gucci Guilty Platinum cologne and sprayed each side of his neck. He checked his beard and decided to grab his beard brush and beard balm. Women loved beards but if your beard was rough that shit could be a turn-off. He rubbed a little of the citrus-scented balm in his hands and rubbed it into his beard. After a few strokes of the brush, his shit was silky and soft. He checked his teeth and breath again to make sure they were still clean and fresh. Although they were, just for good measure he popped an Altoid in his mouth. *Arlene is a hygienist, so your teeth and breath have to be on one hundred,* he thought as he stepped out of the car and checked his reflection one last time in the window of his truck. Since it was a casual night, he opted for dark denim jeans, a black Todd Snyder shirt with a matching baseball cap, and dark blue Nike shoes.

Dorrian was feeling a little nervous as he walked down the sidewalk to the door of her home. He wasn't sure why he felt so nervous. It wasn't like he had never chilled with a woman before. Standing at her door, he inhaled and exhaled a calming breath. His stomach was tight, and his mouth had become dry. He took a few steps back to try to get his shit together.

"Yo, playboy, what the hell wrong wit' you? Shit, you acting like a little nigga going to a shawty's house for his first piece of pussy," he mumbled to himself.

He ran his hand down his beard like he always did when he was nervous, and took another calming breath then rang the doorbell. Dorrian put his hands in his pockets and played with his keys as he waited for Arlene to answer. He could hear the sound of footsteps approaching the door, and his nerves started to increase. The clicking of the locks sent his nervous feelings into overdrive.

"Nigga, get yo' shit together," Dorrian coached himself under his breath.

The door opened, and Arlene was standing there smiling at him wearing a black cotton top that rested above her naval, and dark skinny jeans with black Nike socks.

"Really? Were you watching me through the window or something? Let me find out you were stalking me," Arlene joked, scanning Dorrian's outfit, noticing that they were matching.

Dorrian chuckled. "Nah, not this time, and you would have known if I was staring in your window 'cause a nigga would have been trying to break the shit down trying to see that body getting dressed."

"I don't know whether to be scared or flattered." She laughed as she stepped to the side. "Come on in," she said, motioning for him to come in the house.

Dorrian felt a little more relaxed. Arlene was just as sweet in person as she was over the phone and video chat. "No need to ever be scared of me, ma. I promise you that always," Dorrian said as he stepped in the house with a goofy-ass grin on his face. "I think our selection of clothing just means that we on the same wavelength," he added, giving Arlene the once-over.

"Is that right?" Arlene said as she closed the door and began locking the deadbolts.

"I can't be sure unless I see if our underclothes match as well," Dorrian said mockingly, pulling at his waistband.

"Boy, you are something else," Arlene said, laughing, walking around him. He noticed the dragon tattoo that started at the lower part of her back and wrapped around her waist. His mouth watered as he thought about where the head of that dragon led. The low-rise jeans she had on accented her high ass and tight abs.

"Well, you coming or not?" Arlene asked, extending her hand to him. Her home was spotless and smelled of citrus and lavender. Dorrian was impressed.

Dorrian took her hand, and they walked around the corner to a large room with a soft gray sectional with yellow pillows, and a large flat screen on the wall.

"So, what would you like to drink?" Arlene asked as Dorrian sat down.

"Whatever you drinking," Dorrian said.

"All right. Well, you find something for us to watch," Arlene said as she threw the remote to him. "Do me one more favor and take your shoes off for me, please." Dorrian nodded and pulled off his shoes and placed them beside the couch. Arlene returned with pretzels, popcorn, two glasses of ice, a bottle of blackberry Bai, and a can of strawberry seltzer water.

"Is that what you're drinking?" Dorrian asked, laughing.

"Yep. Why? You want something else? I'm not really big on alcohol, but I do have some

Guinness in the fridge that I keep for people who do drink. Would you like one?" she offered.

Dorrian felt a twinge in his side at the mention of people visiting her. He wondered if "people" meant other niggas. Even though they weren't technically in a relationship, Dorrian already claimed her, and that meant that she was off-limits to other men.

"Nah, this good for now. I don't want you trying to take advantage of me or nothing like that. You scientific types know how to mix shit to knock a nigga out," he joked, and Arlene burst out laughing.

Dorrian loved the sound of her laughter and the way the dimples deepened in her cheeks when she laughed. He couldn't help but laugh himself. Finally, she had stopped laughing long enough to respond to him.

"I will try to restrain myself," Arlene said as she placed the tray on the coffee table.

"I mean, if you behave yo'self, I might give you a taste of this cinnamon brown sugar," he continued, making Arlene shake her head.

"You are a mess." She chuckled as she grabbed a couple of the large pillows from the couch and placed them on the floor. "I hope you don't mind. I'm more comfortable sitting on the floor, but if you prefer the couch, I can—" she started, but was cut off by Dorrian sliding down onto the floor beside her.

"The floor is good," he said as they locked eyes and stared at each other in silence.

Dorrian moved a lock away from her face and gently traced her jawline with his index finger. Arlene closed her eyes, and her lips parted.

"You're so beautiful," he complimented her as he pulled her face to his and kissed her passionately. Arlene's tongue was soft and felt like velvet in his mouth, and as their tongues intertwined, he could feel himself starting to brick up. Suddenly, Arlene pulled back and cleared her throat.

"Whoa, well, let's see what we can watch. Did you find something?" she questioned, trying not to sound flustered.

Dorrian pulled her up into his arms. "Yeah, but what I want to watch ain't on that screen," he said as he planted a moist kiss on her shoulder, causing her body to tremble a little.

Dorrian knew that she was feeling the passion that was burning between the two of them. Arlene gently pulled away from him and took the remote from his hand.

"You are something else, sir." She shook her head then kissed his cheek. "I think we can watch *Queen Sugar* or *Greenleaf*. I hear they're pretty good shows," Arlene stated.

Dorrian chuckled out of frustration. He knew that Arlene wasn't ready to go all the way with him just yet, and his mind told him to stop, but the beast in his pants told him to keep trying his hand. He was slowly wearing her down, and he knew that. However, Dorrian chose to ignore the beast and let things happen naturally.

"Yeah, let's check out that *Greenleaf,* but do you mind if I use your bathroom real quick?"

Arlene felt a little relief in having him separate from her for a moment. The urge to crawl into his lap and rock her way to ecstasy was burning between her thighs, and she was dying to see what Dorrian was working with.

"Umm, yeah, it is the first door on your left," she answered as she scrolled through the list of TV shows.

Dorrian stood, and with his hands in his pockets, tried to hide the fact that his dick was hard as he made his way to the bathroom. He reached the bathroom and was relieved that Arlene hadn't noticed the bulge in his pants. "Damn, nigga," he whispered to himself as he walked over to the sink and ran the cold water.

He splashed the cold water on his face and stared at himself in the mirror. This woman was making him do shit that he had never done before: chase and wait. That just wasn't his style. Any other female would have seen him leaving out the door if they tried this shit with him, but he knew that Arlene wasn't playing games with him. She genuinely was a woman of class, and he wanted to make this work with her. This was new territory for him, but he knew it was going to be worth it in the end. Shit, the way she had him feeling, she was going to be the last stop for him.

He wiped the water off his face with a paper towel, then walked over to the door. He took a few deep breaths, praying that he could keep it together so that Arlene wouldn't think that he was just out to make her another notch on his belt. Feeling confident that he could fight off his urges, he opened the door and walked up the hall and back into the living room.

"A'ight, fix me that nasty drink, and let's watch this *Greenleaf,*" Dorrian said as he entered the living room.

Arlene motioned for him to sit down beside her. He wrapped his arms around her, as she placed her head on his shoulder. For the time, the world felt right to Dorrian, and he wanted to make sure he could make it stay that way.

"You know I can't let you drive like this," Roshon told Natalie when they stepped out of the bar.

"Shhh, please. I ain't that drunk," Natalie shot back.

"Oh yeah? Well let me give you a sobriety test then," Roshon said playfully. "If you fail, you gotta ride around with me all night until you sober up," he proposed.

"Deal!" Natalie eagerly replied, placing her bag on the hood of a parked car in front of the restaurant. "Don't be cheating either."

Roshon laughed, taking eight steps backward, then lined himself up with a long, straight crack in the sidewalk. He gave her commands to stand on one leg, repeat the alphabet, and to touch the tip of her nose with her index finger. She ran through every test, passing them with flying colors.

"Now, I want you to walk this line all the way up to me," Roshon said, pointing at the long crack.

Natalie was cracking up in laughter thinking about how silly she looked.

"Come on, stop laughing. Are you ready?" Roshon asked.

Natalie stood up straight, muffled her laughs, then began to walk the line like it was a tightrope. She playfully leaned side to side as though she were about to fall off, but she straightened back up once she got closer to Roshon. As she looked directly into his eyes for the last few steps, Natalie walked up to Roshon, slowly wrapped her arms around his waist, got on her tiptoes, and kissed him. Her lips pressed softly up against his, and automatically, Roshon kissed her back.

They stood there tonguing each other like they were two lovers standing under the Eiffel Tower on a clear, dark night when the stars were shining. They didn't care who was watching them. Finally, Roshon pulled away from her, feeling his dick beginning to get hard. He looked at her, licked his lips, and smiled.

"You're definitely drunk right now, and if you not, I am," he joked.

They both broke out into laughter. What they shared today was something that the both of them needed and hadn't had in a very long time. It was companionship and the ability to do some of the simplest things like talk, laugh, joke, and just be out. It was like a friendship all the way up until Natalie kissed him, and now Roshon didn't know where it was headed. The one thing he was sure of was that he was feeling the fuck out of Natalie.

They kissed again for a while, and when they let go of each other, they stared into each other's eyes and laughed.

"Come on, let me drive you home," Roshon said. "Where are your keys?" he asked.

She turned around and patted the pocket on her ass. "Come on, don't be shy. Bring it out for me," Natalie said.

He shoved back the groan in his mouth and slipped his hands into her back pocket. All he could think about was how she had a nice ass, and how hard it was for him not to bend her ass over right there in her truck. It didn't help that she wiggled her ass around as he removed the keys from her pocket. Roshon could feel his dick starting to rise again. He knew he had to get her home before he did something stupid. The last thing he wanted was for her to wake up the next morning and regret what they had done. He led her to his car and helped her into the passenger seat.

"Where's your apartment?" he asked.

She mumbled the address then shut her eyes. In a few seconds, she was sound asleep. He checked her purse and got her ID, and was able to locate her home. As he got her out of the car, an elderly woman came up to him.

"Is that Natalie?" she asked, looking at him suspiciously.

"Yeah, we went for a drink together, and she got a little tipsy," he said. He was now glad they hadn't done anything sexually already. He was a black man, with a drunk white woman, in Charlotte, North Carolina.

"It happens," he heard her mutter. She waved her hand. "Don't worry, I can take it from here," she spoke as they reached the front door of Natalie's apartment.

"Good night," the woman uttered as she was shutting the door, letting Roshon know there was no need for him to come in. Although pissed at Natalie's neighbor's behavior, he let it slide. He just hoped she made sure Natalie was put to bed.

As he drove home, he could not help but laugh. He had had a nice time with Natalie, even though the night had ended quicker than he hoped. He had seen her in a new light. He had never fooled around with any of the women in the office, but he was beginning to consider it if Natalie was up for it. He just hoped that she did not come with any drama, because that was the last thing he needed. Brandi was giving him enough hell as it was.

Thinking of Brandi made him think of the call she had made to him. He knew she had not gone to her folks' house to get the kids. *Where the hell is she this time around?*

***

Dorrian and Arlene were watching their third episode of the *Greenleaf* series. Dorrian hated to admit that he was kind of getting caught up in the story line.

"See, this is the reason I don't be going to them big-ass churches. They want them coins just like everybody else and ain't about to pay no damn taxes. One of my boys got a megachurch, a wife, a mistress, a mansion, and all of these fools paying for it."

"So, are you saying you don't have faith?" Arlene asked as she caressed Dorrian's hand, which rested on her waist.

"Naw, I didn't say that. I said that is why I stay away from those churches. I got my faith, believe me. I ain't that stupid. Something be out here looking out for a brotha."

"Okay, I was just making sure," Arlene stated, looking at him out of the corner of her eye; then she burst into laughter.

"What's so funny?" Dorrian asked with confusion covering his face.

Arlene shrugged her shoulders. "I don't know." She chuckled.

Dorrian playfully nudged her. "Let me find out you goofy." He shook his head. "Unless it's something else?" he added.

"What?" Arlene asked in a high-pitched voice.

Dorrian moved closer to her. "I make you feel some type of way. You know, like, you like me. I see how you be blushing and shit. It's cool, ma. You make me feel things too," he stated in a serious tone as he gazed deeply in her eyes.

Arlene twirled one of her locks between her fingers as she held her head down. A sudden rush of sadness washed over her, and she started feeling a little uneasy. It had been over a year since she'd been with a man. Her ex-boyfriend, Tornado, was just as his name promised: a fucking disaster. He hurt her in ways that she could have never imagined.

Dorrian noticed the somber mood that Arlene was in, and thought that maybe he'd overstepped his boundaries. "Arlene, if I said anything to offend you, I'm sorry," he apologized as he took her hand in his.

She looked up at him with tear-filled eyes and shook her head. "You did nothing wrong. That's the problem, Dorrian. You've been nothing but respectful to me. To answer your question, yes, you make me feel things, and I do like you. It's just . . . it's just that I'm not sure if I can be the girl you want me to be."

"And what type of girl is that?" Dorrian asked, looking at her as if she had lost her mind. In his eyes, Arlene was exactly what he wanted in a woman. How could she not see that?

"Perfect. And that's something I can't be."

Dorrian saw the sadness in her eyes and immediately felt her pain. He didn't know what the cause of her pain was, but he wanted to be the one to take it all away.

"Nobody's perfect. Hell, I'm not perfect. Truth be told, I did some fucked-up shit to people who didn't deserve it, but that don't make me a fucked-up-ass nigga. Whatever you did or went through in life shaped you into the person you are, and to me, that person is perfect."

A smile grew on Arlene's face. It seemed as if Dorrian always knew what to say to put a smile on her face. She liked the fact that, even though Dorrian was very attractive and successful, he wasn't arrogant at all, and he'd been nothing but the perfect gentleman all night.

"You hungry?" she asked, trying to lighten up the mood.

Dorrian flashed her a half smile as he nodded his head. "I can eat," he replied.

Arlene reached in the drawer on the table next to the couch and pulled out two menus. "Chinese or Caribbean?" she questioned, holding up the menus.

Dorrian took the menus out of her hands and placed them on the table; then he pulled her into his arms. “You. I’d rather have you for dinner,” he stated seductively as he stroked the side of her cheek then kissed her passionately.

Wrapping one of his arms around her small, curvy frame, Dorrian held her tightly as he used his other hand to caress her body. Arlene threw her arms around his neck and pulled him deeper into the kiss. As their passion grew to a hunger, Arlene could feel Dorrian’s massive erection poking through his pants. Feeling his body next to hers caused her nipples to become erect, and her clit started throbbing. It had been about eighteen months since she’d been this close to any man, and her body was starting to betray her. She climbed on top of him, straddling him, as their tongues continued dancing around in each other’s mouths. The moistness between her thighs rubbed up against his growing erection, and Dorrian could feel the heat. Running his hand up her back and grabbing the back of her neck, he gently messaged her neck, then began sucking and gently biting her neck, as she started rolling her hips and pushing farther into his lap.

“Baby, I want you,” Dorrian whispered into her ear as he licked and sucked on the lower part of her earlobe.

"Mmm, I want you too," she moaned as he slid his hands up her shirt and started massaging her breasts.

"You sure you want this?" he questioned, looking into her eyes as he stroked his thumb across her erect nipples.

Arlene looked at him with lust-filled eyes, and her bottom lip sucked into her mouth. She didn't utter a word, but her eyes were saying, "I want you to fuck the shit outta me."

"If I ask you to be gentle and make love to me tonight, would you?" she questioned in a low voice.

Dorrian gave her a lingering kiss. "Yeah," he answered as he sucked her tongue into his mouth.

"What if I ask you to fuck me hard as if it were our last night on this earth?" she asked in between kisses.

That question caught Dorrian off guard. He wasn't sure if it was her words or her tone, but that shit sounded like heaven coming from her lips.

"Baby, I'll fuck you however you want," he admitted, lifting her shirt over her head.

He cupped her breasts in his hands then sucked on her nipples. Arlene threw her head back and let out a soft moan. Dorrian unbuttoned her jeans and slid his hand down her pants and started fingering her wet pussy.

“Dorrian,” she called out as her heart began pounding in her chest. Dorrian lifted her up and placed her on the couch, then slid her body forward, as he snatched down her pants and panties in one motion. She spread her legs wide as she could to allow him a perfect view of her nicely shaved honey pot.

Dorrian got up on his knees and kissed her right inner thigh, then her inner left. Arlene felt chills through her body. Dorrian used his fingers to spread her pussy lips, then he devoured her pussy, licking, sucking, biting, and kissing until her body started convulsing.

“Shit, Dorrian, I’m about to . . .” Before she could say the word, she exploded into his mouth, and Dorrian lapped up every bit of her sweet juices.

“Damn, baby, you must have been eating a ton of pineapples,” he said, licking the remainder of her cum from his lips.

“I love pineapples,” she replied, pulling his head in for a kiss, tasting her own juices off his lips. Lifting Arlene’s hips and pushing her legs back as far as they could go, stroking his dick up and down her wetness then the entrance to her hole, he teased her as her pussy started to get wet all over again. The more he teased her, the wetter she became. Dorrian dipped the tip of his dick into her warm, moist center.

"Come on, stop teasing me," Arlene whined as she reached her hand on top of his and directed his stiff member deeper inside of her.

Dorrian bit down on his bottom lip, as he thrust in and out of her slowly, her pussy feeling like a glove around his shaft. Closing her eyes tightly, Arlene loudly moaned. Continuing his stroke, he gripped her thighs, pushing her legs back farther into the back of the sofa, and he plowed deeper inside her.

"Oh shit," he hissed, loving the way her inner walls tightened with each stroke, driving him crazy. He had to take his mind somewhere else so he wouldn't bust prematurely and look like a minute man, but her pussy had him hypnotized and was like nothing he'd ever felt before. It felt like it was a perfect fit for him.

Arlene started rolling her hips and moving up and down, matching Dorrian's rhythm. "Damn, baby, you're so fucking good!" she groaned, digging her nails into his arms.

"Shit," was all Dorrian could say as he grabbed the back of the couch for leverage and rose to his feet.

Damn near squatting, Dorrian lifted Arlene's hips in the air and started drilling in her like he was digging for diamonds.

"Ahhh, ahhh, ahhh." Arlene panted aloud as if she wanted to scream.

Her body stiffened and started trembling. Dorrian knew she was about to cum, so he wrapped one arm around her waist to hold her in place while he switched up his stroke. Lifting her up off the couch a little more, he thrust in her quick and fast.

"Oh fuck," he grunted as his body let him know that he was about to cum too. After a few more strokes, Arlene screamed, latching on to him, as he thrust one hard stroke, and they both climaxed at the same time.

Dorrian had never climaxed with a woman at the same time, and it was an indescribable feeling. He wiped the sweat from Arlene's forehead as he gazed deeply in her eyes. He knew in that moment that this girl was gonna change his life.

Roshon smiled to himself as he sat at the red light, thinking about the kiss that he and Natalie had shared. The way her tongue massaged the inside of his mouth almost made him bend her ass over and make her pay for teasing him. The loud honking of a horn behind him caught his attention, bringing him out of his thoughts. He didn't realize that the light had turned green. He waved his hand in the rearview mirror to signal the driver to let him know that he apologized.

As he drove down the street, his phone started to ringing. He looked at the screen, and Mrs. Covington's name appeared on the display. Tonight was a good night for him, and he really wasn't in the mood to be bothered with any of Brandi's drama. Letting the call go to voicemail, he tuned his radio to 92.7 and cranked up the volume.

No sooner than he started to feel the music, bobbing his head and reciting the lyrics, his phone rang again. He shook his head and rejected the call. A few minutes later, his phone pinged, alerting him that he had a text message. He picked up his phone and opened the text. It read: Answer your phone!

The text was in all caps meaning that it was either something important, or Brandi was acting a damn fool. Either way, he wasn't interested in Brandi's bullshit. He continued down the street, listening to the music, trying to get his ass home. Again, his phone rang again. This time it was Brandi's cousin Jarvis's number.

"What the hell?" Roshon mumbled to himself before answering. "Yeah?"

"Hey, man, this Jarvis. Auntie been trying to get a hold of you. We need you to come to the house ASAP." Jarvis's voice quivered, and Roshon could hear Mrs. Covington sobbing in the background.

Roshon became alarmed. "Yo, Jarvis, what's going on? What's up with Mrs. Covington? Why she crying? What Brandi do now?" Roshon was firing off question after question before Jarvis could answer.

"Yo, man, Brandi's dead," Jarvis blurted out. Roshon stopped abruptly, causing the large SUV behind him to run up on the curve to avoid hitting him.

"What you say?" Roshon asked.

"Hey, man, what the fuck wrong wit' you!" the driver from the SUV yelled as he pulled around Roshon.

"Man, Brandi's dead," Jarvis repeated. "Yo, Shon, just come to the house, please," Jarvis said, this time with a tinge of annoyance and anger in his voice.

The air in the car became thin, and Roshon found it hard to breathe. For a brief moment, he wasn't even sure where he was.

"Roshon? Roshon, man, you still there?" Jarvis yelled.

"I'm here," he answered, still trying to process what Jarvis had just said. "Did you say that Brandi was dead?" he asked for clarity.

"Yeah, man. The police are here, and we really need you to stop through, Shon. Auntie's straight losing it, man," Jarvis said.

Roshon's heart dropped to his feet. As much drama as Brandi caused him, he never wanted to see any harm come to her. That shit was fucking with his mental. The first thought that came to mind was Roshon Jr. How was he gonna tell his son that his mother was dead, and how in the hell was he going take it?

Letting out a sigh, Roshon responded to Jarvis. "I'm on my way," was all he said before he ended the call and pulled back onto the road.

Mrs. Covington's house was only fifteen minutes from where he was, but time seemed to slow down with each stoplight. They had to be mistaken. Brandi wasn't dead. She was just out on one of her tangents. The girl was annoying as fuck, flighty as hell, but dead? No. She was too crazy to be dead. She couldn't be dead. She had her other kids and their son to think about. All of these thoughts were jumbled, scattering through Roshon's mind. His stomach tightened, and his head began to pound. He was hurt, angry, and confused all at once, and he began to feel numb.

Roshon turned down Gallagher Drive. The tree-lined street with its modest homes looked like it came from one of the stories from the Investigation Discovery channel. People were standing in their well-manicured yards, staring down at house number 15502. Three police cars were in the driveway along with several other cars. Roshon parked behind a blue Dodge Charger on the street. He opened the door and felt a wave of nausea overcome him. His mouth began to water as he inhaled through his nose and sat back in the seat for a moment.

"Fuck, get it together," he mumbled to himself. After a few moments, the sick feeling he was experiencing passed. He stepped out of the car and began walking up the driveway. As he approached the door, Jarvis appeared from the side of the house.

"Hey, man," Jarvis said as he wiped the sweat from his face with the back of his hand. "Glad you here. Shit, Auntie and Unc to' up fo' sho. I just called Mama, so the rest of the family should be here in a minute, too."

Roshon shook his head and opened the glass door. His breathing became labored as he glanced around, seeing pictures on the wall of Brandi as a child and some in her adult years. *This has to be a dream. It has to be.* As he walked farther into the house, he could feel eyes on him. Mr. Covington sat stone-faced on the couch, staring off into space.

"Yeah, they had to give Aunt E something to calm down. Man, this is—"

"I know, man, I know," Roshon replied shaking his head.

A female detective walked over to Jarvis and Roshon. "Excuse me, uh, Jarvis. The medic said that your aunt needs to rest, so is it all right if I ask you some questions?"

"Yeah. She's not going to be able to help you with anything in that kind of state," Jarvis said, rubbing his forehead. "This is Roshon. He is Brandi's oldest son's father. This is Detective Adams."

"Roshon?"

"White. Roshon White."

"Mr. White, when was the last time you spoke with Ms. Covington?"

"She called me a couple of days ago," Roshon said as he sat down on a white chair.

"Can you be more specific?" Detective Adams asked with a tone that made Roshon look her up and down.

"It was a couple of days ago, like I said. She called asking me to pick her up, and I told her I was busy. A friend of mine was in the hospital."

"How did she sound?"

Roshon exhaled and stood. "She sounded like she was drinking or something. She asked me to come pick her up." Roshon could feel the detective's and Jarvis's eyes on him.

"Why didn't you pick her up?" the detective asked, eyeing Roshon suspiciously.

"As I mentioned, a friend of mine had been hurt, and I was at the hospital. Brandi was just always being dramatic. I told her to call her mother and to pick her kids up. If I had known she was really in danger, I would have gone to pick her up, but I just wasn't in the mood for her mess that day."

"Well, Mr. White, if you had been in the mood, she might be alive," Detective Adams said, taking a closer step to Roshon.

"Now wait a minute, Detective, that is fucked up," Jarvis said. He didn't really have any use for the police, and this bitch was straight out of fucking line. He knew Roshon, and he knew his cousin. Roshon was a good dude, and although he loved his cousin, she was always doing stupid shit. Hell, if she had called him, he probably would have cussed her ass out.

"See, this the kind of shit that make people handle their own business instead of involving y'all stupid asses. I bet if we were white, you wouldn't have said no shit like that!"

Roshon touched Jarvis's shoulder. The last thing they needed was for him to go to jail.

A tall, slim man walked over. He wore a dark navy suit with a light blue shirt. "Everything all right?"

"Nah, everything ain't all right. Your partner here is being really disrespectful. You best check her ass," Jarvis said, not dropping his eyes from Detective Adams, who now stood in an offensive position.

"Hey, Adams, why don't you head on over to the scene? I can handle the rest from here."

Detective Adams smirked at Jarvis. Roshon looked at her stone-faced. His lack of response made her even more suspicious of him.

"Adams," Detective Marshall said with a little more bass in his voice.

"Yeah, I'm going. I'll take Dover with me."

"Man, what's her fucking problem?" Jarvis asked as he walked back out to the porch. Roshon and Marshall followed him. He took out a Newport. "She over here accusing motherfuckers of shit when she need to be finding out who did this to my damn cousin."

"What did she say?" Marshall asked Roshon, handing Jarvis a lighter.

"She asked me when was the last time I talked to Brandi. I told her a few days ago when she asked me to pick her up, and I refused. I told her to call her mother, and to pick up her kids. Thinking back now, she wasn't drinking. Maybe she was scared. But you got to understand that Brandi was always full of drama, and I just thought it was another one of her episodes. One of my boys was in the hospital, and I just didn't have time for her nonsense." Roshon's heart was aching as he thought back to how she sounded on the phone.

What he once thought from the sound of her voice was her in an inebriated state, he now realized was fear, and she had reached out to him for help. He had let her down in the worst way, and now he was going to have to tell his son that his mother was gone. Despite how she behaved, RJ loved his mother, and like any good son, he was very protective of her.

That was one of the main reasons he wanted custody of RJ. He felt like RJ wasn't being a child. Brandi leaned on the boy almost like a woman would lean on a dude. He was young, but he knew how to wash clothes, cook dinner, put his siblings to sleep, and at times, console his mother. Roshon had to get him out of that situation. He was a child, and he had seen too many women like Brandi raise boys who became resentful at having to grow up too fast.

Childhood is short. Hell, RJ had the rest of his life to be an adult. He wanted to make sure that he had the chance to enjoy being a fucking kid.

"So, what do you guys know?" Roshon asked, leaning against the column of the porch.

"We got a call from a bicyclist about seeing a large, ripped duffle bag on the side of the road. He stopped to look at it because he said he could smell a foul odor coming from it. He opened it up and saw her inside. She had to be there at least two or three days. We ran her prints, and that is how we identified her. So, when she called you, what exactly did she say?"

Before Roshon could answer, the front door of the house opened. Mrs. Covington walked out. Her hair was pulled back in a bun at the nape of her neck. She looked at Roshon, and tears began to flow down her cheeks.

"They killed her. They killed my baby, Shon. Lord, help me, please!"

Roshon rushed over to her and caught her before she fell to her knees. He guided her over to the wicker couch.

"Come on, Auntie, you should be resting," Jarvis said, kneeling down beside her.

No amount of drugs or sleep was going to take this pain away. "Lord, my baby. They killed her and threw her away on the side of the road like she was trash. Like trash, Shon!"

Roshon held her close to him. He wanted to absorb the pain she was feeling as she sobbed. He felt his soul break as Mrs. Covington cried out for her baby girl. He thought of the love he had for RJ and how his world would implode if something happened to him. The thought of losing a child was something that he knew he would not be able to bear.

"She was my baby, Shon, mine. Nobody had no right taking her from me. I just wanted her to come home, just come home and be with me and her babies. She wasn't trash, Shon. My baby wasn't trash!"

Mr. Covington appeared at the door. He seemed to have aged ten years. "Evie, come on inside and lie down. Come on now," Mr. Covington said gently as he put his arms around her waist.

"I don't want to lie down! I want my baby. I want my baby!"

"I know, honey, I know. Me too. But we are going to find out what happened. I can't lose you too, so please come back inside with me." Mr. Covington kissed her forehead. She put her arms around his shoulders and stood.

"Shon, you know my baby wasn't trash," Mrs. Covington said again. "She was loved, she was smart, and she was a little broken. We all are a little broken. Some of our cracks just go a little deeper is all," she mumbled as Mr. Covington led her to the door.

The door opened, and Brandi's little girl stepped out. The little girl's large brown eyes felt like two heat rays hitting Roshon's heart. Roshon looked down at her little face. In that moment, he realized how much she looked like Brandi.

"Hey. Come on, little mama, you hungry? Let me fix you something to eat," Jarvis said as he picked up the child.

Roshon buried his face in his hands. His mind was reeling him in to believe that Brandi would some staggering up the driveway, high and drunk. The sad part was he would give anything right now to see her even in that state. At least that way he could be pissed off but would not feel the aching in his chest that he now felt.

"So, what was your relationship to the victim?" Detective Marshall asked.

"I'm the father to her oldest child, RJ. Fuck! What am I going to tell him?"

"I know this is hard on y'all right now, but I do need someone to come down and identify the body," Marshall said, studying Roshon's body language. Roshon shook his head.

"Yeah, just let me call the nanny and let her know I'm going to be late." Roshon's legs felt like they had fifteen-pound weights on his ankles as he walked down the long driveway. As he reached his car, his stomach cramped, and he vomited on the sidewalk.

Marshall watched from the porch. He had been a detective for going on ten years, and one thing he trusted was his gut. The type of reaction Roshon displayed was not one of a person who was guilty, but one of someone who was hurting and in pain. This wasn't his guy, but he was going to question him just to be 100 percent sure.

Chapter 7

Sunday was the crew's catch-up day. The guys always met up at the Cracker Barrel at Concord Mills. Today, Los was sitting outside in one of the white rockers when Ant walked up wearing a black Adidas warm-up suit with the matching white Adidas sneakers.

"What up, boy? Shit, how that leg doing, man? You supposed to be out walking around?" Ant asked, bumping fists with Los.

"Shit, I'm good. Had to get away from Keera's crazy ass. She been at my spot since she shot me. I had Moe drive me up here," Los said, standing. The truth was he was supposed to be home with his leg elevated, but he needed to get the fuck out of the house. He had told the police he didn't want to press charges against the crazy bitch, and now she and the baby were always at his place.

"You got it, dawg?" Ant asked as he watched Los struggle with his crutches.

"I'm good, man."

"Where everybody else at?" Ant asked, opening the door.

"Well, I spoke with Doe yesterday. He stayed over ol' girl's house last night, so you know he going to be late since he been eating pussy all night. I ain't heard from Shon. I been calling him. Man, they will show up. I'm hungry as hell! Need me some of them pancakes and bacon, baby!"

The men walked inside, and the short hostess with the huge tits walked them to their table. Ant winked at her as she handed them their menus.

"Your server will be with y'all in a moment," she said, smiling at Ant. He noticed she put a little extra switch in her ass when she walked away.

"She look back, brah?" Los asked as he looked at the menu.

"You know she did," Ant said, licking his lips. "Doe's ass been missing a lot lately. I ain't ever known a bitch to have his nose this fucking open, man. Shit, you could drive a damn semi through his nose it is so open right now!" Both the men laughed.

"Fo' sho, nigga. Ol' girl got his ass twisted up. Shit, it is too much pussy out here to be getting caught up in one. Speaking of getting caught up, what up with you and old girl? Doe said you was with his little cousin Janelle, the one with the fat ass. How you mess up live-in ass, man? Shit, you got cooking, cleaning, and on-demand pussy."

"Man, I know that's Doe cousin, but she's a piece of wet paper when it comes to fucking. I can't believe I made it as long as I did with her boring-ass sex game."

"Nigga, she sexy as hell, and that damn body is dangerous!" Los said as the server walked up. The men placed their drink orders and ordered their food. "Man, it was that bad?"

"Nigga, I been locked up, and the first night I was just grateful to get my dick wet. The second time, I was like, what the fuck is this shit? All this ass and you don't know how to move? Then you got all this mouth and shit, but you can't give a nigga some good head."

"Damn, man," Los said, shaking his head. "That is a fucking waste." The waitress placed their drinks on the table.

"Man, she only knew two positions: on her side and missionary. She couldn't ride a dick to save her life. Most of the time, I had to think about other bitches to get my shit off. I even had this little Dominican chick who wanted to join us, but her ass wasn't feeling that shit. Talking about she wasn't sharing her dick."

"Damn, I would have never thought that 'bout shawty. I just hate you got up outta there before I could ask you to plug me in with her sister Carly. Now I know she a go-getter, because this nigga who hair I used to cut was fucking her at one time, and the dude swear that was some of the best pussy he ever had."

"Well, on that, my nigga, I gots to say two things: one, I wasn't going to be plugging you in on shit, and two, your boy wasn't lying. That pussy is that snapper."

"What! You been fucking Carly?"

"Hell yeah, I was fucking both of them at the same time, in the same house, just not together. Shit, if I could have had them together, a nigga might have stayed." Ant and Los both burst out laughing and gave each other a high five.

"Damn, I should have known your no-good ass was busting down both of them hoes. Ass broke as shit, but slinging dick to cop a place to lay yo' head. I ain't mad at you," Los commented.

"Damn, Los, you stay trying to come for a nigga. You see I'm trying. I haven't said a word about your Down syndrome–ass kid you been lying on and denying," Ant retorted, and Los tossed his hands up in surrender.

"Nigga, so how the fuck you gon' pull that shit off? Where you squatting at, fool?" Los asked.

"Nigga, I found another sponsor, and that's all the fuck you need to know," Ant replied with a laugh.

Ant had actually convinced Pam of the lies that he told himself. She agreed to let him stay with her, bill free, until he saved enough money to get his own place. She was just as gone over the sex as Carly was.

"So on some real shit, was it worth it? You know damn well Dorrian gon' flip the fuck out if he find out you been smashing both of them."

"Fo' sho it was worth it, and he ain't gon' find out cause yo' ass ain't gon' say shit," Ant said.

His phone buzzed in his pocket. Carly's face flashed on the screen, and he hit ignore and sipped his tea.

Roshon entered the restaurant. He'd made it home to check on RJ, but he hadn't told him about his mother. He sat up all night thinking about Brandi's phone call to him. He was going to head down to the police station later today. He was too tired to do it yesterday. He saw Los and Ant sitting at the table, shooting the shit, and he walked up toward them.

"Damn, nigga!" Los said, looking at Roshon's red eyes. "What the fuck? Snow bunny tore that ass up or something? You look like shit."

"Damn, dog. I told you them white girls got that crazy drive and head game."

"Y'all niggas are so fucking disrespectful," Roshon said as he sat down. Los could see that Roshon was genuinely fucked up. His clothes looked like he had slept in them, and the bags under his eyes were not from banging a chick all night.

"Yo, dawg, what up, man?" Los asked.

"Yo, man, they found Brandi on the side of the road, dead in a bag, man."

"What! Yo, dead?" Ant said, nearly dropping his glass.

Los looked at Ant, and then back at Roshon. "What you mean, man, they found her in a bag? What the fuck?"

"Jarvis called me yesterday evening. I went to the house, and her mother was broken, man. I don't have all the details. I was supposed to go down to the station, but shit, I just went home, man. I had to hold my son. I called them and told them I would be down there this afternoon."

"Shit, they looking at you, man?" Ant barked. He had been in the system, and going into an interview room with motherfucking pigs always ended with him not walking out the same day.

"Shit, all I know is that the female detective didn't pull no punches. She fucking flat-out accused my ass of killing Brandi. I had to hold Jarvis back off her ass."

"Yo, ain't nothing worse than having a bitch cop on your ass. Them bitches mad 'cause they always feeling like they got something to fucking prove," Ant said as he thought back to the female detective who was always on his boy Tito.

Tito made his moves underground. He was one of them niggas who got loot but didn't flash it. Dude was ruthless as shit, too. Not the type Ant wanted to hang around, but the kind you needed in case some shit jumped off. Tito's little brother had gotten caught up in some shit, and when he was locked up, Ant looked out for the kid. When he got out, Tito told him that he would never have to worry about shit. Ant was cool with having old dude in his corner, but he knew that he needed to keep his distance. Ol' boy had bodies dropping around him and Fed heat on him. Shit, at times when Janelle was fucking getting on his nerves, he was tempted to call ol' boy and get himself set up right. But he was tired of going to prison, and more importantly, he liked breathing air above ground. This local bitch detective approached him a few times about Tito, and he cussed her ass out. He sent word to Tito about the chick and left it at that.

"Yo, man, we will come wit' you to the station," Los said.

Ant took a long swig of his tea. "Ay yo, dawg, I love you, but I can't be going to no station. That shit—"

"I got you, man," Roshon said. He couldn't blame Ant for not wanting to go to the police station, considering he was out on parole and had just gotten his freedom less than six months ago.

"Did they say what the fuck they think happened, or they too busy trying to hang your ass?" Ant asked as he put butter on the biscuit the waitress had placed on the table.

"I don't know nothing yet. They said they wanted me to come down and identify the body. I know the Covingtons can't handle that shit right now, dawg. Her mother is just messed up, man. I tell you, it was hard watching her break down. I can't help but think that if I had listened to Brandi when she called, this shit wouldn't have happened."

"What you mean, man?" Los asked as the waitress handed him his plate.

"Sir, what can I get for you?" the waitress asked Roshon.

"Just some coffee," he addressed the waitress, and she wrote it down on her tablet and flashed Roshon a warm smile and walked in the opposite direction. Roshon took in a deep breath and then continued his talk with his boys.

"Brandi called me a few days ago, begging me to pick her up. I was pissed at her. She had left her kids on me, and she went out partying. I left a message telling her I had taken her kids to her mother, and she didn't call her mother for days. I figured she was out of money and just wanted some more to keep partying. So I told her that I didn't have time for her and hung up," Roshon said, swallowing the lump that was in his throat.

"Shit. Well, man, how was you supposed to know she was in trouble? I mean, we talking about Brandi. She was always into some shit. Don't blame yourself, dog. Hell, any of us would have done the same thing probably," Los said. He could see the shit was eating away at his boy. He wasn't good with empathetic shit, and he wasn't sure exactly what to say to Roshon to make him feel all right.

"Man, you tell the cops what you just told us?" Ant asked. "If you did, they looking at you. You might want to talk to a lawyer before going down there, man."

"I don't think I need a lawyer. That shit would make me look guilty. I haven't done anything."

"Dude, you black. You ain't got to do shit for them to fuck with you. Call Michael, man, and see what he tells you. Don't walk in that muthafucka unprepared," Ant said.

"What am I going to tell little man? For all the faults that Brandi had, RJ loved his mother. This shit right here is going to devastate him, man." Roshon buried his face in his hands. His head was pounding, and his stomach was bubbling. Ant and Los looked at Roshon, neither really knowing what to say to him. The three of them sat in silence. Brandi was a little crazy, but she didn't deserve to go out like that.

"All of this talk about Brandi got a nigga head fucked up. So when I walked up, y'all was talking about this nigga smashing two bitches. Who the fuck you tapping, Ant? What two hoes dumb enough to let yo' broke, weak-stroking-ass hit?" Roshon teased. Los and Ant just looked at each other for a moment before Ant spoke.

"Just some hoodrats. Nobody you would know." Although Roshon was their boy, they knew that he and Dorrian were closer and that he would tell Doe the first chance he got. Ant didn't want Dorrian to know that he was fucking both of his cousins, and Los already knew why. They both understood that Dorrian wouldn't allow his family to get played like that, and it would drive a wedge between the bond they had.

"Man, forget them rats he messing with. What's up with the white chic at work? Give up the dirt. Have you hit that yet or what?" Los asked.

"Man, I'm not about to discuss my sex life with you guys. Just know that she has called my name out in three different languages and that everything they say about white girls swallowing is one hundred percent true. Crazy shit is, I ain't even hit yet. She sprung off the tongue alone."

"Oh shit. That's what's up, kid. Before you hit that, you better make sure she on some type of birth control, because your no-pussy-getting ass probably gon' fill up two or three condoms," Ant joked.

The three of them sat for a moment while Roshon filled them in on his newfound relationship. Los made sure to add a few recent war stories of his own, and he also couldn't help but throw in a breakdown of his last sex session with Keera. It was another forty-five minutes before Dorrian finally arrived.

"Damn, my nigga, you smiling too damn hard," Los cracked.

"Nah, this nigga got that morning afterglow, like chicks be having," Ant added, and the guys all started laughing.

"Y'all leave my boy alone. He just looks like a man in love, that's all," Roshon chimed in while laughing at the previous statements. Dorrian couldn't do anything but keep on smiling. He was truly happy and in love.

"Y'all niggas can say what you want, but truth be told, if you could cop a lady like this, y'all would be the same way."

"Oh, wow. She not a chick, not a ho, not a female, but a ladyyy," Ant said in his Martin/Shanaynay voice.

"On the real, shawty is pretty as fuck. I can't lie," Los stated.

"Yo, I know you got some pics of ol' girl. Let me see what she look like," Ant said. Dorrian pulled out his phone and scrolled through his photos and turned the phone so Ant and Roshon could see the picture of Arlene.

"Damn, she is cute. You got any money-shot pics of her?" Ant asked.

"Yeah, I need to see them myself. I was wondering what that body look like outside them work scrubs," Los added. Even Roshon's eyes widened, ready to see some sexy nudes of Arlene.

"Nah, niggas, that's not happening," Dorrian answered.

"Damn, that's fucked up, kid. Shawty ain't sent you no real flicks of her?" Los asked.

"Nah, she did, but I ain't showing them to y'all thirst buckets. This my baby here. I'm talking wifey. These pics are for my eyes only." Los, Ant, and Roshon looked at each other. They had never seen their boy act like this about any female. Dorrian had been in a couple of so-called serious relationships and loved showing his boys pictures of his women. Hell, a few times he had even shared videos of them performing sexual acts. This was truly some new shit from him, and his friends now knew how serious this new relationship really was.

After clowning Dorrian a little longer about his newfound relationship, Roshon caught him up to speed on the situation with Brandi. Like Los and Ant, Dorrian was in shock and couldn't believe it. He could only imagine how his boy felt, knowing that he turned her down the day she needed him the most. What concerned him even more was how little RJ was going to take it.

Janelle and her girls ran inside their home. She was finally able to bring her babies home where they could sleep in their own beds. Staying with Phaedra was cool, but there was nothing like being in your own place just to be yourself. She was so happy to be back in her own space. She was relieved when Carly said that Ant had gotten his things and left. The girls ran to their room as Janelle walked into the kitchen.

"Trifling nigga done ate up everything and didn't replace shit. Oh yeah, you gotta have a fucking job to buy food and shit," Janelle said to herself as she slammed the refrigerator. She walked upstairs to her bedroom. As she entered the room, there was a faint musty scent in the air. She looked over at her bed to see the covers and sheets crumpled on the bed. She moved closer to examine the dark navy blue sheets and the dried stains they had on them.

"I know this muthafucka didn't!" Janelle yelled as she began ripping the bedding off the bed. "I know this nigga didn't bring some ho to my house and fuck her in my bed!" Janelle ran down the stairs to the kitchen and grabbed a large black garbage bag. As she ran up the stairs, she stopped in the door of the bedroom, tears flowing down her face. She knew Ant could be a bastard, but this shit was beyond disrespectful. He had done this to intentionally hurt her, and he had succeeded.

"I got you, nigga. I got you. You gon' pay for this shit!" Janelle said as she stuffed the bedding in the garbage bag. The nigga was ungrateful! After all she had done for his black ass, this was the way she was repaid?

Carly appeared in the doorway. She watched Janelle grab the Lysol and spray down her mattress. She smirked as she saw tears flowing down her sister's face.

"What you in here yelling about? Damn, Ant ain't here for you to yell at, so what's wrong wit' you now?"

"Did you see that nigga bring a bitch in my house?" Janelle asked as she walked into her bathroom.

"He ain't have nobody over here while I was here. Why?" Carly asked, sitting down in the chair by the door.

"I can smell that ho's stankin' pussy, and the nasty bastard didn't even have the decency to wash the sheets. Why would he do that, Carly, after all the shit I've done for this nigga?"

"I don't know, sis. That's messed up," Carly said, trying to hide her smile. "You sure that ain't the way you left your bed?"

"Hell yeah, I'm sure! You sure you ain't seen him bring someone here?"

"Girl, I ain't got time to be watching your man. I was out most of the time. I came back to make sure he was gone like you asked. I been out hanging with my peeps."

"You need to be looking for a better job so you can get your own place. Evidently, that job ain't paying you much of shit!" Janelle snapped.

"Damn, I guess you throwing everybody out, huh?" Carly said, standing. "Don't worry. I won't be here much longer, and then you can have this government mansion to yourself!" Carly stormed out.

Janelle thought about apologizing, but fuck it. She was tired of these grown-ass people living off her. She slammed the door to her bedroom and sat down on the floor, staring at the bed. "I will make you pay for this, nigga. I promise you that.

"Kalani and Tiana, clean up your rooms and straighten up the downstairs," Janelle yelled as she pondered her next move. Ant played her for the last time, and it was time that he learned the meaning of never biting the hand that fed you.

Fucking Carly in Janelle's bed was Ant's final act of disrespect, and also his way of saying that it was over. It wasn't just disrespectful, but he was hoping that it was hurtful. After all she had done for him and everything she endured during the course of their relationship. Get back was a must and there wasn't nobody better at the get-back game then Janelle. Before she could do anything, her first order of business was to finish cleaning her bedroom and getting rid of all the remnants of Ant and his slut who had violated the sanctity of her home.

"You gon' pay for this shit," Janelle mumbled, heading for the bathroom cabinet to grab some latex gloves. "I'm on ya ass now, muthafucka," she promised. "I'm on ya ass."

"We appreciate you coming down, Mr. White," Detective Marshall said as he pressed the elevator's down button.

"Yeah, sorry I didn't make it yesterday. I needed to get to my son," Roshon said.

Los had texted Dorrian, who met them at the station. "Hey, man, I'ma wait for y'all right here. My leg is killing me."

"I told you not to come, man. You need to stay off that leg," Roshon said, shaking his head.

"Hey, I would still like to speak with you with regard to how you were shot," Detective Adams said, looking at Los.

"Nah, I'm done talking about that shit, man. It's over, and I ain't pressing charges. It was an accident," Los said, sitting back and getting comfortable in a chair. Roshon glared at Detective Adams. Los waved him on, letting him know he had the bitch under control. Dorrian and Roshon followed Detective Marshall down the hallway.

"All right, here we are," Detective Marshall said as the doors of the elevator opened. The bright fluorescent light flooded the hallway.

Roshon's stomach tightened, and he felt dizzy as they approached the two large metal doors. They entered the small room with the large flat-screen television on the wall. Detective Marshall picked up the white phone that hung on the wall, and the screen flickered. Brandi's bruised and swollen face showed on the screen. She was unrecognizable. The tattoo of the humming bird behind her left ear was the only way that Roshon knew for sure it was her.

"Fuck," Dorrian mumbled under his breath as he looked away from the screen. Roshon ran out of the room, searching for the restroom. He managed to make it inside a stall and began throwing up.

"Shit, Brandi, got damn it!" Roshon said as he hovered over the toilet. "Who did that to you, baby?" Detective Marshall and Dorrian were standing outside the stall. Roshon walked over to the sink and splashed water on his face.

"I'm sorry for your loss, Mr. White. Let's go upstairs," Detective Marshall said handing Roshon a few paper towels.

The men walked to the elevator. Once Roshon and Detective Marshall were in the office, as promised, Detective Marshall began asking Roshon a few questions to see if he could hem him up. Although he did not believe that Roshon was guilty, he knew how people could feign hurt at the news of a loved one dying, yet be guilty the entire time. He didn't think this was the case with Roshon, but as a detective, it was his job not to make assumptions.

After an intense half hour of questioning, Detective Marshall was satisfied that he was correct all along. "Mr. White, I just need you to sign some papers saying that you have identified Ms. Covington. It will only be a few more minutes," Detective Marshall said.

Outside of the office, Dorrian and Los were conversing about what Dorrian saw on that screen. "That is some real *The First 48* shit, man," Dorrian said, fighting the bile in his throat. "Brandi didn't deserve no shit like that, man."

"Damn, man, it was that bad?" Los asked. Dorrian began pacing the floor. "These pigs need to get on their fucking job and find the muthafucka before we do, man," Los added as he continued to watch Dorrian. Both his boys were a shade darker in the face. He got a glimpse of Roshon before he walked in the office, and Roshon was pale, and Dorrian looked like he was about to explode.

"Yeah, fo' sho," Dorrian said, taking out his phone. "They best get on it, 'cause we sho ain't waiting around."

"We will handle this, and we don't need any help," Detective Adams said, walking up to the two men.

"Yo, ain't nobody talking to you. Instead of y'all finding the fucka who did this shit, you trying to hem up my boy," Dorrian said between his teeth.

"Look, I know you guys are upset, but let us do our job. Believe me when I say we want to find the killer just as much as you guys."

"Yeah, that is why we ain't seen shit on the news, huh? If it were a fucking snow white broad, it would have major coverage. But it is just another dead black woman, huh?" Los said trying to stand up.

Detective Adams's face turned red. They had intentionally not released anything to the media as of yet. They were patrolling the area, hoping that the killer would return. "Look, there is a reason we have not involved the media yet," Adams began.

"Right," Los said as he hobbled toward Dorrian. The door to the office opened, and Detective Marshall and Roshon walked out.

"Like I said, y'all need to get on this shit before we do," Dorrian said as they began walking toward the exit.

"They are going to be trouble," Detective Adams said, crossing her arms.

***

RJ walked into the bedroom with his suit and tie on, ready to attend his mother's funeral. He still did not understand fully that Brandi wasn't coming back, and Roshon found it difficult trying to explain it to him. "Come here, li'l man," Roshon said, waving RJ over to him. "I wanna talk to you about something."

"About Mommy again?" RJ asked in a sad voice as he stood in front of his dad. "Can we see her today?"

This was why Roshon was having so much trouble with this. What was the right way to tell a child that he would never see his mother again? It was eating Roshon up, but he knew that it had to be done.

"Well, yes, we're going to see Mommy today, but after today she's going to heaven. We won't be able to see her again for some time. But she will always be looking down on you from the clouds," Roshon explained.

"I don't want my mommy to go to heaven," RJ cried.

His little tears were like acid on Roshon's skin when he wiped them from RJ's face. He was at a loss for words for a moment, only able to hug his son as a form of comfort. Roshon wanted to cry too, but he couldn't right now. He had to be strong for his boy. "Come here, li'l man," Roshon said, lifting RJ onto his lap.

"I want my mommy!" RJ cried out uncontrollably, planting his little head into Roshon's chest. RJ could feel it in his soul that his mommy wasn't coming back. His loud cries could be heard throughout the whole house, causing everyone who was there to cry even more than they were.

Roshon tried so hard, but even he was unable to hold back his tears. He felt helpless in his unsuccessful attempts to take RJ's pain away. He wanted to tell him that he was going to be all right and that things were going to get better. But the truth of the matter was it wasn't going to get easier anytime soon. RJ was going to miss her; not just now, but throughout the remainder of his life.

"Aww, see, he loves his daddy," Keera said, watching as baby William rested his head on Los's chest while he sat up in the bed with him. Los wanted to make it to Brandi's funeral to show his support to Roshon and RJ, but he was barely able to move about within his apartment due to the pain his leg was causing him. However, he did manage to call Roshon earlier that day to give his condolences for their loss.

"I know I said this before, but I'm really sorry for shooting you," Keera said, kneeling down next to the bed.

Now that Los had acknowledged William as his son, she regretted having to do what she did. The doctor said that the cast was going to be on Los's leg for eight to twelve weeks, meaning he wasn't going to be able to go back to work or do just about anything until he could walk again. The only good thing that came out of this was that Los was getting to know his son a lot better.

"Look, Keera, all this is new to me, so you're gonna have to give me some time to get used to being a dad of a special-needs child. Our son is going to require lots of attention, considering his condition, and once I get back on my feet I'ma have a lot of catching up to do."

"So, what are you trying to say? I don't understand," Keera questioned, tensing up.

"All I'm saying is don't expect me to be this perfect dad. I still have goals and things I wanna accomplish. Just be patient with me and continue to be the best mother you can be for him."

In so many words, Los was trying to give Keera a forewarning that he wasn't about to put his life on hold and become a family man just yet. He still wanted to enjoy life and the freedom of being a single man. As far as he was concerned, he wasn't in a relationship, and he didn't want to give Keera the impression that they were together now that it had been proven he was the father of William.

Keera frowned. She did not say a word as Los turned around with William in his hands. She wanted to push him so he could see how disappointed and pained she was. As a matter of fact, she no longer regretted shooting him. He fucking deserved it. She had thought that when she proved to him that William was truly his child, he would not only open up to his responsibilities, but that they would become a perfect family, living happily together. But he just had to go ahead and kill her joy.

He was always like that: always hurting her happiness. *It's a wonder why this man I love always seems to cause me so much pain.*

"You okay?" Los asked.

Keera smiled. "Why wouldn't I be?" But when Los turned his back to her, she stared daggers into him. He was not going to ruin her vision of a perfect family. She was not going to let her child grow up out of wedlock, unrecognized. She knew Los. She had seen what he did with his other children. He would continue to slip every day, and soon, he would forget all about his son and her. He would ride on with another bitch and knock her up, then get married to her. She wasn't gonna be another one of his babies' mamas. She wasn't gonna be that woman who was gonna be asking for child support. She wasn't gonna be crazy like that.

No! She shook her head as she had visions of some ratchet bitch trying to take her man from her and pinning him down. She fucking knew women, and she also knew that Los was a catch in her eyes. Any bitch who came into his life was going to make sure he forgot about her and William. What she had to do now was make sure that he did not have any stupid thoughts of abandoning them. She had to make sure she and William were a part of his life, forever and always.

Family and friends poured into the church for the viewing of Brandi's body. People still couldn't believe how she died. She had been a carefree person all her adult life, but everyone had expected her to stick around for a while. Two days ago, Detective Marshall came to Brandi's mom's house and informed the family that the autopsy reports determined that a single blow to her head with a blunt object crushed her skull and killed her. The detective went on to say that it all happened during a robbery attempt in a trap house she and her boyfriend were selling drugs in. She had died instantly, and the drug-induced state she was in did not help matters. Those were the only details they had available.

They told Mr. and Mrs. Covington that they were looking for the people who had robbed the trap house. They had asked the Covingtons about Brandi's current boyfriend, but they had little to tell him, as they had never really met him. Detective Marshall promised he would try his best to find their daughter's killer, but in the back of his mind, he knew the chances were slim. Nobody really talked in situations like this. Mr. and Mrs. Covington couldn't believe it. They knew their daughter had gone off track, but they were not aware to what extent.

Roshon made a conscious decision not to allow RJ to see his mother lying in a casket for his last time seeing her. He didn't want it to be the last image he had of her, especially with him being so young. He, along with his other siblings, were taken to the far rear of the church where they could only hear the service and not see their mother.

"Damn, that's crazy," Roshon said, looking down at Brandi's pale face. "You gon' really leave me with li'l man like this. I swear I didn't want it to happen this way. I fuckin' hate you for this," Roshon said, shaking his head. "You gon' die on me though. You gon' leave me and li'l man behind like this," he said as he held back his tears. "This is some fucked-up shit, baby girl, but I still got love for you. Bye, Brandi," he said then walked off.

He walked over and gave Mrs. Covington a hug then gave Mr. Covington a handshake. He could see how sad they were. They probably blamed themselves for what happened, but all the blame was on Brandi. She had been the one to ruin her life, not giving a shit about anyone else, not even her children.

Before he could walk off, Mrs. Covington grabbed a hold of his hand. "Sit down for a second," she said, patting the empty seat beside her. "You know, despite what you know and wanna believe, my daughter loved you. She lost her way, but it was no denying how she felt about you, and, babe, she loved you and y'all child."

Roshon couldn't lie. At one point in his life, Brandi meant everything to him. He always thought that they were going to stand the test of time and live the happily ever after of a life. She was the mother of his first and only child, and he was grateful for that. He would never be able to forget about all the good times they had together, but at the same time, Roshon could never forget about all the pain and suffering she had put him through. The lying, the cheating, the disrespect, the thirst for money. Roshon really wished that things could have been different, but Brandi was who she was, and this wasn't the time to judge her. There was nothing left for him to do now but move on and try to give RJ the best life that he could possibly have without Brandi being around any longer. It was going to be hard, but Roshon had no other choice but to do it. It was time to start afresh on a clean slate, and he was going to continue making sure his li'l boy was raised right.

Chapter 8

Ant pulled up in the driveway of the small house and sat in the car, wondering if he was making the right choice. It had been a long time since he'd been here, and he wasn't sure if he would be welcome or not. It was hot as hell sitting in the car as Ant stared at the house. The sun beamed down on the little house, and the swing on the front porch creaked as the wind blew. Ant shut the engine off, then sat there thinking. After realizing he was tired of living off of women, he had finally gotten a place of his own, and Dorrian was letting him hold his Jeep so he could get back and forth to school. After all the shit that went down with Janelle, he decided that it was time to buckle down. Don't get it twisted. Buckling down did not include not continuing to sex Carly. He just realized he needed to be a man and stand on his own two feet for once in his life.

Cutting hair was something that he knew how to do well, and it was the best way to stay out of trouble, so he enrolled in barber school, and he had managed to get a part-time job at the mall working at the Sugar Shack making cookies. The owner didn't seem to care about his record, and he understood what it was like trying to start over. In addition, a blessing for Ant, he felt that everybody deserved a second chance.

Ant loved the fact that he worked in the back, away from all the temptation that came in and out of the shop. Shit, twelve dollars an hour wasn't bad either. His shift ended at one, just in time for him to get to class and have a few hours after that to relax before going to his second job, which consisted of him working for Dorrian at night at the club. He finally felt as if his life was getting back on track.

Ant got out of the car and started walking toward the house. He paused, and took a deep breath, then made his way up the cracked concrete walkway and knocked on the door.

A woman opened the door with a scowl on her face. Her hair was in lemonade braids, and she was wearing a low-cut white cotton shirt, and black capris.

"Hey, Ma. Happy Birthday!" Ant said, smiling and handing her the bag with the festive picture on the front.

"What you doing here?" his mother asked, stepping outside and closing the door behind her. Ant knew what that meant: the same thing it always meant since he was a child. She had a nigga in there, and she didn't want him messing up her chances with him.

"Whose car is that? Boy, don't be bringing no trouble to my house. I told you I can't be dealing with your shit," Karen said, placing the bag on the chair.

"Ma, I just wanted to stop by for your birthday. I ain't bringing no trouble. That's my car. I been doing real good, Ma. I even got my own place."

Karen looked him up and down. She shook her head. He was as handsome as his father and as useless, too. "Boy, you must think I'm stupid. What dumb little ho done gave you that car to use? You don't know nothing about getting your own shit."

Ant sighed, trying to not show how much she hurt him. "Can I at least come in so you can open your present, Ma? I don't want nothing. I just thought I could take you out to dinner for your birthday, and catch up."

Karen laughed. "Take me out to dinner? With what money?"

"I'm working, Ma, two jobs. One at a bakery and at a club."

"Oh, you working now? Like real work?" Karen smirked. She opened the bag to see the Michael Kors handbag. "Boy, this shit looks real!"

"It is real, Ma. You like the color?"

Karen took out the handbag and sniffed the leather. The dark blue color was smooth and sleek. "Well, it is nice. You got the receipt? I can take it back and get the money to help pay some bills around here. What the hell am I gonna do with a damn four hundred dollar bag with nothing to fucking go in it?"

Ant began to grind his teeth. His mother always found a way to make him feel like shit. He felt like her hatred for him started in the womb. He always tried to make her happy, but it was never enough. Hell, he started dealing just to try to make her happy that he was paying all the bills for her. When he got arrested and sentenced the first time, she didn't show up to his hearing. He had been locked up about three months when she visited him, asking him where the rest of the money was. He had put back some stacks for when he got out. He left her with about fifteen stacks to help her out, but she went through it within weeks. He remembered her threatening that if he didn't get her some cash, she'd tell the DA that he had stashed money.

He had tried to convince her that he had given her all he had, but she was like a fucking bloodhound when he had money. He ended up giving her what she wanted. He told her to go to his boy in Jersey to get the money he had left with him to flip for him while he was locked up. He wanted to call Monte to tell him not to give her all the money, but he knew calling from the prison phone would be foolish. At that time, he didn't want or need no more time added to his sentence. Monte had a soft spot for folks Mama and even drove down to give her the $30,000. He kept the $20,000 for Ant and did as he promised and flipped his shit for him.

When Ant got out, he couldn't leave the state, and Monte had gotten caught up himself with a murder charge. He got sentenced to fifteen years, and Ant's money was still with Monte's boy, Rider. Monte told him that Rider was a good dude and when he was ready, he could come and get his loot. Ant never made it. He had been locked up twice since then. Ant knew that his stacks had definitely multiplied by now, but he had too many eyes on his ass to get it. He had Rider wire some loot to his boy Doogie so he could pay for his tuition, and a little extra for some shit he needed. He was going to wait until his probation was over then go scoop up all his shit from old boy.

"Ma, you want to go to dinner? You can pick anyplace you want," Ant said.

"Boy, I ain't got time for that. I got company. You gon' pay for both of us? Sho look like you can by the looks of that Jeep. Taking me to dinner. You sure as hell owe me a lot more than that with the shit you put me through."

"Ma, I'm trying to do better. I just wanted to talk to you and celebrate your birthday with you."

"Oh, I see it is a gift receipt. Well, they should still give me money back if I tell them I already got one, right?"

Ant clenched his fist, which shocked him. He had never in all his years thought of hitting his mother, but today she was pushing all the wrong buttons.

"Happy Birthday, Ma," Ant said as he turned to walk down the steps. Karen looked him over and noticed the shoes, jeans, and bracelet on his wrist. He really was doing better than he normally had been doing.

"Wait. Come on in," Karen said, thinking of the things she wanted and bills she needed to be paid. "Let me get dressed, and you can take me to Chimas. I will tell Andre I'm going to spend some time with you." Ant smiled and ran back to the porch like a little kid. Karen shook her head and opened the door for him.

Ant walked into the living room and noticed a man sitting on the couch watching TV. He looked Ant up and down with disdain. Ant returned the look and sat down on the love seat. His mother went into the kitchen and then walked down the small hallway to her bedroom. A soccer game was on, and the announcers were speaking Spanish.

"So, who you like to win?" the man asked in broken English.

"What?" Ant asked. The man pointed to the television.

"Da game. Who you like? Who ya tink will win?"

"I don't really watch soccer, man. I watch basketball. I can't even tell you who the hell is playing right now, and I'm looking at the screen."

"Oh. Ya want a beer or something?" Andre asked, standing and going to the kitchen. Karen walked out wearing a navy blue halter jumpsuit, and pink open-toe stiletto sandals.

"Where you going?" Andre asked as he sipped his beer.

"My son is taking me to dinner," Karen said, checking her reflection in the mirror. "Come on, boy, I'm hungry." Ant got up from the love seat and walked over to the door.

"I'll see yo' ass in a minute," Karen said as she kissed Andre; then she whispered something in his ear that made him laugh.

Ant shook his head as he opened the door. He looked back at Karen just in time to see Andre smack her on the ass, making her giggle. Ant winced at the sight but pretended not to be fazed by it. Growing up, he witnessed so many men coming in and out of the house. Men had always treated his mother like a piece of meat, and for some reason, she enjoyed it. Some of the men even would tell him about things that his mother did to them sexually—like old man Roberson. That's what he was called in the neighborhood.

He was an old-ass man who thought he was a young boy. He popped Viagra like they were Tic Tacs, then wanted to find some young girl to pay to fuck. Karen was one of his many choices. Ant heard sex sounds coming out of her room when he was supposed to be sleeping. After a while, he learned to block out the sounds, but this one particular day, Ant was sitting in the living room watching cartoons when old man Roberson came knocking on the door.

Karen came out of her room wearing a skimpy little dress and no panties. She opened the door, and old man Roberson didn't waste no time grabbing her up and feeling on her ass. He noticed Ant in the living room and smirked.

"Boy, this right here is grown folks' shit. You see this ass right here?" he asked, grabbing a handful of Karen's ass and jiggling it.

Karen giggled and playfully slapped him on the arm. "Now you stop that, Willy. That's my boy you talkin' to." She chuckled.

"Shit, one day he gon' be a man, and he gon' need to know how to handle a woman like you. Boy, yo' mama got that pussy that make a nigga wanna live in that shit. Pussy like that can get you in trouble. That's why I got to get the fuck outta here after I bust my nut. Yo' mama been done made my ass marry her, and I ain't doing that shit. Hell naw. I did that shit one time, and the bitch hurt my heart. Take my advice, son: never fall in love. Bitches don't give a fuck 'bout yo' heart. Ain't that right, Karen?"

"Yeah, Willy, you right. Shit, that love shit is for them damn birds."

"I know that's right. See, that's why I like yo' mama. She understands the dick and pussy game. Ain't no love in this shit. Now you listen to old man Roberson and yo' mama, and don't let no bitch tie you down. Oh, and fuck all the bitches you can before yo' dick fall the fuck off. Now go on and finish watching that TV and let me and yo' mama go take care of business."

He slapped Karen on the ass again, making her squeal; then they hurried up the steps. A few minutes later, Ant heard the same sex sounds and squeaking bed noises that he'd been hearing all his damn life. He turned the TV up louder to try to block out the sounds, and he sat there thinking about everything old man Roberson was saying, and picturing his mother hanging all over him, kissing his neck, and agreeing with everything he was saying.

It was that day he decided that he would never fall in love with a woman like his mother. Although he loved his mother, Ant had always been disgusted by her. His childhood was the reason for him abusing women emotionally the way he did. As much as he tried to or at least thought he wanted to love Janelle, he couldn't, because in his mind all females equated to the scandalous woman who birthed him.

"Take care of my woman, boy," Andre said, watching Karen walk toward the door. Ant was about to set his ass straight about calling him a boy, but Karen's glare stopped him.

"Let's go, Ma."

"See ya later, baby," Karen said, winking at Andre and blowing him a kiss, and that disgusted feeling that Ant always had for her returned.

***

Janelle placed her food in the microwave and began checking her social media. Ant had been gone for a while, but she was still keeping tabs on his ass. He had really fucked up sleeping with a raggedy ho in her bed, and she was not going to let him get away with disrespecting her or her damn house like that. She checked his Instagram page, and it was full of pictures of him with his boys and some bitches.

"Oh, this nigga done got his own crib now?" she mumbled to herself.

The entire time he was with her, he never made an effort to do anything. Someone had told her that he was working at the cookie place in the mall, and going to school. She had sent Carly to the Sugar Shack to see if the rumors were true, but she said that she didn't see him. Yet, lo and behold, he was in a picture on social media with a chef's apron and a hat with the Sugar Shack logo on it, holding up a tray of cookies with the hashtag MyCookiesAreLikeCrack. As much as she fussed about him getting up and getting a job, and the nigga wouldn't get off his lazy ass and do shit. Now he was working and going to school. Janelle was pissed. Slamming her laptop down, she let out a frustrated sigh, then laid her head on the table.

"What's wrong with you?" Tasha asked as she walked into the break room, and went into the refrigerator. She walked over to where Janelle was sitting then flopped down in the chair.

"Shit, girl, it's fucking Ant's ass, but that shit ain't important. You look like shit. What's wrong with you?" Janelle retorted as Tasha took a tissue from the box and wiped her eyes. She looked like she had been crying, and this caused Janelle concern.

"Girl, you all right?" Janelle asked as she looked closely at Tasha's face. Her left cheek was swollen, and she had a large bruise on her forearm.

"Yeah, girl, I'm good. Just tired of fucked-up niggas, that's all."

"What happened to your arm?"

"Mike happened, girl. I'm so embarrassed. I'm so tired of this shit," Tasha said as he began to sob. Janelle grabbed some more tissues and handed them to Tasha.

"Oh, my goodness, Tasha, what happened?" Janelle asked, putting her arm around Tasha's shoulders.

Tasha wiped away her tears then exhaled. "I was looking through Mike's phone the other night, and I saw all these text messages from some other bitches. Keep in mind that I pay for the phone service 'cause he ain't worked in over a year. Shit, to be honest, I don't see the nigga even trying to find job. So, I confronted him about the text messages, and he slapped me in the face with the phone." Tasha burst into tears, and Janelle's heart broke.

Tasha continued telling her stories of all the abuse she'd taken from Mike, and as she listened to Tasha talk, she couldn't help but think about her own relationship with Ant. Just like Tasha, she was a good woman. Both women were loyal, smart, and hard workers. They deserved good men, and for some reason, the ones they fell in love with were just not worthy of having them. Ant didn't appreciate anything she had done for him.

"I got you on that shit, baby. Ant fucked a bitch in my bed. This nigga wanted me to know what he did 'cause he left the nasty-ass sheets on the bed. Dried wet spots and all."

"I don't know what we are doing wrong. We are good women, and we don't deserve to be treated this way. Thank God I ain't got no kids by this dude. I don't know what keeps me with him. Shit, when I think about it, my lifestyle went down after I got with him."

The door to the break room opened and Victor, a coworker, walked in. He waved to the two women and opened the refrigerator door.

"Oh, y'all ain't got to stop talking 'cause I came in here," Victor sang as he switched over to the microwave.

"Boy, we not talking about nothing but these trifling men we got, or should I say had."

"That's cause y'all hoes be settling for the first thang who speaks to you. Chile, ain't no way no nigga gonna be lying up in my shit while I'm out here busting my ass. Fuck that. His ass better flip a damn burger or something. Shit, y'all bitches let these ain't-shit-ass niggas dick you down the right way and y'all fell in love. Thought y'all ass had that forever thing. Now y'all sitting here looking stupid and mad 'cause y'all ain't kick that nigga to the curb the first time y'all saw that he wasn't shit. Any nigga I fuck with know from the gate: if I have to roll all this fabulousness out the bed in the morning, his ass better not be too far behind me!" The microwave dinged. Victor batted his eyes as he got his food out of the microwave. "I'll talk to you hoes later," he said then walked out of the break room.

"That right there is the reason we can't find any decent men," Janelle said, laughing and dapping up Tasha.

"So, he left the dirty mess in your bed? That is beyond fucked up!"

"Oh, I didn't tell you everything. You know he had me put out of my place for days, right? I had to stay with Phaedra 'cause the police took his side. I found out he was talking to some chick and I smacked him a little bit. He told them he didn't have a place to go, and they told me since I did have a place to go I had to leave."

"Are you kidding me? What kind of bullshit is that?"

"I know, right. So me and my kids had to stay with Phaedra, and then my mama, and you know how she wrecks my damn nerves. When I was finally able to go back home, I found those nasty, filthy sheets on my bed. It was so fucking disgusting." Janelle shook her head just as Romona, another coworker Janell and Tasha were close to, walked in.

"Hey, ladies," she spoke, walking over to the table with a bottle of water. She sat down and crossed her legs. "What's going on?" she asked.

Tasha shook her head. "Girl, the same shit. Fuck-boy-ass niggas," she replied, showing Romona the bruise on her face.

"Girl, I been told you to leave that nigga alone. His ass gon' seriously hurt you one day."

"Naw, we done. This was the last straw. That nigga slapped me with a fucking iPhone, like for real. He had messages from other bitches talking about fucking and shit, and he slapped me with the fucking phone."

"Shit, it was no different from the time he stole you in your face when you found a girl's nasty-ass thong in his pocket, or the time he damn near broke your jaw when you found a picture of him and a bitch at a concert the day he was supposed to take you out in your car. I mean, I hate to bring up old shit, but you acting surprised that he smacked you with his phone."

"For real, Romona, that's what you doing? Throwing shit up in my face?" Tasha asked as she rolled her eyes.

"Tasha, you know I love you like a sister, but I have to be honest. You let this nigga get away with way too much shit, and I get it. I been there too, but you got to know when enough is enough. Shit, I wish I had somebody telling me shit like that when I was going through it with my ex. Maybe I wouldn't be in the situation I'm in now."

Tasha took the last bite of her lunch. "What situation?" she asked with her mouth full of food.

Romona inhaled and exhaled a deep breath before answering. "My ex used to do that same type of shit that Mike and Ant did. I took care of his ass. I fed him, clothed him . . . hell, I even wiped his ass if he asked me to."

Romona's last statement made Janelle and Tasha both look at her like she was crazy.

"Oh, hell naw. I ain't wiping a nigga's ass unless his ass was sick or injured and couldn't do it himself. Shit, I might just get a nurse for it then," Janelle said, and Tasha agreed.

"That's how stupid I was for this nigga. Trust me, it got worst. He used to beat on me and fuck around on me. I had threesomes for him, with either me and another girl or him and another nigga. Mostly his boys. They would talk shit and slap fives and shit while they were fucking me. It was humiliating. But he didn't give a fuck. It took something drastic for us to break up. He gave me genital warts around both holes. Check this out. When I told him, he said I was a trifling ho and I must have been fucking someone else. I knew he was gon' say that shit, so before I told him, I went snooping and found his paperwork. When I showed it to him, he beat me so bad that I thought I was gon' have to go to the hospital. Then the nigga left me."

"Damn," Janelle and Tasha said in unison, staring at Romona with a look of shock plastered on their faces. Silence filled the air, as the three women sat there not knowing what to say. Finally, Tasha broke the silence.

"I got an idea. We gonna get these niggas back! Make them pay for the shit they done put us through."

"Girl, you talking crazy. I ain't trying to go to jail now. I can't be going to jail!" Janelle said, shaking her head.

"No, Janelle, I'm not talking about nothing like that, but I'm talking about something that will make their asses suffer!"

After pondering it for a moment, Janelle said, "I'm listening." She looked at the clock to make sure they were not going to be late. She really was not in the mood to hear their supervisor's mouth.

Tasha got up and walked over to Janelle and placed her arms around her neck. "I say we hit them where it hurts," she stated, and Janelle and Romona were confused.

Tasha let out a chuckle. "Romona, you were never able to get yo' ex back for giving you an STD that you can never get rid of. Why not help us get revenge on our dudes?"

"What you mean?" Romona asked.

"Both of our fuck boys like fucking other women, and they both love big asses, and Romona, you know you got ass for days. I want you to hook up with Mike and Ant, and give them a gift that keeps on giving." A devilish grin appeared on Tasha's face as the wheels started turning in her head.

Janelle sat in silence, thinking. If Ant got an STD that he couldn't get rid of, he'd probably kill himself. One thing he couldn't do was go without pussy.

"Tasha, something is seriously wrong with you. You telling me that you want me to fuck y'all niggas?" Romona questioned in disbelief.

"That's what exactly what I'm saying," Tasha answered.

"I don't know about that." Romona was still shocked that finally opening up to her friends about her situation would lead to her fucking their niggas.

"Yeah, Tasha, that does sound a little crazy," Janelle said, and Romona agreed once again.

"Listen, I know that this sounds crazy and a little farfetched, but just hear me out. That's all I'm asking."

Janelle and Romona looked at each other as if they were asking for each other's approval.

"Okay, Tasha, I'm all ears," Janelle said. "What about you, Romona, you down?"

Romona looked back and forth between the two. "Fuck it, I'm down. These niggas need to learn not to keep fucking with women's hearts."

Tasha smiled. "Good, so all we got to do is basically stalk these niggas and find a way for them to meet the lovely Romona. Once they meet her, the rest will be like taking candy from a baby."

Janelle and Romona both nodded their heads in agreement, as smiles appeared on their faces.

Los couldn't walk fully normally yet, but he got around by way of crutches. He grew tired of sitting in the house and decided to go down to the shop for the first time since he'd been shot. He wanted to check on business and shoot the shit with his regulars. Falicia had stepped up in his absence and held the shop down, making sure all the barbers paid their rent on time as well as keeping the place cleaned and manicured.

Los pushed the door open with his crutch. He was hit by a standing ovation along with warm welcomes, and loads of hugs and kisses from the people in the shop. Los felt loved.

"Damn, boy, I'm glad you're back. Ya boy Pablo been fuckin' my head up, and pushing a nigga hairline way back." Dorrian laughed, pointing at his crooked hairline. Los couldn't help but laugh with him. That shit was fucked up for real.

"Nigga, you laughing, but I'm dead ass. I got a party tonight, and I need you to tighten my shit up, brah," Dorrian said with a straight face. "You think you can do that?" he asked.

"Shit, my leg is fucked up, nigga, not my hands. Hop yo' ass in my chair," Los said, leaning his crutches up against the wall. "I'm feeling good right now, so I'm up for whatever," he added.

"Yeah, we gon' see about that later," Rhonda teased, giving Los a wink of her eye. He looked from Rhonda to Falicia, and they both had a seductive look on their faces.

"Yo, I saw that crazy-ass chick Keera the other day. I thought she would be in jail by now," Rhonda stated, looking at him questioningly. It was not news that Rhonda and Falicia didn't like Keera and her craziness.

Yeah, Los would have liked that to happen. Keera had gone overboard by shooting him. The worst part of it all was that Keera didn't think that she had done anything wrong, blaming shit on him. He would sure love to see her pay for the pain and embarrassment she had caused him. The only reason Los didn't get her locked up was because she was the mother of his son. With her being in jail, the full weight and responsibility of baby William would be left to him. Los couldn't hack it right now and chose not to implicate her in the shooting.

After a long talk, a mutual agreement took place between Keera and himself. They decided not to see each other anymore in a sexual way. The only relationship they would have now would be in their parenting. Of course, Keera hated the idea, at first, but after some convincing, she gave in to Los's demands. Well, she really didn't have a choice if she wanted to keep her crazy ass out of jail so that she could raise her son. A part of Los still couldn't believe that William was his. His life had changed tremendously over a short period of time after finding out that baby William was indeed his. Even though he knew he had no choice but to accept it, mentally dealing with it had been a burden of its own.

"Good morning, Mrs. Johnson," Roshon greeted her, walking into the kitchen. "I'm going out tonight, so I'm gonna need you to watch RJ for me."

"Roshon, we need to talk," Mrs. Johnson said in a serious tone. "It's about RJ."

Mrs. Johnson walked over and took a seat at the table, then motioned for Roshon to do the same. What she had to talk to him about was going to take a little while, because RJ had some serious issues.

"Your son is crying out for some attention, and he doesn't want it from me. That boy is starting to become destructive," Mrs. Johnson told him.

"I'll talk to him, Mrs. J," Roshon replied.

"No, I don't need you to talk to him. I need you to spend some time with your son. He needs you right now."

Just about every weekend for the past month, Roshon and Natalie had been inseparable. He was always out all day either at work or on dates with her. It left RJ with little to no time to spend with his dad. Funny thing was that Roshon didn't even realize it until Mrs. Johnson pointed it out to him. He was having so much fun with Natalie that she was all he could think about.

"And what's going on with you and that little white girl you keep going out with? Don't you end up like Tiger Woods."

"Nah, Mrs. J, she's cool. We're just having fun right now."

"Yeah, well you better be having fun using condoms. Don't be coming up in here with no more babies," Mrs. Johnson playfully hissed then got up to finish the rest of the dishes. "Oh, and make sure you give Mrs. Covington a call. She's been trying to reach you. She might wanna take RJ for the weekend or something. Go on and let that boy see his grandma and his brother and sisters. No matter how bitter you felt toward his mom, those people are still his family," Mrs. Johnson added.

"Yeah, I know, Mrs. J. I just don't want him getting too comfortable around them. He's my son, and I have full custody of him now."

Mrs. Johnson turned around and looked at Roshon with a straight face. He knew she was about to say how she felt no matter how he would take it. She was like a second mother to Roshon and had babysat him when he was RJ's age, and there had never been a time when she hadn't told Roshon when he was or was not doing something right or wrong. Today wasn't going to be any different.

"Yes, Roshon, you do have full custody of that boy, so my suggestion to you is that you need to start acting like it. I love RJ just as much as you do, and he is a special child. But he ain't no more special than them other children, and I don't like the tone you giving off, like he too good to be around his siblings. Now them young'uns deserve to see their brother just as much as he deserves to see them," she said then walked out of the kitchen.

Roshon sat there, throwing his head back in frustration. Mrs. Johnson never told a lie, and Roshon knew that her words were genuine because she always had his best interest at heart. That was why he loved her so much. His frustrations were directed toward Brandi, and it was times like this when he hated her for leaving him out there with RJ by himself.

He had never thought it was going to demand such time from his work. In the past, he had always scolded Brandi for not living up to being a mother, but now he was learning firsthand what it meant to be a parent. He had promised himself that he was going to make sure RJ got a good and happy life. Now he seemed to be doing the opposite. He had to get his priorities straight and own up to his responsibility.

"Oh shit, Janelle here," Carly ran into the room and told Ant, who was lying in Carly's bed with only his boxers on. "Get yo' dumb ass up, boy!" she yelled, scrambling around the room to grab Ant's things.

The fact that Janelle had a few bags from the grocery store gave Carly and Ant a little bit of time to work with. Carly was panicking and didn't know what to do. It was too late for him to sneak out the back door, and if he climbed out of Carly's window, Janelle and just about all of the neighbors would see him. Ant was trapped in, and if Janelle caught him inside of her house, she was going to flip out. Even worse, if she found out he and her sister were fucking, somebody was going to get killed this morning.

"Get in here and don't make a peep," Carly said, pushing Ant into the closet. "You gonna have to stay here until she goes back to work." As soon as the closet door closed, Ant felt like R. Kelly when he did the *Trapped in the Closet* series. Janelle could be heard coming through the door yelling for Carly to help her.

"Damn, bitch. What you up in here doin'?" Janelle said, lugging the remainder of the bags off to the kitchen.

"Girl, I was lying down. You know I gotta go to work in a few hours. And why you using your lunch break to go food shopping?" Carly asked as if she was concerned with Janelle not eating during her break.

"Because it's less crowded. Now move so I can go to the bathroom," Janelle said, heading for the steps. Carly watched nervously, hoping Ant kept his dumb ass in the closet. Janelle was like a hawk and could sense when something was out of the ordinary.

"Are you still gonna do my hair tomorrow?" Janelle yelled from upstairs. "I'm going to get three bundles of hair after work."

"Yeah, I told you I got you. And don't get that cheap shit," Carly yelled back, creeping to the bottom of the steps to hear which bathroom Janelle was using.

Hearing the toilet flush, Carly could tell she was using the bathroom in the hallway instead of the one in her bedroom. She felt relieved as she walked back toward the kitchen before Janelle could exit the bathroom.

"What the hell!" Janelle said, stopping at the top of the steps.

She looked up and down the hallway at all of the bedroom doors, then took a deep sniff. She could smell an all-too-familiar fragrance in the air, and it wasn't one that a woman would wear. It was stronger and more masculine, like that of a male's cologne. She didn't want to be nosey, but her woman's intuition was begging her to check it out. She knew the kids wouldn't have a man in their room, and Janelle damn sure would have remembered if she'd left a nigga in her bed this morning when she went to work, so the only room left in the house was Carly's. Her door was closed, too. When Janelle walked up to the door, the scent got stronger; then, after looking up and down the hallway one more time, Janelle cracked the door open.

"I know this shit ain't happening," she mumbled under her breath as she took another whiff of the scent.

Her first instinct was to go downstairs and beat the shit out of Carly, but she decided against it. If Carly wanted to play with fire, then she too could get burned. Janelle slowly closed the door and went back downstairs as if nothing had happened.

Roshon pulled up to Mr. and Mrs. Covington's house in the late afternoon, hoping that somebody was home. RJ really wanted to see his grandma and his siblings, and Roshon didn't realize how much he'd neglected RJ by not spending time with his mother's side of his family. He now really felt bad about it.

"Grandma, Grandma!" RJ screamed when she opened the door.

Mrs. Covington looked beat, like she hadn't slept in days. Her eyes had huge bags under them, and it looked as though she'd aged tremendously since the last time Roshon had seen her, which was only a few weeks back. Her hair even looked grayer. *The aftermath of her daughter's death isn't doing well for her, but then which parent would it do well with?*

"I'm so glad you're here, baby. I really need to talk to you," Mrs. Covington said, stepping to the side so Roshon could enter.

RJ darted by, running right upstairs where he could hear his brother and sisters playing around. Seeing the distressed look on her face, Roshon could feel the blitz coming on. He just wasn't sure from what angle.

"Roshon, I'm not gonna beat around the bush with you. My husband is sick," she said, taking a seat on the couch. "His diabetes and blood pressure won't go down, and we're not sure how long he's going to live. This is the third time it's been out of control, and this time it's worse than before."

"I'm sorry to hear that, Mrs. C. If there's anything I can do—"

"I need you to look after the kids for me," she said before Roshon could finish his sentence. "I know I'm asking for a lot, but me and Donald don't have anybody else to turn to."

"How about their daddies? It's high time them niggas start stepping up anyway," Roshon responded with a serious look on his face. That sounded good, but even Brandi wasn't sure who her baby daddies really were, aside from Roshon and the youngest child's father.

"Roshon, these kids will have to either be split up among what family I have left on my side, or they will have to go into foster care. And even in foster care, they will be split up."

"Come on, Mrs. C. I can't take on that kind of responsibility. RJ is enough. I just can't do it. They can't come stay with me," Roshon spoke.

RJ walked into the room just in time to hear Roshon's last remark. He had Olivia with him, but he turned around and ran off up the stairs, leaving his little sister standing there with an innocent look on her face. Roshon sighed then sat down on the couch, dropping his head down into his cupped hands. He had said the first thing that came into his mind, but never in a million years did he want RJ to feel like he didn't care about his brothers and sister. *Damn Brandi.* Even in death, she was still causing problems.

She had ruined not only her life, but the lives of those around her. Roshon pitied her mom, he really did. She did not deserve all the shit that was happening to her. She was such a nice woman who shouldn't have to spend her golden years raising children. He really wanted to help, but four kids? It wasn't as if they were teenagers. At least then he could maybe deal with the thought that they would be soon going off to college. They were just little kids. How was he supposed to take care of them with his work and lifestyle? *There is no way I can do it.*

RJ was upstairs changing his infant brother's diaper when Roshon walked into the room. He looked up at his dad then turned back to finish doing what he was doing. Baby J was cooing and giggling at his big brother, trying to pull the Pampers off while RJ tried to put it on.

"RJ, we gotta get ready to leave," Roshon said, standing at the entrance of the room. "Did you hear me, RJ?" Roshon asked when RJ didn't respond.

"I'm staying with my little brother," RJ said.

"Come on, RJ, I don't have time for this. It's time to go," Roshon demanded.

RJ was firm on his position, and if Roshon wanted him to leave that house, he was going to have to drag him out of there.

"I gotta stay and help my grandma," RJ told his dad. "Don't make me leave my brothers and sister," he pleaded.

RJ's words shredded Roshon's heart into pieces. His son was so brave and so thoughtful when it came to his siblings, and the stance that he made showed that he was willing to sacrifice getting his ass whooped in order to get his point across. In a sense, Roshon was proud of his son for standing up for something that he felt was right. But at the same time, RJ had no idea how hard it would be for Roshon to take on raising three extra kids without any help. That wasn't something Roshon could see himself doing.

"What nigga you done had up in yo' room?" Janelle playfully asked when she walked back into the kitchen. "And don't lie. I can smell him."

The question caught Carly off guard, and she wasn't sure if Janelle had seen Ant and was just trying to make small talk before she unleashed an ass whooping on her, but in any event, she played it cool.

"Nobody special. Just some guy I know," Carly answered nonchalantly.

"Well, do I know him?" Janelle asked, walking over and leaning up against the sink right next to her. That scent had been damn familiar, and though she knew where she could place it, she didn't want to believe her sister would be that trifling. It started to feel a little like an interrogation, but Carly stayed calm with short and sweet answers. She knew Janelle. If she acted all defensive, she would figure the shit out, and blood was bound to flow.

"Nah, just a friend from work." Carly smiled then went back to the dishes.

Before Janelle could probe any further, Carly changed the subject to a more interesting topic: one that she knew Janelle would be happy to hear about.

"On another note, I found a place. The landlord wants to run a credit check on me to make sure I pay my bills, but after that, I should be moving into the apartment. It's over off Milton Road, and it is so nice," Carly said.

"Dang, girl, you really wanna move? I was just getting used to having you around," Janelle spoke. "You know you don't have to leave."

"Yeah. As much as I like living with my little sis, I need my own space. Besides, I see you and that nigga Kareem starting to get close, so it's only a matter of time before you two become an official couple. Y'all are definitely gonna need y'all space in a minute." Carly smiled, play-humping the air to simulate having sex.

Most of what Carly said was true about now wanting her own space, but her main reason for doing so was to be able to fuck Ant without always worrying about being caught or him having to come and leave at a certain time. She was also tired of hearing all the shit her sister talked about Ant. Janelle would go on these rants about how she was glad to have the asshole nigga out of her life, and how the next woman to have him was gonna be unfortunate. Carly could tell her sister was still in love with Ant.

Janelle smiled, shaking her head. "Who told you me and Kareem ain't already do it yet, huh?" she asked.

Carly swatted her. "You slut! Tell me what's really real. He good right?" she asked.

"Oh yeah, he good. He hit all the spots, even a better lover than Ant," she added with a frown.

Kareem and Janelle had been seeing each other for the past month. Though it was nothing serious at the moment, Janelle could definitely see it getting there.

Kareem was one of the guys who had once stayed in the complex. Back then, he was always hollering at Janelle to be his woman, but she wasn't interested. He had gone away for a while and returned while Janelle was dating Ant, and once again she told him she wasn't interested. If only she'd known that Ant was going to turn out to be such a jerk, she would have let go of him and become Kareem's woman. He was a hard worker and not a deadbeat like Ant. He was well dressed, educated, and knew how to provide for a woman. *Who wouldn't want to be with a man like him?* It had only taken some time for her eyes to be opened to see that she had been wasting her time with Ant.

"Girl, let me get my ass back to work," Janelle uttered as she was heading to the door. "I'll hit you up after I pick up the girls and am headed this way."

Janelle hopped in her car and pulled out of the parking lot. Her stomach was tight, and she didn't think she was going to make it around the corner to the other parking lot without throwing up. The scent of Ant and her sister fucking lingered in her nose. She swore it had gotten in her mouth as well. She parked the car in front of the other building and ran to the bushes to vomit. She walked back to her car and grabbed a bottle of water. She was disgusted and hurt. Molly was walking up the sidewalk, smoking her black.

"Hey, baby girl, you a'ight?" Molly asked, flicking her ashes.

"Yeah, I'm good, just got a little sick."

"Mm-hmm," Molly said, sizing Janelle up. "Pray to God you ain't pregnant." Molly laughed. Janelle half chuckled and sat down in the car.

Janelle had left the house hoping to make it back to work before her lunch was up. That's what she wanted Carly to think anyway. Janelle was like a private investigator mixed with a bloodhound. Well, that and the fact that her neighbor had pulled her aside a few days ago to have a talk with her. After that exchange, she knew that people had been talking.

"Hey, boo. How you and the babies doing?" Shay had asked her, smiling. Shay was the neighborhood gossip chick and knew everybody's business. If there was tea to be spilled, Shay was the bitch to go to. "You a cool chick, you work, take care of your babies, and mind your business. So, I just like you, and I ain't gonna keep letting them fools that stay with you keep playing you."

Janelle was lost for a moment. "What fools? I put Ant out, and the only other person staying with me is my sister."

"Babe, can I give you some advice? Your sister ain't nothing but a li'l ho, and she is fooling around with that lazy bum you called a man," she had said in plain words.

At the time, Janelle didn't think much of it. She knew how ghetto people were always trying to cause trouble, especially among family. But as she observed her sister's moves, the more she noticed that things seemed to be off. Carly had never been the type before to hide her men. It was just the opposite. She normally liked to flaunt them in front of Janelle. But there was something about this new man that wasn't the same. Carly would hang up the phone whenever she came into the room. There was a lot of texting and snickering.

If she was going to flip on her sister, it was going to take more than the word of some old, nosey neighbor. Janelle needed to catch her in the act, and she felt like today she may have gotten what she'd been looking for. Though it had appeared that nobody was in the house when she was snooping around upstairs, she felt like somebody was there. More than likely, it had to be Ant, because the strong scent of his cologne lingered in Carly's room. Living with Ant for so long, Janelle knew the smell all too well, and she knew he was too cheap to buy some new cologne.

Janelle drove up the street a few blocks, then got out and walked back toward the house. The whole time, she was contemplating what she would do in the event Ant was really there. She brought her pocketbook with her just in case, which concealed her knife and Mace. She wasn't sure which one she would be using, but she was ready for the perfect opportunity for either.

When Janelle walked up to the house, she quietly opened the screen door then pressed her ear up against the front door, listening for any voices. Music was the only thing that could be heard. She used this to her advantage when she stuck the key in the lock. Her heart began beating fast when she walked into the house. The downstairs was empty, and the music was coming from Carly's room. Janelle put her bag down on the table, grabbed her Mace, and headed for the stairs. She crept up the stairs slowly and quietly. The closer she got to the top, the more she could hear the sounds of Carly's moans along with a man's grunts coming from her room. This was it: the moment Janelle had been waiting for.

In between songs, Janelle could hear Carly calling out Ant's name. *No-good muthafuckas,* Janelle thought as she walked up to Carly's door. Instead of kicking in the door like she had planned to, Janelle slowly turned the knob and cracked the door open about an inch.

"Fuck me harder. Harder, baby!" Carly yelled out.

Ant was on top and had her legs so far back her toes touched the pillow. He was pounding away, long-stroking Carly viciously. She ripped the sheets off the bed, taking all his dick.

"Ooooh, cum all in this pussy, nigga," Carly encouraged him.

Janelle became sick to her stomach and didn't even have enough energy to do what she had planned on doing to them. Everything had changed, and in an instant, Janelle went from being angry to being hurt. It was a feeling she had never felt before. Knowing what was going on was totally different from actually seeing it. She saw Ant in a different light. This was a man who always complained about her sister, how he thought she was so lazy and trifling, and how Janelle needed to put her out. And now he had her stretched out wide while he drilled her. She had been taken for a ride, and it hurt badly.

Janelle quietly closed the door, going undetected, then headed for the bathroom because she knew she wouldn't make it out of the house in time to vomit. She sat there on her knees in front of the toilet allowing everything she had in her stomach to come up. She thought that flushing the toilet a couple of times would get Carly's and Ant's attention, but it didn't: not by a long shot. When Janelle exited the bathroom, she could still hear Carly yelling and screaming.

As bad as she wanted to bust in the room and kill the both of them, she had to resist. She had a better plan for the two of them. She just had to see the two of them with her own eyes. Revenge was what she now needed, and Janelle wanted it on her terms. She crept back up to the bedroom door, cracked it open, then reached into her back pocket to grab her iPhone. She snapped a couple of pictures before softly closing the door, then walked down the hallway and crept down the steps, leaving the house without either of them noticing that she was there. She got in, found what she was looking for, then got out, and not once did Ant skip a beat or miss a stroke.

Feeling angry and hurt, Janelle got in her car and headed back to the office. As she was sitting at a red light, she started thinking about how selfish and ungrateful Ant and Carly were. Of all the people she knew and loved, they were the two people she had done the most for. She had taken Ant's bastard ass in when he was released from jail and no one gave a shit about him or was willing to take him in. The nigga had eaten her food without dropping a dime, she had paid his bills, and yet, he could still do this shit to her. Then, to add icing on the cake, her own damn sister. She would expect that from a nigga, but not her big sister, Carly. They were blood. Fucking blood! It was fucked up.

"I can't believe this shit," she said to herself as she thought about what she had just seen.

This was her sister she was talking about. They shared the same dad and mom. They had grown up together and been through shit together. She had welcomed her into her home, and what had she done? Thrown her kindness in her face by fucking her man. She was the greatest traitor between them. She had done the unthinkable: she broke the sister code and had destroyed their relationship. Janelle was the one they had considered a fool, the one they were subjecting to heartbreak. Even though it was over between her and Ant, it still hurt like crazy. As sisters, you aren't supposed to fuck your sister's boyfriend or her ex. It was a code. But she had gone ahead and fucked her boyfriend, in her house, and on her bed. There was no way she was not going to hold them accountable for their actions.

If it was the last thing she did, she was going to make them both pay.

"Baby, you gotta relax. I told you my people are gonna like you," Arlene said as she got out of the passenger's side of Dorrian's car.

"Yeah, I hear you, baby," Dorrian responded, getting out of the car and fixing his clothes. "What if they don't?"

It had only been a few weeks, but from the outside looking in, it seemed like Dorrian and Arlene had been together for a couple of months. They had hit it off instantly, and the connection that they had was simply amazing. Though their difference in age was about ten years, with Dorrian almost forty and Arlene almost thirty, they shared some of the same stories and struggles in life. Dorrian had never been the type to believe in love at first sight, but he was really feeling like that was indeed what he and Arlene had. A few times he had almost slipped up and told her that he loved her, but he would catch himself and just say that he missed or needed her so much. It became their signature line before they got off the phone every night.

"Baby, they're going to like you because I love you," Arlene responded. The words caught them both by surprise.

"I love you too, baby." Dorrian smiled as Arlene used her key to gain entry into her parents' home.

She just looked at him and smiled. Her family was just as dysfunctional as any other family, and Dorrian was in for the shock of his life, starting with Big Jeff. Arlene entered the house and ran straight upstairs past Jeff, leaving Dorrian in the living room.

"Who da fuck you done brought up in this house?" Jeff asked, coming down the steps. "Hey, Milly, yo' daughter got a nigga down here!" he yelled back up the stairs. "Who da fuck is you?" he asked, walking up on Dorrian with his fists balled up.

Dorrian knew that this had to be her brother, who she had warned him about, and he was a little nervous because she described him as being crazy and bipolar. Arlene had run up the steps, so it was only them two downstairs having a staring contest. Finally, Dorrian introduced himself.

"What up, brah? My name is Dorrian," he said, sticking his hand out for a shake. Jeff looked at his hand then twisted his face up. He looked young and fit, so if it was about to go down, Dorrian was about to be in for a run for his money. Jeff stared Dorrian in the eyes and then out of nowhere, he burst out laughing.

"Aww, my nigga, I was just making sure you wasn't no bitch." Jeff was cracking up as he smacked and shook Dorrian's hand. Dorrian didn't laugh right away. He was more relieved Jeff wasn't trying to go at it. Fighting his girl's brother on the first day they met wouldn't exactly make a good impression on the family.

"Dad, would you leave my friend alone?" Arlene said, coming back downstairs. Dorrian looked from Jeff to Arlene with a confused look on his face. He had to make sure he heard her right.

"Dad?" Dorrian asked when she walked up.

"Yeah, Dorrian. This is my dad, Jeff. Daddy, this is my friend, Dorrian," Arlene introduced the two. Jeff didn't look a day over thirty-five, nor did he have a head full of gray hair, just a few strands. At the age of forty-eight, Jeff carried his age well.

"Damn, he's fine," Milly, Arlene's mother, said as she came down the stairs. She was clearly older than everybody in the room, but even at her ripe age of fifty-nine, she too looked good for her age. She was a MILF and still had a vibrant aura to her, along with a great body.

"Now what do you want with my daughter?" Milly asked as she looked Dorrian up and down. "You ain't too old for her?"

Dorrian looked from Milly to Jeff with one eyebrow up.

"No, he didn't," Milly said, knowing what he was thinking. "I was twenty-nine, and he was eighteen. He had game and a big package I couldn't shake." She laughed.

"Mom!" Arlene cut her off as she described Jeff, justifying the large age gap between the two of them.

"You already know," Jeff bragged and boasted as he slid up behind Milly and wrapped his arms around her waist.

Dorrian couldn't believe how hood and cool Arlene's folks were. Even though they joked around about the age difference, they weren't really tripping about it. In their eyes, Arlene was a grown woman and had the right to date whoever she wanted. They of all people knew that love could come in all shapes, forms, and sizes, so who were they to judge? Meeting and winning Arlene's parents over was going to be easier than what Dorrian thought, and it was a plus, because as long as he had their approval, the sky was the limit for him and Arlene.

"Oh my God," Natalie said, walking into Roshon's office. "When your secretary told me you were still here, I didn't believe it," she said, walking over and taking a seat on his desk.

"Yeah, ya boy Mr. Humus got me working on a new account. You ever heard of Whitman Industries?" Roshon asked as he wiped the corners of his eyes.

"Sure have. It's one of the fastest growing distribution companies in the country right now. Is Humus trying to take them on as a client?" Natalie asked excitedly.

The Whitman account wasn't as big as the Oya account, but it was the next biggest thing on Wall Street. People predicted that, in 2020, Whitman Industries would overshadow other distribution companies like Goya, Chicken of the Sea, Maruchan, Jozev, and Keefe Supply Company. If Roshon were to land this account, it would put Global at the top of the food chain and have other investors knocking on the door. Mr. Humus only trusted one man with the job, and that was his go-to man: Roshon.

"Well, congratulations," Natalie said, getting up and walking around to Roshon's side of the desk. She leaned over and kissed him on his forehead then proceeded to the window in order to check out the view.

"Every time you come in my office, you look out my window," Roshon said, spinning his chair around so he that he was facing her. "I got one of the worst views in the building."

"You got the best view in the building," Natalie corrected him. "Come here," she said, waving him over.

Roshon got up and stood behind her, looking out of the window over her shoulder. On this side of the office, all you could see were a few buildings and several housing developments being constructed in the distance. It was nothing like the west wing of the building where you could see Charlotte's skyline clear as day. The west wing was reserved for the executive staff only.

"If you look right over there, you can see my house," she said, picking up the binoculars Roshon had on his file cabinet and putting them up to her eyes.

Roshon wasn't thinking about the view of Natalie's house right now. Every time he got this close to her, it did something to him. They'd been hot and heavy a few times, but Natalie never let it get to the point of Roshon getting inside of her. One thing was for sure: it never deterred him from trying, and often. Damn, he wanted to be with her so bad. He could not count how many days he had gone home to have a cold shower to take care of his blue balls.

"How long are you gonna make me wait?" Roshon asked, shifting her long blond hair over her right shoulder. A kiss to the back of her neck almost melted Natalie. If Roshon didn't know anything else, he knew that her neck was a weak spot on her. He kissed it again, then wrapped his arms around her waist.

Natalie rolled her eyes, putting the binoculars back on the file cabinet. "Don't do this, Roshon," she moaned, placing her hand over his on her stomach.

Natalie wanted Roshon so bad, but she was afraid of how things would change once their relationship turned sexual. She wasn't the type to just sleep around with men with no strings attached. With Roshon, she was swimming in dangerous waters, because she actually liked him and oftentimes thought about being with him in a more serious relationship. Giving up the goodies now could ruin those possibilities, but tonight wasn't one of those nights she could be strong. She was horny and vulnerable to Roshon's words and his touch.

"I think you're ready," Roshon said, reaching down and grabbing the ends of her skirt.

Natalie was paralyzed but could feel him lift her skirt over her waist. Roshon got down on his knees behind her, palming and massaging her ass with both his hands. Moments later, her panties were pulled down, ass cheeks spread apart, and Roshon's face was planted into her soft, warm, and very wet box. She gasped for air, feeling his long tongue twirling around inside of her. "What are you doing to me?" Natalie whined.

She reached down and began rubbing on her clit, at the same time grabbing a handful of her breast. Her face was planted up against the window, deep breaths fogging the glass, and an orgasm was on the rise. She could feel it in her stomach. He went from the inside of her pussy to licking and sucking on Natalie's asshole. She didn't want him to stop. It felt too good.

"Oooooh, Roshon, it feels so good. I can feel it," she whined, reaching back and grabbing the back of Roshon's head.

She pushed his face into her ass, bending over slightly so she could feel his whole face in it. As her orgasm began to erupt, her knees started to buckle. Roshon held her up against the glass, allowing for her juices to drain into his mouth.

"Come here," Roshon said, grabbing her hand and pulling her to the floor. "I want you to feel me inside of you," he told her, laying her down on the floor between his desk and the window.

He sat up on his knees between her legs, stroking his hard dick while watching Natalie unbutton her blouse. She looked sexy as hell, and without further ado, Roshon lay down on top of her, slid the head of his dick up and down her soaking wet pussy, then pushed his thick, long black rod inside of her.

Natalie grunted, then let out a deep sigh. "Ohhh, Roshon," she moaned, pulling his face down to hers so she could kiss him. Roshon took his time too, slowly stroking and going in as deep as he could. He wanted his dick to touch every inch of her insides. As they lay there on the ground engulfed in each other's passion, Natalie's body submitted itself to Roshon's will. This was the very thing Natalie was afraid of, but at this point, it was far too late to turn back.

Falicia texted Los's phone telling him that Keera had posted a picture today on Instagram of her and baby William in the hospital. Los immediately called her phone and got the information pertaining to what hospital she was in and what room number.

"You want me to go in with you?" Rhonda asked when she pulled up to the children's hospital with Los.

Los instructed her to park in the deck, come in, and wait for him in the waiting room. He didn't feel like having any awkward moments when Keera saw that he'd brought a female with him. When he got up to the north wing where baby William was, Keera was standing outside of his room looking down at her cell phone. It took a little time for Los to get down the hallway, but when he finally got close, some dude went to Keera and wrapped his arms around her waist. The guy didn't even notice Los coming up the hallway, but Keera had. She detached herself from the guy's bear hug and walked over to try to tend to Los.

"Is my son in there?" he asked, nodding in the direction of the room where the guy had come out and was standing in front of.

"Yeah, the doctor said that William's condition is getting worse—"

"That's ya nigga?" Los asked, cutting Keera off.

Keera ignored the question and began trying to explain what was going on with William, but Los insisted that she answer his question.

"He's my friend, Los," Keera said with her head down in shame like she'd betrayed Los. "But let me finish telling you about William."

Los looked at her then across the hallway at her so-called friend. Though they weren't together, Los felt some type of way about her being with someone else and moving on so fast. Not just that, but she had another nigga around his son while he was hospitalized. He felt disrespected.

"It's bad enough I had to find out through someone else that William was in the hospital, but to get here and see you got a whole other nigga up here . . . It's all good. I see you got everything under control here, so I'ma go ahead and get out of y'all way," Los said.

"Come on, Los, don't be like that. Go in there and see your son."

Los gritted his teeth at her. He wanted to slap the shit out of her but decided against it. He mugged dude, then hobbled off down the hallway.

"Los. Los. Don't leave," Keera call behind him, but Los ignored her and continued down the hall, and before Keera knew it, he had disappeared into the elevator.

The guy she was with tried to walk over and console her, but Keera stuck her arm out to stop him. The only man she wanted consoling her at the moment was Los. She went back into the room to watch over her baby. She was pissed as she tried to hold in her tears, but she couldn't hold them in any longer. Her body began to quiver, and her legs started to feel like jelly, causing her to lose her balance and drop to her knees.

She hated seeing her son in this condition. What the hell had he done to deserve this?

William was a sweet baby, and she knew he would have been sweeter if not for his sickness. He didn't get the chance to play like kids his age. She had to be extra careful with him. *Why didn't God give me a healthy baby?* she questioned as she buried her face in her hands. Seeing him in such a state weakened her. He was so little, and she could feel his pain. It hurt her to the core. If she could switch places with him, she would not hesitate. She needed him to have a healthy life. She wanted to teach him so much, and to have memories with him. She wanted William to be happy.

She pulled herself off the floor then sat beside William. Holding his hand, she started thinking about Los. She hated Los even more. She would have liked to revel in his jealousy, but it was just plain stupidity. Couldn't he see that his son was hurting? That he needed him more than ever? When he said he was willing to learn to care for his son, she had not expected this. Why would he leave her alone at such a trying time for their child? She needed him by her side. She knew there were no longer any sexual relations between them as agreed, but why couldn't he just be a father to her child? She hated that, despite everything that had happened between them, she still loved him, and that she had trusted and believed in him. Her love for him was beginning to wane as William's had become a part of her. She had thought she would never love anyone like she loved Los, but she was wrong. The day she gave birth to William and held him in her arms for the first time, she knew that William would forever hold a place in her heart. The love she had for him was greater than any love she had felt for anyone.

Keera closed her eyes. It had been a real long time since she spoken to God. Right now, she needed Him to intervene. "Lord Jesus, please don't let my baby die," she prayed. She would die if William was taken away. He was just a baby and needed her, but she needed him as well. He was the only thing that mattered now.

Roshon pulled up into his driveway singing Jon B. and Babyface's "Someone to Love."

It's because of you I was able to fall in love again. You give me someone to love, someone to touch, someone to hold. . . .

Roshon sang that song all the way into the house, stopping periodically to hit his high notes. Natalie was the first white woman he had sex with, and it was even better than what he thought it would be. He was wide open, but just when he thought life was good to him, his happiness diminished as soon as he walked through his front door. Mrs. Johnson sat on his couch wiping tears from her face with a Kleenex.

"What's going on?" Roshon asked, looking around the house suspiciously. "Where's RJ?" he asked.

"He's upstairs asleep now. Roshon, RJ tried to run away from home tonight. I caught him sneaking down the driveway," she said between tears. "I was so scared for him. I don't know what I would have done if he had—"

"Damn, RJ," Roshon said, taking a seat on the couch next to her.

"He said that he didn't want to live here anymore. He said that you didn't love him," Mrs. Johnson explained.

Roshon scratched his head. He knew this had to come from the other day when he wouldn't allow Brandi's other kids to come live with them. But to run away didn't sound like something RJ would try to do. "I'll be back," Roshon said, getting up and heading upstairs. Mrs. Johnson probably thought that RJ was asleep, but he knew that he wasn't. When he got to his room, RJ tried to throw the covers over his head, but Roshon caught him.

"Li'l man, come out from under there," Roshon said, taking a seat on RJ's bed. RJ's little head slowly peeked out from under the blanket.

"You wanna talk about what happened earlier?" Roshon asked, turning to face his son. "Why would you try to run away?"

"I don't want to live here anymore. I want to live with my grandma now," RJ's soft voice said.

"RJ, we talked about this already. Your grandma is sick and—"

Roshon couldn't even finish what he was saying before RJ started to cry. His little head went right back under the blanket.

Roshon was heartbroken hearing his son cry out, "You don't love me," from under the blanket. It hurt so much that Roshon became frustrated.

"What do you want from me, RJ? I give you everything you want. What am I doing wrong?" Roshon snapped, jumping up from the bed.

"I want my brothers. I want my sister!" RJ cried.

RJ went crazy, kicking and screaming in his bed. "I want my mommy. I want my mommy!" he continued screaming.

When he yelled out for Brandi, Roshon felt his pain. This was the first time RJ cried long and hard for her since she had died, and he was letting it go. It was all finally coming out, and a sense of guilt rushed Roshon's thoughts as the last words he had heard from Brandi were her pleas for him to come get her. He started to feel somewhat responsible for her death, knowing that he had a chance to save her life but didn't.

"Shhhhh, li'l man," Roshon said, sitting back down on the bed and wrapping RJ up in his arms. "I'm sorry, li'l man. I'ma fix it. Just give me a chance, and I promise you I'ma fix it," Roshon said, rocking his son in his arms.

In a few minutes, RJ, with a tearstained face, was sleeping. Roshon looked at him. He was so innocent and small. He hated that he had hurt him, even though it had not been a deliberate act. He scolded himself. He should have known better. He should have realized that RJ was missing his mom, no matter how bad a mother Brandi had been.

He had been so occupied that he had forgotten all about his son, who was his first priority. What if he had managed to leave the house without Mrs. Johnson noticing? His blood ran cold as he thought of the things that could have happened to him. He could have been hurt by a speeding car or one of those sick child molesters out there. And what if the cops had seen him out there roaming about? He could have possibly lost custody of his child for his negligence.

He knew without being told that his relationship with Natalie, as well as work, was overshadowing the needs of RJ. All this time, he had been so into Natalie that he had forgotten the most important person in his life: RJ. *How could I have been so stupid?* he berated himself. He needed to put things in order, or he was going to lose his son.

Keera sat at William's bedside watching his little stomach go up and down with every breath he took. The doctors didn't know how much longer he was going to be able to breathe on his own because, thus far, one of his lungs had collapsed. She tried to call Los, but at first, he didn't answer his phone. Then, after a while, he turned the phone off altogether. He really didn't feel like being bothered, and the more Keera sat there thinking about it, the more her mind let her lean toward Los's point of view. Maybe her friend Tim shouldn't have been at the hospital with her and William, especially since she had only known him for a couple of weeks. He was a good guy and treated Keera good. *But it is way too early to have him around William, and that is probably why Los was so upset.*

The truth was that Los was just upset at the fact that Keera had somebody else in her life. It was truly selfish. Since Los had accepted Keera as his baby mama, he didn't want to see her with anybody other than him, even though they weren't together. Keera was so confused and didn't know what to do at this point. She was still in love with Los, but at the same time, she wanted to move on and try to see what life would be like with somebody who might really love her. Tonight, it felt like she and Los were pulled apart even further than what they were, and any chance of them ever getting back together flew out the window the minute Los saw another man wrap his arms around her.

Keera's thoughts were interrupted when the doctor walked into the room to give her an update on William's condition. Though Los was invading her thoughts, baby William was more important, and Keera's attention needed to be focused on him right now.

"And what are you smiling about?" Natalie's babysitter, Hellen, asked when Natalie walked through the front door. Natalie had a full glow on her face, and she didn't even have to answer the question for Hellen to know that something had happened, and it involved a man.

"Wouldn't you like to know?" Natalie replied, kicking off her heels then joyfully sashaying her post-ravaged body into the kitchen. Hellen hopped off the couch and followed her, thirsty for all the juicy details of what went down.

"Sooo. Spill the beans," Hellen said, taking her seat at the island in the middle of the kitchen.

Natalie gracefully walked about through the kitchen, putting together a quick meal before she headed for the shower. She could still feel Roshon's body pressed up against hers, and the scent of his cologne was saturated in her clothes.

"Well, if you must know, my nosey best friend slash babysitter, I was touched by a gentleman tonight." Natalie smiled, sliding a plate of pie onto the island before taking a seat.

"Oh shit, you banged him." Hellen laughed. "You totally banged the guy. You whore," she said as she continued to laugh.

Natalie stuffed her mouth with a forkful of apple pie, listening as her friend cracked all kinds of jokes on her. After swallowing what she had in her mouth, Natalie rinsed it down with the glass of milk she had poured. She looked at Hellen with a mischievous grin on her face and held her stare for a moment before confessing. "I let him bang me," Natalie spoke, then burst out laughing with Hellen, who was up in arms. "It was amazing, too," she got out before stuffing her face with yet another piece of pie.

It had been a long time since Natalie allowed another man to touch her. After her divorce, she made a vow to herself that she would not have just casual sex. She wasn't that type of person, and she was adamant about making sure that the next man she gave the goods to would at least be her boyfriend. Roshon somehow came along and took her by surprise. He gave her exactly what she yearned for, exactly what she needed, and at the end of the day, Natalie wasn't even mad at him.

Chapter 9

Mrs. Covington's whole body was aching, and just a walk to the kitchen had become a mission. Brandi's kids wore her out so much it seemed like she was dying. Constant running around behind the toddlers, changing baby J's Pampers, and only getting a few hours of sleep at night was taking its toll. Mrs. Covington didn't want to put her grandchildren in foster care, but she was at the point where she didn't know what else to do. She wasn't sure how much more her body could take before it shut down.

"Olivia, please don't eat that, baby," she warned, taking the crayons out of her hand. "Samuel, can you go and get Grandma a diaper and wipes for your little brother?" she asked the oldest of the three. Olivia tried to make a break for the steps in an attempt to get the Pampers for her grandma herself. With a little bump from Samuel, she fell face flat on the stairs, busting her bottom lip in the process. Her ear-piercing cries sounded throughout the house, and it only became louder when she walked her little body over to Mrs. Covington. Hearing Olivia's cries started baby J up, and before you knew it, he was also crying. She shushed and rocked him, all the while using his blanket to wipe the blood and spit coming from Olivia's mouth.

It was so loud Mrs. Covington could barely hear the knocking on the front door. Mr. Covington, sick as he was, managed to make it down the stairs to see what was going on. He too didn't hear the knocks on the door until he got to the bottom of the stairs. As he went to answer the door, he looked over at his wife sitting on the couch with a defeated look on her face. He felt so bad for her and wished he could do something to help, but he was too weak physically to do anything.

"Pop Pop!" RJ yelled when Mr. Covington opened the door.

Roshon, RJ, and Mrs. Johnson looked like they had wings and a halo over their heads in Mr. Covington's eyes. Roshon could see the stress and tiredness written all over Mrs. Covington's face when he walked into the living room where she was. At that very moment, she was at her breaking point and had begun to cry herself. Mrs. Johnson ran over and attended to little Olivia while RJ took baby J from her arms.

When she stood up, Roshon wrapped his arms around her and gave her a much-needed hug. At the same time, he whispered in her ear some words of comfort. "I'll take it from here, Mrs. C."

She was so happy to hear those words come from him. It was the relief she'd been begging God for all these nights. Ever since she had started taking care of her grandchildren, she realized why she and her husband only had Brandi. She was their only child and had caused them so much turmoil. If they had known things were going to end this way, they would have pulled a tighter rein on her. Instead, they had allowed her to run wild, causing the problem they were in. She loved her grandchildren, no doubt, and she was glad they were around, but they were quite demanding. She wasn't as young as she used to be, when she could control them with an iron hand. Now she was weak and tired, and she needed some rest.

"You two go upstairs and get some rest. I'll send somebody over here in the morning to clean the house up," Roshon said.

Roshon and Mrs. Johnson loaded the kids into Mrs. Johnson's minivan and took them with them. Mr. and Mrs. Covington could finally hear their own thoughts now that the kids were with Roshon. They weren't sure how long he would keep them, but for however long it was, they were going to enjoy every second.

Los hobbled his way through William's hospital room door, taking a seat in the empty chair by his bed. Keera had gone to get something to eat, so for the moment, it was just him and his son in the room. He looked over at his child's little body and all the tubes sticking out of his mouth and nose. Even for Los, it was painful to see William like this. At the end of the day, this was still his son, his own flesh and blood. Roshon had given Los a good cussing out about him not going to see his child because Keera was fucking with some other guy. Dorrian had followed up, and even Ant told him he was tripping. Los knew that when Ant said you wasn't shit, you really had to be low, because Ant didn't give two fucks about many people and wasn't shit himself.

"I'm sorry for acting like a bona fide ass," Los said, sitting up close to William in hopes that he could hear him. "I know I could have been a better father, and I swear that if you pull through this, I will be. It's just, I never had a father, and all this stuff is so new to me. I don't know the first thing about taking care of you," Los said, shaking his head. "I just need you to pull through, so I can at least try. I owe this to you, if nothing else."

The rare lung disease was trying its hardest to claim William's life, and if it weren't for the fact that Los's lungs were too big for his infant body, he would have given William one of his. He had not realized the extent of his son's sickness until now. It was staring him right in the face. Although he had not wanted this child at first, he felt something for him. Maybe it was love. Maybe it was the realization that he could be the father to him he had never had and wanted so much.

At that moment, Los made up his mind that he was going to start being a better father to all of his kids. He had three beautiful, healthy little girls, daughters he hadn't seen in nearly a year. Their mothers not only deserved the child support he had been dodging, but also a break. Los knew it was time to grow up and be the man his father never was.

"Always know that your daddy loves you, and no matter what me and yo' crazy mama go through, I will be here for you," Los continued. "Just don't die on me, son. Fight for me," Los pleaded. Feeling the presence of somebody in the room, Los turned toward the door. Keera was standing there with her food in her hands and tears running down her face. She had heard just about the whole conversation Los was having with his son. All she had ever wanted Los to do was love and care about her and their son. To hear him speak in the manner he did was touching. She had never heard him speak so gently.

"Can I come in?" Keera asked, not wanting to interrupt this father-and-son moment.

"Yeah, come on in," he replied then turned back to face William. "But tell that nigga of yours to wait outside. This is family business," Los demanded, seeing the guy coming toward the room with his food.

Keera jumped up and walked to the door, stopping Tim before he could enter the room. She pushed him back out into the hallway, said a few words, then came back into the room. Los didn't know what she said to him, but Tim walked off with an attitude, throwing his food on the chair sitting outside the room.

"I'm really sorry about that," Keera said, taking a seat next to Los. "I swear I didn't mean to disrespect you—"

"But you did." Los cut his eyes over and told her. "So, because we agreed to stop seeing each other, that means you go out and fall in love with the next nigga? You got this nigga around my son."

"I know, I'm sorry. I fucked up, Los, but that nigga is not my boyfriend, and you know I'm not in love with him. Shit, I didn't even give him the pussy yet," she admitted.

"Well, I don't even care anymore. I have come to realize that it's not even about you anymore. It's about him," Los said, nodding toward William.

Keera didn't believe him. She knew that Los had some feelings for her. If he didn't, he wouldn't have acted the way he did when he saw her with another man. "Los, look at me," Keera said, nudging him in the side. "Come on, Los, look at me," she begged, now grabbing a hold of his arm and pulling it.

"What do you want, Keera?" Los inquired, turning to face her.

"Can you please give us a chance? We're not the same crazy young people," she said with all sincerity. "We have both changed. He has changed us," she spoke, looking down at their child.

Los had to admit he could see the changes in her attitude and in the way that she carried herself now. No more yelling and being ratchet in public, no more resulting to violence when things didn't go her way, and no more stalking and posting crazy comments online about him. She had changed an awful lot in a short period of time, and he knew he was changing. Maybe it was time for the both of them to show and prove.

But he knew more time was needed before they could commit to anything outside of their son.

"Man, whatever kind of weed that doctor is prescribing for you must be some good shit," Los joked, knocking on Keera's forehead like it was a door. "Listen, Keera. Aside from the fact that you crazy as hell and you shot me, I think you're a good woman. I'm not sure if either one of us is ready for a full relationship. I think we both still have some growing up to do. So, in the meantime, let's just be parents and help our son get through these rough times. We don't need to be arguing and fighting. And as far as you having a boyfriend—"

"Stop right there," Keera said, cutting him off. "I'm not gonna have any boyfriends. I'ma wait on you, Los, and I know it might seem crazy and people will say that I'm stupid, but I don't wanna be with anybody but you. My heart belongs to you, and that's how I plan on keeping it until you either turn in yo' playa card or check out," Keera told him.

She leaned over and kissed the side of his mouth then got up and walked over to William's bedside. Her heart was so content with loving him, nothing else really mattered. Los believed every word that she said. It was words like those that made him think maybe, just maybe, he could really learn to love her. Maybe one day in the near future, Los might decide it was time for them to be together exclusively. Only time could tell, but one thing he felt for sure was Keera was gonna be there waiting on him.

Ant walked down Summers Street on his way to his mother's house. They had begun trying to form a relationship since the day he showed her the wad of cash he had. Initially, he thought about asking her could he stay at her house, but the memories of his childhood came back and changed his way of thinking quickly. He also decided to stand his ground and not freeload off another female, his mother included.

Ant was a little startled when he walked up on the steps and Janelle was standing there on the porch. She looked sexy as hell, rocking a floral thigh-high dress, and a pair of Yves Saint Laurent sandals that matched the dress. She kept a Gucci bag on her arm, and her hair was laid down all the way around.

"Long time no see, stranger," Janelle said, standing pigeon-toed.

“Yeah, it’s been a while. How did you know I would be here?” Ant asked, leaning up against the wall.

“I didn’t. Since I didn’t know your address, I decided to stop by your mother’s and see if she’d be willing to give it to me. Running into you was a bonus,” she answered, shaking her head. “Another bonus was my prediction of what my man would do actually being correct. I predicted you would fuck my sister if you ever got the chance,” Janelle said, catching Ant off guard with that.

“You trippin’, Janelle. Ain’t nobody fucked Carly’s whore ass,” Ant denied, shooting her a glare to make his denial more effective.

Janelle went into her bag and pulled out her phone, scrolled through her photos, and showed Ant the one of him and Carly from the day she saw them fucking in her house. He still tried to deny it, saying it wasn’t him. “It ain’t me,” Ant said, shaking his head. “I know he look like me, but he ain’t me.”

“Just like a typical nigga. You’ll lie ’til the very end.” Janelle laughed, shaking her head. How stupid did he think she was?

“I’m not here for that, though. I just wanted to see if you wanted to make some money,” Janelle said, putting her phone back into her bag. She knew that if anything could get his attention, it would be money. Even though he had a job and seemed to be doing okay for himself, she knew that money was his driving force behind anything and everything. Looking at Ant, she felt disgusted with herself. What the hell had she seen in him in the first place? Love indeed was blind. She was so thankful to God that He had removed the sash from her eyes. She would have still been working and taking care of his trifling ass.

"Make some money how?" Ant responded, raising one eyebrow.

Carly wasn't the only one in the family who could be slimy. It wasn't in Janelle's character to be this way, but when pushed, she definitely knew how to get down and dirty. She just did it at a higher level, and she made sure that when she hit, she hit hard. Carly had no idea what Janelle was about to do to her, and if everything worked according to plan, Ant too was going to feel her wrath. They both were stupid in thinking that they could get away with having an affair under Janelle's roof.

The confidence of Carly irked her, that she could do such a thing. She was beginning to think that maybe it had not started with Ant. For her to be so confident, then it had to go a long way back. The bitch could look her in the eyes, laugh, and talk to her as if she hadn't done shit.

"You really outdid yourself this time, Roshon," Mrs. Johnson said, passing him the warm bottle of milk so he could feed baby J. The amount of respect she had for Roshon could not be explained with words. It was rare in these times to see men make the sacrifices that he did taking in Brandi's three children.

"Well, don't go congratulating me so quickly." Roshon chuckled. "You might as well cancel your weekends also. I'm thinking maybe we can get the kids every weekend."

"Oh dear, four kids, three nights a week? I don't think you can afford me." Mrs. Johnson laughed.

"I'll give you whatever it takes: free food, a new car. I'll even have you added to my medical plan," Roshon joked. He knew Mrs. Johnson would never leave him and those children stranded. She loved him like a son, and it didn't matter if he had ten kids to raise, she wouldn't let him do it by himself. This was a part of the promise she had made to his mother right before she passed away: that she would always look out for Roshon no matter what.

"Boy, I wanna be paid every week, and I need to go to the doctors to get these corns and calluses shaved off my feet if you expect me to be chasing these kids around all day." Mrs. Johnson laughed, agreeing to stay and help Roshon with the children.

"Thanks, Mrs. J. I owe you big time." Roshon jumped up, passing her baby J and the bottle. "And don't worry about those corns. You soak your feet, and I'll shave 'em down myself." Roshon laughed, giving her a big hug and a bunch of little kisses to her forehead.

Without her, Roshon didn't know how he would make it, and even with Mrs. Johnson being there his problems were far from over. He couldn't just let her do it by herself, so he was going to have to put time in with the kids. Helping to raise three other children, and the time he was going to be away from the job, was definitely going to affect his pockets. Close friends and family members probably wouldn't understand his reasons for doing what he was about to do. When it came to relationships, the first person who popped up in his head was Natalie. He had an early prediction that she would last every bit of five minutes after seeing he had a houseful of his dead ex-girlfriend's children. There wasn't a woman in her right mind willing to come into a relationship under those conditions.

Time, money, friends, family, and companionship were what Roshon was sacrificing for this cause, and those were just a few of the things he'd sacrificed, compared to the overall bigger picture. His life was about to change dramatically, and Roshon knew it.

Roshon's eyes narrowed as he stared at a mark on his son's arm, wondering why hadn't he seen it before. Even though it was faded, he could clearly see it. Someone had touched his son in a forceful way. If Brandi had done it, he was going to make sure he dug her up and gave her a resounding slap.

"What happened to you, RJ? Who did this to you?" he asked as he grabbed RJ's arm to see the mark up close.

RJ's head lowered, and he shook it. "Nobody."

He knew his son all too well, and he knew that was lying. As much as he wanted to grill him and get the name out of him, he knew that he couldn't because RJ would only shut down. RJ was just like him when he was younger. He rubbed RJ on the top of his head then kissed his forehead.

"A'ight. Go outside and play with your sister and brother. I will meet you in there in a minute," he said. He was angry and needed some time to calm himself down before joining the kids. Someone had harmed his son, and he was seeing red.

"I promise that whoever touched my son is dead."

Mrs. Johnson had overheard a little bit of the conversation, but she didn't want to pry until Roshon told her what was going on. She had seen the marks on RJ before as well, yet she didn't inquire about them. Roshon didn't know, but Mrs. Johnson was not the only one who overheard him asking RJ what happened to him. Samuel poked his head around the corner.

"I know who hurt RJ," he said, immediately gaining Roshon's attention.

"Come here, Samuel. Come sit beside me," he told him, patting the spot beside him. "So who hit your brother?" Roshon asked him.

"It was Joe. Joe hit RJ. Please don't tell him I told you. Mama told RJ not to say anything, and he would be mad if I said something," Samuel begged.

"Pinky promise," Roshon said.

Samuel smiled. "Joe was angry with Mama that she was not able to shut Olivia up, so he wanted to hit her to make her shut up. But RJ stopped him. He stood in front of him and stopped him from hitting her. But Joe ended up hitting RJ. He was shouting at RJ, calling him stupid and names Mama said we shouldn't say."

"How long had Joe been hitting Olivia?" Roshon asked, trying to keep his calm.

"Been a long while. He didn't like her and always liked keeping her quiet," Samuel informed.

"Thanks, Samuel. Your secret is safe with me," Roshon said, ruffling his hair. The boy smiled and ran back outside. Roshon's blood was boiling. He could not believe that this had been going on under Brandi's watch. She was a junkie, no doubt, but to sit still while some deadbeat hit her children was something else. He knew the asshole called Joe, but not too well. He was a crackhead as well as an upcoming rapper who didn't know how to throw a punch line. He also knew the deadbeat had been living off Brandi for a while.

"If the nigga wanted to whoop somebody's ass, then he should've confronted me like a man, not no woman and some little kids," Roshon mumbled to himself.

He could only assume that if Joe put his hands on his son, and Brandi told RJ not to tell, then he had to be putting hands on her as well. Roshon became pissed at Brandi for letting this shit go on. If only RJ had told him, he would have taken him from there a long time ago. He was more than glad that RJ and the rest of kids were no longer in that environment. It was no good for them.

Roshon could not imagine leaving the situation alone. Joe was going to pay for what the hell he had done to RJ. He began to pace the floor, and Mrs. Johnson became extremely nervous knowing that once he was in the state of mind he was in, it could become deadly for someone.

"You need to calm down, Roshon," Mrs. Johnson said in a panic.

Roshon ignored her and moved about in rage. He was going to kill Joe's bitch ass if he had a hand in hurting his son.

Chapter 10

Dorrian grunted a final time and exploded in Arlene before he pulled out. He patted her ass as he moved away from her. The only thoughts running through his mind were how good their sexual encounters were, and how he couldn't get enough of her. He went to the toilet and disposed of the condom then returned. She was spread naked on his bed, and his dick rose again.

He loved everything about her: her intelligence, her sexiness, her understanding. Every single thing about her was the shit. Sex with her was damn great. She wasn't a log of wood, and she knew when to take control and when to surrender to him. She was the kind of woman he had been searching for. He had gone through many women, there was no doubt about that. Since he was a rich, hardworking brother, the bitches threw themselves at him. He could not count the number of bitches who wanted to give him a lap dance or suck his dick during the club parties. They all wanted a piece of him. Black bitches, white bitches, Puerto Rican bitches stayed trying to hook, line, and sink him in.

Dorrian wasn't stupid, however. He had not made it as far as he had in life by being stupid. He could spot desperate bitches a mile away. And while he humored some of them, he knew he was not going to have anything worth holding on to with them. It was all about sex and head. They all wanted to tie him down, but he wasn't interested. He knew one chick who had ruptured a condom so he could get her knocked up. She had brought the packet from her purse, swinging it at him, but Dorrian brought his to the party and wasn't about having some bastard out there. Another had blamed some shitty baby on him, coming to the club to shout shit on him to own up to his responsibility. He had put the bitch in her place when he did the DNA test.

He liked Arlene a lot. He liked her more than any woman he had been with. She was fun to be around. She didn't judge him, his past, or anything like that. She was classy, but at the same time down to earth. He also freaking loved her folks. They were cool as well. If there was any woman who could deal with his mess, it had to be Arlene.

They had been dating for a few months now, and he knew it was time to move things further. He would be stupid if he thought that, if he let go of her, he would find a better woman. You only came upon such a woman once in your lifetime. He knew if he let go of her, he was going to regret it later in life. That was why he needed to stamp their relationship and make her his for good. Let the whole world know she was his woman.

She made him a better person. He knew he had changed since he met her. Shit he used to care about before didn't matter to him in the least bit, and he knew that Arlene was the cause of this change. He had always been a womanizer, not caring if the bitch was married or single. He fucked them all. Dorrian saw a change within himself long before his boys saw it. There used to be a time when he would be out with his boys, and all he could do was look at women and fantasize about what he would do to them. Once he had his eyes set on a woman, he would find a way to fuck her every which way and turn her out to the max.

The moment he connected with Arlene, the old Dorrian began to fade. He had not bothered to look at another woman. Arlene was more than enough for him, and he showed her by his actions and never his words. The other day, some skanky bitch had been all up in his business in the club trying to twerk on him. He had let her, but afterward, when she followed him to his office, begging for him to fuck her, he turned her down. He thought about it later on. The Dorrian he was before would have fucked her ass on that table and not given a shit. But now that he was with a woman like Arlene, the last thing he wanted to do was hurt her. Even though she would not have found out, he knew his conscience would not be at peace. His conscience was an asshole he had not worried about before; then Arlene had come along. She was a treasure, and he was going to take good care of her.

"What are you thinking about, baby?" Arlene asked, her hands sliding around his chest.

"Us," he confessed.

"What happened to us?" she asked.

"About how good we're together, you know," he said.

Arlene laughed. "I'm the good one. You, on the other hand, are the naughty one," she said with her hands palming his dick.

He chuckled and lifted her up, making her straddle him. His hands palmed her boobs, and she moaned, as her head stretched back and that natural arch hit her back. "You are so fuckin' sexy. Ride that shit, baby," he said in a panting tone.

"With pleasure, handsome," she replied as she slid her panties to the side and welcomed his dick into her awaiting dripping wet pussy.

Is it because we finally crossed the line and fucked that he is no longer interested in me? Natalie wondered. It had been quite a while since she'd had sex with Roshon, and he had not called her once. It was as if they had never shared a moment, never had sex, or never even went out on a few dates. It was as if he had used and dumped her. She hit the desk softly. She knew she should have held out the cookie much longer. But instead, she had ignored her heart and allowed her body to give in to the temptation. Now he was out of her life.

She was greatly disappointed in him. How could he do such a thing? She needed a good explanation for what he had done. She got up and went to his office, but it was locked. He had not come in.

"Did you see Roshon?" she asked their colleague.

"He just came in for a few minutes to talk with the boss and left. He has been doing that for the past week now," the guy said.

Is he avoiding me? she wondered. He was not a coward, but then she had not expected him to treat her in such a way. Maybe something was wrong at home. She had not called him and instead expected him to call her. She returned to her office and called him. He answered after two rings.

"Hey, Nat," he said.

"Roshon, what did I do to you?" she asked, getting straight to the point.

"Huh? What are you talking about?" he questioned, not understanding what she was getting at.

She pulled the phone from her ear when she heard a scream followed by several cries.

"Look, Nat, I am really busy right now. Got to go. I will talk to you later," he said before hanging up.

She looked at the phone, annoyed. She knew he was a good guy, but had she been wrong? Was he playing her? She shook her head. He was not that kind of guy, and something had gone wrong somewhere. She picked up her purse and headed outside. If he was too busy to talk to her, then she was going to pay him a visit.

Roshon knew he had acted like an asshole with Natalie, but how did you tell someone that you liked them a lot but now was not the right time? With the kids, there was no way he could bring a woman into the equation. It was just too much drama, more than he could handle. Especially since he decided to keep the kids more than on the weekends, knowing how hard it was for Mr. and Mrs. Covington. It would be a huge problem if he dated her. He had so much going on that it would only be a source of problems for their relationship. He was a single father with four kids. That would make any woman run and scream in the other direction.

Where the hell is Mrs. Johnson? he wondered as he looked around the house, which was in chaos. The woman had stepped out for a church meeting in the morning and had not come back. In her absence, the kids had run amok, screaming and shouting just because they felt like it. He had tried to calm them down, but the hide-and-seek game he'd started had ended in bickering when they accused each other of cheating. He closed his eyes and sighed. There was no way he had been this way as a kid. He knew that he was calm and collected. Nothing he said or did calmed them down. It was as if he had no authority.

RJ climbed his back, squealing, and he got up, giving him a ride. The other kids gathered around him asking for back rides as well. The bell rang, and he froze. *Please let it be Mrs. Johnson,* he prayed silently. Her presence was long overdue.

He opened the door and froze. Natalie stood at his doorstep, glaring at him. "Natalie," he said in disbelief.

"Roshon, you sure know how to treat a lady," she said, annoyed.

"I can explain," he started but was cut short by the noise in the house. "I will be right back," he said, rushing back. He groaned when he saw the boys arguing, with baby J crying in a high-pitched voice.

"What is going on here?" Natalie asked, confused.

Roshon sighed. "It is a long story. Kids, cut it out! There's a lady in the house."

That stopped their bickering, and they smiled shyly at Natalie who smiled back at them. She surprised him by picking up baby J, who immediately kept quiet a few seconds later.

"Where's his bottle? He's hungry," Natalie asked.

RJ ran to the kitchen and returned with a bottle, which Natalie fed to him. She turned to the boys. "Okay, kids, it is time to have a nap."

Roshon's eyes widened more when he saw them headed upstairs. He turned to Natalie. What the hell had she done? She was like a child whisperer. They were like putty in her hand.

"See you later, Dad," RJ said, heading upstairs.

"What did you do?" Roshon asked. He got a glare in reply from Natalie who pointed at baby J who was eating quietly. When she was done feeding him, baby J drifted off to sleep, and Roshon showed her the cot, which she placed the baby in.

"What's happening?" Natalie asked when they returned to the living room.

Roshon sighed and broke down all that had happened with Brandi's folks. "I can't leave them like that with them. They are really old and tired, especially with their only child gone. Caring for four kids is no joke. It is fucking hell."

"And this is why you have been avoiding me?" Natalie asked.

He took her hands in his. "I'm sorry, Nat, I never meant to hurt you. I know I should have called you, but see what you walked into? I'm feeling you, hell, a lot, but I can't drag you into this, and this will require too much dedication and time. If we have something going on, the kids have to come along with us, and it is not fair to you to treat you in such a way, so it is better I free you now before things get complicated."

Natalie was relieved as she heard his words. More than ever, she was sure that Roshon was a good man. Where the hell had he been when she met her fucking ex? The scene she had walked in on had been quite surprising. The last thing she had expected was children running around. She could see the toll it had taken on him. He already had bags under his eyes as well as beard growth. And although she understood him, she was not willing to let go. There was just something about him she loved.

Any other man would have said it wasn't his business, might as well let foster care take over the situation, or he would have even employed a full-time nanny to take care of them without giving a shit. But Roshon was interested in the kids, and it showed. He was spending huge money on them and their care, and it was going to increase as they got older, but he was willing to take it all on. She wasn't going to run away from him and his responsibilities. They were what made him.

"I'm not leaving you because of this," Natalie said, surprising Roshon.

"What? Are you seeing my shambles of a life right now?" he asked.

"Yes, I am, and I understand. Remember, I have three kids. They are worse than your kids, I assure you. I understand where you're coming from, but you don't have to give it all up. You can care for them and still have your life on track. You deserve happiness as well, you know.

I am not leaving. We're going to go through this together."

"But—"

She stopped him with a kiss. He realized as he explored her lips that he had missed her so much.

"Are we good now?" she asked when they separated.

He nodded. Her reaction was something he had not been expecting, but then, he had judged her wrongly. He should have known she was stronger than she looked.

"Now when was the last time you had a decent night's sleep? You look like shit," she said.

Roshon laughed. Getting sleep around the kids was a hard thing to do. "I can't remember," he admitted.

"Then go to your room. Don't worry about the kids. I will check up on them and join you," she said, dismissing him.

He went to the room to lie down. She joined him a few minutes later on the bed. His hand reached for her, and they cuddled.

"Thanks," he muttered into her ear.

Natalie shook her head amused. "You're welcome, and know this: a hundred kids can't drive me away."

Roshon chuckled. For the first time in a few days, he fell asleep without worry.

The tears did not stop pouring from Keera's eyes as she stared at the body of her lifeless son. It was over. He had taken his last breath. For Keera, being a hands-on mom, it was tough for her to be able to watch her son take his first breath and to stand, and then watch him as he took his last. She shook her head in disbelief as her body jerked in sorrow. The pain that Keera was feeling was indescribable. It was as if the life she had in her own body was slowly but surely leaving. Her son was her life, and he began to change her in ways that she never thought would be possible.

"No, God, why? He's just a baby. I would have taken care of him forever. He was my gift, my miracle, my angel. Please, God, I'll change everything about myself. Send him back," she cried. She just wanted to wake up and see that it had all been a dream, that William was still alive. "Why, God?" she begged. Why had He not given her baby boy a fighting chance? Instead, He had taken her baby away. How was she going to cope in the world? She had no one except William, and now he was gone.

A hand touched her shoulder, and she looked up to quiet yet welcoming Los. He had been quiet, and Keera wondered what had been going through his mind. Did he think he was free at last, from the baby he never wanted to have? *How happy he must be to be a free man.* Any hope of being with him had gone down the drain. She had not only lost a son, but also the love of her life.

"You should go. You don't have to stay. I know you don't want to be here," Keera said, wiping her tearstained face.

"Na, you need me, Keera. Don't try to push me away. He's my son too," Los said.

She shook her head. "No, Los, just go away. I don't want or need your pity. I know you never wanted him. Just go. Leave me. He was all I had, and now he's gone."

He ignored her and pulled her into a hug. She burst into tears even more and cried on his shoulder. "I want my baby back, Los. I just want my baby back. Help me bring him back, please," she begged.

"I wish I could do so, Keera. I wish I could bring him back for you, but he's in a better place. Wherever he is, he's well and happy," Los said as he comforted her.

She shook her head. She just wanted to hold him in her hands, to see that smile of his. The door opened, and Dorrian walked in with some woman. He gave Keera a hug, and she tried to clean her face. She was at her weakest moment, and she hated they could see how weak she was. She was not the strong Keera with the ratchet and bipolar attitude.

The doctor soon joined them, and they took baby William away. Her heart wrenched in pain as she silently said good-bye to her son. She had no idea what to do, but Los said he would take care of the funeral preparations. She was glad. She doubted she could go through with it. She knew her baby was sick, but in the back of her mind, she thought she would never have to bury him. He was going to get well and one day bury her. She fought so hard for Los to be a part of William's life, and she thought had he been there sooner, her son would have fought hard to get better.

Los had never seen Keera so weak and drained. It was as if she were high and out of the world. He shared a look with Dorrian who shook his head as well. Los wanted to wrap her in a hug and make everything go away. "I need to take her home," he told Dorrian.

"I don't want to go. I want my baby back," she said, shivering.

"She might be in shock," Arlene said.

He lifted her head and noticed her eyes were dilated. It was as if she were absent in the mind. He wondered when the last time was that she had taken her pills, considering she had been by William's bedside for days. "Help me. Go get the doctor," he told Dorrian who hurried away.

He made the right decision as, a few seconds later, she began to struggle against him. "Get me my baby. Get me my baby!"

He tried to hold her down, but damn Keera had sharp claws and fought hard against him. Nurses and a doctor burst into the room and rushed to her. She fought hard against them as they injected her with some substance. In a few seconds, she became limp and unconscious.

"We have to admit her for a while," the doctor told him. "The shock of the loss of her son has affected her. She needs some time to accept it and move on."

Damn, Los thought. Shit was just getting real. What the hell was he supposed to do now? He knew he had not wanted William to be his child before, but after finding out he was indeed his and accepting the fact, he couldn't help but feel some love for his son. But was he glad he was no more? In a way, as harsh as it may have seemed, yes. Caring for such a child was going to drain not only him, but also Keera. In years' time, it was going to kill her, reduce her joy, and affect everything she had going on. At least now she was free, and so was he. He could move on. Or could he? He could not leave her at this point in time. She needed him more than ever. He knew he did not want to be tied down to a woman, but he could not leave her hanging. He needed to be there for her.

Chapter 11

A week had gone by, and Roshon had to admit every day that Natalie had the magic fingers when it came to the kids. He wondered why he had never asked for her help. The kids loved her as well and were always looking forward to seeing her. Even Mrs. Johnson had jokingly said that Natalie was stealing her spot.

He rang the bell and moved to the side, so she could not see him through the keyhole. He was at Natalie's house. This was the first time he was going to be here since the night he had brought her home, the night Brandi had died, and yet, it seemed like forever. The door opened, and Natalie stepped out. She looked at him surprised then smiled. "Come on in," she said.

"Nice home," Roshon said, looking around. It was simple but beautiful, just like her. A young girl ran down the stairs screaming, and he could not help but smile.

"Theresa," Natalie scolded. "No running down the stairs."

She was pretty and looked so much like Natalie. "Who are you?" she asked, looking at him curiously.

He knelt down and smiled at her. "I'm Roshon, your mommy's friend."

"Oh, you're the Roshon Mommy is always talking about. 'Roshon is so cute,'" she mimicked in her mother's voice.

The adults laughed, and Roshon looked to Natalie, who was blushing and shaking her head in amusement. Another girl ran down the stairs, followed by a small boy. Sonia was ten, Theresa was eight, and Gabriel was five. They seemed like pretty cool kids, and they squealed in excitement when he gave them the chocolate he bought for them.

"Thanks," Natalie said when the kids ran upstairs.

He shrugged. She had done more than enough for him, so he felt it was just right for him to pay it back by paying her a visit. He had no idea what was going on between them. They had just shared a few kisses since they'd had sex, but he would be lying if he said he did not want to have sex with her again. All he could think of when he lay at night alone was her body, and how he could make her scream his name over and over.

The bell rang, and he looked at her curiously when the kids came down the stairs with bags. "They are spending a few hours at a friend's place. It is a Saturday routine," she explained.

"Bye, Mr. Roshon!" they screamed, waving at him.

When Natalie returned, she stretched, and a wide smile spread on her face. "We're all alone."

"Yeah," he whispered, pulling her to him. He had missed her warmth so much. He kissed her, and she pulled him closer to her. "I have missed you so much," he said.

"Me too. I can't stop thinking about that day, you know?" she said.

He laughed. "Me too. Now show me where your bedroom is. I want to see you naked."

She led him to the room, and their lips met again. He squeezed her breasts, and she shrugged the shirt off of her.

"I fucking missed this," he said, palming them. "You got a condom?" he asked.

She nodded and pointed at the bedside cabinet. He pushed her gently to the bed and pulled down her skirt, ready to give her the pleasure of a lifetime.

***

"Antttttt, where the fuck is you? Come get your shit from here. I ain't your motherfucking slave, you asshole!" his mother screamed from the kitchen.

Ant sighed. He didn't even know why he bothered to come visit her. He felt himself on the verge of strangling her every time he came over, even though she was his mother. She never saw any good in him since he was a little kid, no matter what he did. Even the time he got the highest grade in middle school, she had only told him his mates were doing better and that he was still a dumbass.

It didn't matter that he loved her and was trying to do everything he could to make her love him. He had gone so far as to serve time because he had been in a robbery because he needed the money to get her a new house. And what had she said when they came to take him away? That she had expected the shit from him. He wondered if she would ever be able to love him. If he died tomorrow, would she even cry? He doubted it.

Dorrian had said once that it was his mama's behavior that made him not take bitches seriously. Ant thought it was stupid, but Dorrian was right on the mark. His lack of love when he was a child, and now that he was grown up, had affected him. He didn't have love for women, and he was an awful boyfriend. None of the relationships he had been in lasted a year. As a matter of fact, the shit he had with Janelle had been the longest relationship he had been in, and it was because he was getting another cookie on the side. But with his niggas, it was another deal. He was loyal to a fault, and he was a damn good friend.

He walked to the kitchen and nodded at his mother who glared at him. Even though she was hitting fifty, she still dressed like she was in her twenties. She had on a short skirt and some tank top with her boobs spilling out, with some terrible wig, which he wanted to fling off her head, as well as some nasty-ass red lipstick he wanted to wipe off. But he knew if he did shit like that, he was gonna end up with a broken tooth and knocked on his ass.

He went to the sink and washed the plate he had used. His mother's phone rang, and she screamed into it, "Sheila, stop calling my phone. I'ma be there in a minute. You know how Ant is: the idiot doesn't know anything. So I got to make sure this shit is clean before I bring someone home tonight."

"Where you going, Ma?" Ant made the mistake of asking.

"What is it any of your business, huh? You come by when you feel like it, eat my food, use up my lights, even wash your nasty ass over here, and you think you got a right to question me, boy?" she screamed.

"I was just asking," Ant muttered.

"Keep your fucking asking to yourself, you piece of shit."

Her stilettos thumped against the ground as she went to her room. He heard a car pull up in front and he went to the window. He rolled his eyes as he saw Sheila and Patricia, his mother's friends. He guessed they were going to pick up some men. His mother had been a hooker when she was younger, and although she was a bit comfortable at this time in her life, she still refused to stay off the streets. Man after man kept on coming into the house when he was a little boy, and to this day it had not stopped. His daddy had been one of those men, and when his mother told him that she was pregnant, he had denied it. She could not do anything, as he was a married man whose wife was crazy as hell.

The door swung open, and Sheila and Patricia stepped in. Sheila whistled as she saw him. "Ant, you are looking fine today. Where your mama at?"

He gestured at the room, and Patricia went to join her. In the absence of both women, Sheila moved up to him and grabbed his dick. "When are you going to give me this dick again, huh? I have missed you so much, you know. Why don't you drop by my place tomorrow?" She kissed his ear with her nails trailing his neck.

He watched her ass sashay away. He shook his head. She wanted him just as much now as she did when he was a child. Sheila had been his first. He was eight years old when his mother left for the weekend, leaving him at Sheila's. It had been a week of fucking between him and Sheila, although he had no idea what was happening. As he grew older, he understood what the hell was going on and had taken revenge by screwing the fuck out of her. From time to time, he would give in and go fuck the hell out of her. She stayed thirsty for the sex between them.

He could hear his mom complaining about him to her two friends. He didn't understand why he continued to deal with the abuse from his mother. Although she wasn't abusive to him physically, his mental had been crushed because of her. A woman was supposed to show her son how to treat women. That was not the case with his mother. She was like the mother from hell. But regardless of everything he endured with her during his childhood and even as an adult, he still craved the love and affection from his mother. That's why he continued to come by and check on her as much as he did. He felt that if he could salvage his relationship with his mother, it would somehow right the wrongs he inflicted on other females. However, everything came with a price.

Chapter 12

"So, there I was being all polite to this bitch, and she calls me a ho. I'm like, you crazy, right? You really trying to get that ass beat? I pulled her fucking hair out and beat the shit outta that bitch," Carly said, laughing hard as shit.

Janelle smiled. She sure would have loved to beat the shit out of a bitch right now. Most importantly, the bitch who was talking to her. Well, hers was just around the corner. The bitch was going to know that you did not mess over family, especially when they were always there for you.

For weeks now, she had continued to fuck her ex-boyfriend in her house without remorse, while laughing and talking in her face as if she weren't a ho. She would even go so far as joining in with talking shit about Ant, how he's all types of assholes, yet she was riding his dick the other day. Not only was she a backstabbing-ass sister, but she was a lying, two-timing bitch. Janelle sat there and continued to feign interest in the story her sister was telling.

Her phone buzzed, and she looked at the screen. "Why the fuck is Ant calling?" she asked aloud, knowing that Carly was all ears. The reaction from Carly was fast, but she saw it.

"Hey, Ant, why the fuck you calling?" she asked.

"Carly is there, right?" he asked, knowing she was acting.

"Yes, what?"

"I'm in on it. You need to tell me exactly what you need and want me to do. You gotta understand that I ain't doing this shit for you. I just need the dough."

Of course. The bastard was as cheap as a pack of beer. "I might be interested in meeting up with you. I'll call you with the details," she said, knowing that she was feeling like Tupac: all eyes on her. Janelle was playing the hell out of her role. She began biting down on her bottom lip and twirling her fingers in her hair while bouncing her crossed leg. Ant had already disconnected the call, and Janelle started acting very flirtatious knowing she was pissing Carly off. After a few rounds of "see you soon" and "no, you hang up" and "on three hang up," Janelle placed her phone on her side and then smiled. Looking at Carly, she said, "I'm sorry, what were you saying?"

The look on Carly's face was priceless. If there was a going rate for her ass right now, she would have sold hers for a penny. Janelle was enjoying this torture. It was her pleasure to piss Carly off just as much as she was pissed off as she watched her sister bounce and contort into multiple positions on her man's dick.

"What did he want?" Carly asked.

"Who, Ant?" Janelle replied while internally laughing at her sister's despair.

"Yeah, bitch, Ant. What did that nigga want? What did he say?"

"Carly, I had no idea you were this interested in my love life," Janelle stated looking Carly deep into her eyes.

"I'm not. It's just that he's a dog-ass nigga and you up here cheesing like you just won the fucking lottery. I'm trying to find out what the fuck he say to make you all giddy and shit," Carly retorted with a frown.

"He said he missed me and needed to see me, and said that he was sorry, and he will never fuck with another ho again because I'm all the woman he will ever need," Janelle said with a smile.

"And you believe that shit? This nigga lived off you, never would contribute anything to the household, and please let's remember you stayed with Phaedra because of his ass. Nigga just wanna fuck, but I know you not falling for that shit. Nigga ain't shit! Fuck he mean you're all the woman he need?" Carly said.

"Damn, sis, is it wrong for him to learn and realize the error of his ways? Look, he said he was sorry, and if you know Ant, he never apologizes. I think he means well now," Janelle said.

"But what about Kareem?"

"What about him?" Janelle responded coldly.

She could see the anger on Carly's face. She was so going to talk about it throughout the day to make sure she rubbed the shit in her sister's face. She was going to teach her ass not to fuck over family. In the meantime, she needed to think about getting her revenge. She was going to deal with Ant, although he was working with her, but Carly's case was different. Carly was her sister, and she betrayed her when Janelle had been the only person to give a damn about her. When all else failed, it was Janelle who opened her arms and her doors only to be made a fool of. She was more pained as she had come to discover that Carly was also making a move on Kareem. He had said it in passing, jokingly, that Carly was making the moves on him. It had not been funny to her as she knew the kind of bitch her sister was.

She had gone over to one of her ex's and confronted the hell out of him, out of suspicion, and what had the bastard told her? He had fucked Carly, and he knew of another ex-boyfriend of hers who had fucked Carly as well. The bitch was going down! She could not begin to trace all her asshole boyfriends, but she was sure it was the same thing: Carly had fucked all her men. And to think she had cried on the bitch's shoulder. Just yesterday, she had been in the kitchen and wanted to use the knife to stab her in the eyes. That was the kind of hatred she felt for her sister. Whatever remorse she had felt for Carly was gone. She was going to make sure that no man ever fucked Carly when she was done with her.

"Hey, Los, how's Keera doing?" Dorrian asked from the chair in the shop.

Los sighed. "She's doing fine. I dropped by her place last night. She is no longer crying, but she's still not the Keera I know."

"Shit happened to my aunt," Falicia added. "Her baby died. What they call that shit again, you know, when the babies die in their sleep?"

"SIDS, sudden infant death syndrome, but most people call it crib death," Dorrian provided.

"Yeah, crib death. Now, Aunt Malik was a strong woman. The bitch got a strong hand and could whoop your ass good. But her baby's death killed her. She started talking to herself, not sleeping and shit. She was even on pills."

"What happened to her?"

"She killed herself," Falicia said.

"What?" Los asked.

"Yeah, she did. Mama went one morning to go check up on her, and the bitch overdosed. Didn't even write one of those shit people do, you know, a suicide letter. Mama said it was for the best, only way she could move on. So, if I were you, I would keep a close eye on her."

Los exchanged a look with Dorrian, who merely shrugged. Now Los was worried. He knew Keera was a strong woman, but the way he had seen her after William's death was unbelievable. She was a shadow of herself. He had no idea if she was fully in her bipolar mood. She barely talked to him and continued to stare at nothing in particular. The other day, he saw her clutching William's blanket. To him, he thought it was normal behavior because she'd just lost her child, but after listening to Falicia, Los didn't know what to believe. He was fucked up. The shit going on was disturbing the hell out of him. He suddenly felt the need to protect her. He had not been there for her when she needed him, but now was another opportunity, and he was going to be around even when it was time-consuming.

"Dorrian, how's your lady?" one of the customers asked, changing the mood of the shop.

Los was glad for the change of topic and jumped right in on the conversation. "Yeah, how's Arlene?" he asked.

At least something good was happening to one of them. He'd never seen Dorrian hooked over a woman before, and it was funny to watch. He treated her like a fucking egg. Dorrian used to talk to this older guy named Ray who used to pass down wisdom while he was attending his father's church. Ray told Dorrian when he found a good woman to treat her like an egg. Dorrian was confused. In his mind, he only ate eggs, and during that time, all Dorrian could think about was that maybe Ray was telling him to eat his woman pussy to keep her happy. Dorrian was tired of the egg analogy, and since he didn't know what Ray meant, he asked him, and Ray was happy to explain.

Ray placed an egg in Dorrian's hand and told him to run around, up and down the pews of the church. Dorrian did as he was told and then, when he was out of breath, Ray told him to toss it in the air and catch it. Dorrian was hesitant and then told Ray that he didn't feel comfortable that he could do that without breaking it. Ray smiled and told him good, then explained to him that when he found the perfect woman, to treat her as he would an egg. Treat her heart with kindness because it was just as fragile as an egg. Dorrian was blown away by the analogy and always held on to those words of wisdom by Ray.

When Ray passed away five years ago, Dorrian stood at his casket and told him that he hadn't found his egg, but when he did, he would treat her heart with kindness and understand that it's fragile.

Dorrian smiled. "My lady's good. Going over to her folks' place tonight."

Everyone laughed. Dorrian told them all about Arlene's folks and how strange they were. "So, you going over to her folks' place on a regular basis? Sounds serious," Falicia said.

"Maybe it is," Dorrian said.

The guys laughed at him, and Los shook his head. "Damn, I never knew the day would come when Dorrian would be taken. We should have bet on it."

"She's a good girl, makes a wild man calm down. I ain't getting any younger. Need some babies," Dorrian said with a smile.

Los patted him. His nigga was long gone. He only hoped his bubble of joy wouldn't burst. Arlene was a good girl, but life didn't work that way. Not everyone was happy all the time. Who would have told him he was going to be going through this shit with Keera?

"When you gonna take her over to your folks?" Los asked before catching himself.

"Don't even start," Dorrian said. It was no news that Dorrian's folks were dysfunctional. Although he was close with a few of his siblings, there was a severed relationship between them. Dorrian's dad was a pastor, yeah, a preacher man who had a son who ran a club. His dad had one of the most popular churches on this side of town. Daddy Victor was his preacher name. His church was always filled to the max with many of the members ready for miracles. His mom was the perfect preacher's wife in public, who everyone looked up to. But behind it all, out of the cameras, so much was going on.

Daddy Victor was a preacher who had several baby mamas and mistresses. His mother was no better off, as she was a drug addict and an alcoholic. The strange thing was their self-righteousness for every act they did. His father, Daddy Victor, always had a Bible scripture to back up his actions. He, however, wanted his children to live pure and just. Dorrian could not count the amount of beatings and the isolation he had received as a kid from his parents. Although he had the most privileged background among them, he had been emotionally abused. But Dorrian was a strong man who had seen beyond his parents to the future. His parents had made it in a way that they were all to depend on them.

When he turned seventeen, he left home. His parents started demanding that he return home, but Dorrian had his mind made up.

It had started as an act of rebellion. He had gotten a small place and turned it into a bar. With the success of it, he had turned it into a club. For a while, there was news of it in relation to his father's church. The older man had demanded he close his club or be disowned. But Dorrian stood his ground firmly. For too long had he been controlled. Now he could do what he wanted to do.

His club had turned into a success, and he had continued to expand, making a name for himself. In the years since he left home, he barely visited his parents although he kept in touch with his siblings. Yet and still, they were his parents. One of these days, he would have to drop by with Arlene to introduce her to his folks. He needed them to see the woman he was going to end up with. He was more convinced of this as days went by: she was the woman he was going to get married to, sooner rather than later. He was glad as well that his niggas liked her. There was no way he could hook up with a woman who his boys did not like. That was a recipe for disaster.

His phone rang, and it was Hakim: one of his good customers and a renowned jeweler. He was the one to go to whenever you needed top-grade blings as well as grills. Dorrian had hit him up to get a ring made. He needed it on hand for the moment he was going to propose to her. Never had he been sure of a lady the way he was of her.

"Hey, Hakim. How you doing, bro?" he asked.

"I'm doing fine. Your ring just came through, and damn it is a masterpiece. You are gonna love it, I swear."

He knew Hakim wasn't exaggerating. The guy was damn good at his work. "So, I can come around today?"

"Sure, bro. Hit me up in the evening. Got to discuss shit with you. Got some fellas coming from Cali soon. They need bitches, lots of bitches. Told them you can deliver any type of bitch they want. Black, white, skinny, fat, just give a call to Dorrian."

Dorrian laughed. "Thanks for the faith, man. We'll get up later this evening."

"Hakim?" Los asked, lifting a brow. "What you going to him for? You don't use blings."

Although Dorrian rolled in huge cash, he didn't use shit like that. He considered them to be used by small boys. He was always in a well-tailored suit and an expensive wristwatch.

"For something else," Dorrian said.

Understanding dawned on Los's face. "Oh shit! You gonna pop the question to her? Man! You really got it bad for her!"

The store went into an uproar as it dawned on them the once-bachelor for life was going to get hitched.

"Come on, guys, keep the noise down before the whole street knows. No one got to know this shit, understand? Proposals are supposed to be a surprise, and if anyone outside this store knows, I am going to hunt the person down who told and make sure he dances in the club naked for the weekend." They all knew Dorrian wasn't kidding. He was a man of his word.

"Come on, we understand. Our lips are sealed," Falicia said, zipping her lips close.

"Really? You want to do this?" Los asked, still wearing a surprised look on his face.

Dorrian laughed. "Why is everyone so surprised?"

Los shrugged. "Giving up your lifestyle? Your freedom? I mean, we all know you, Dorrian. It just shocked us all."

"I'm surprised as well. But people change. I guess I just realized that I really want to share my life with someone. We can all run free, but there comes a time when we're done sowing our wild oats. It is my time, so don't think too much about it. I am not dying, idiot, only getting married."

"What's the difference?" Los joked, making Dorrian swing at him playfully.

Los shook his head in disbelief as he headed back inside. He was surprised that Dorrian was thinking of making the big move. Dorrian out of all of them? He and Dorrian were really tight, and he knew who his friend was. If Dorrian was thinking of settling down, then he guessed it was time for him to do some reevaluation of his life.

Some time had passed, but Roshon was still upset about knowing Joe had been putting hands on his son. He jumped in his car headed over to Natalie's. On his way, he decided to make a detour and head over in the direction Brandi used to live. He wanted to see if he would see Joe out there anywhere. Coming up empty-handed, he continued to Natalie's house.

Once he rang the doorbell, Natalie opened the door and greeted him with a bright smile, warm embrace, and a passionate kiss. He followed her to the living room but was halted in his steps.

A knock came at the door, and Natalie told Roshon to go get it while she ran upstairs to check on the kids. Roshon opened it to find some white dude standing there. Both men looked at each other confused.

"Who are you?" the man asked, breaking the silence.

"Roshon," Roshon said, stretching his hand forward for a shake, which the other man ignored.

"And what are you doing in my house?" he asked.

So, this is Natalie's ex-husband. Natalie joined him and peeped over his head. "Oh, it is you, Chris," she said.

"Who's this man?" Chris asked, his voice getting louder.

Natalie glared at him. "You will not come to my house and yell at me."

"So, what the neighbor said is true. You have this . . . this whatever he is around my children," he spat out.

Natalie sighed. "Not now, Chris. Can we not do this?"

"We will fucking do what I want to do. I won't let my kids be around some man. Some fucking stranger! You're a useless excuse for a mother!" he yelled.

"Hey, man, chill out. Don't talk to her like that," Roshon said. "If there's anything I am sure of it is that Natalie is a damn good mother to her kids!"

"Shut the hell up, you nigger. What the fuck do you know about children? Where the hell did she pick you up from? Some strip club, huh? Now get the hell out of my way and let me get my kids!"

Roshon glared at him. "Nigger? Nigger? Are we really going there? Look, you don't know me, and I don't know you. Out of respect for Natalie, I'm warning you not to address me as a nigger. I introduced myself to you as Roshon, but if you disrespect me or Natalie again, I'm going to introduce you to my foot diving deep into yo' ass. Make no mistake, I don't go around handing out threats. I promise you, I'll fuck you up. Play with me if you want."

Roshon was a man of few words and didn't tolerate disrespect. He knew that Chris was trying to flex because his feelings were hurt seeing Natalie with a real man. Roshon's words put fear into Chris's heart, but Chris didn't want to look like the punk he was. He shook his fist in the air. "Don't think this is over, bitch. You won't lie up with a nigga and having my kids calling this coon 'Daddy.' I am coming back, and I promise you I am going to be taking the kids away from you," he threatened Natalie, and true to Roshon's word, he knocked Chris to the ground with one punch.

Wham!

"Get yo' punk ass outta here. Come back around when you got some sense." After Roshon slammed the door, Natalie and Roshon watched from the window as Chris staggered and rose to his feet. They watched him get in his car, and Roshon hugged Natalie, who was trembling. It tugged at his heart to see her fearful about Chris's threats and to also see her burst into tears. He led her to her room just in case the kids came downstairs and saw her crying. He could not believe she had such an asshole of an ex-husband. He remembered her telling him about how her ex-husband had cheated on her, but judging by the way he just acted, Roshon was sure that there was more to the story.

"Natalie, I'm sorry. I didn't mean to make things complicated for you, but your ex-husband is a jerk. He was asking for that punch. He better be glad I didn't beat his ass. I didn't want to chance the kids seeing that shit," Roshon admitted.

Natalie laughed and wiped the tears off her face. "Yes, he has always been, but I never noticed it. Until it was too late. You should have beat his ass. It's that type of prejudice that destroys our society, and I'm raising my kids to not see color. Chris is just a fucking moron, and I can't stand his ass. My blinders are off, and I see him for who he really is. "

"What the hell happened between you two? I mean, you told me about the cheating, but what's yo' story?"

"Chris and I started dating in high school. Then we went off to college and gave it a break. We met again, and our relationship reignited. I should have known he was not the Chris I knew when we were younger. I guess I saw the signs, but I was too much in love to notice the obvious. A couple of months into our marriage, I found out he was cheating on me. It was a torment for me because, by this time, I was pregnant. He promised it was a one-time thing and that it did not mean a thing to him, and I fell for it. He knew then that he had to be extra careful, but no matter how hard he tried to hide it, I kept finding out about other women. But that was only part of it. For years, our marriage was going down the drain. We argued a lot."

"Did he hit you?" Roshon asked. His fingers went into a fist when she nodded. He wished he had killed the son of a bitch.

"Just a couple of times, and as usual, he blamed it on me. Then I found out about the threesome thing, and I guess I had had enough and called it quits. He said all sorts of things to make me stay, promised to change, but I knew it was going to be the same story over and over.

He has always used the kids to fight me. This is not the first time he has seen a man in my life and threatened me with the kids. I just feel he's going to make good on it this time," Natalie said.

Roshon cuddled her. "If that muthafucka come around here again, he gon' wish he hadn't. I say we go to court, get an order of protection, and put something in motion for visitations. He can't keep coming around here making you live in fear and continue to threaten to take your kids. There's nothing he can do to take the kids away from you. Everyone knows you're an awesome mother, so ignore him," Roshon said. "We're in this together."

Natalie smiled at him. She was glad he was here with her when Chris arrived. He was right. She should not let him get to her. That was the thing about Chris: he knew how to manipulate people and make them scared. *Not anymore,* she decided.

Chapter 13

Arlene shook her round, plump, juicy ass to the music. Dorrian could not help but admire her. He sucked in his bottom lip as he waited to devour her the first chance he was given. She looked amazing in the white bikini that hugged every curve of her sexy, blemish-free body. He was glad that such a hot-looking woman was his. Yeah, he was a proud man, and he didn't care who knew how infatuated and captivated he was by Arlene. She was different, special, and almost too good to be true. Dorrian knew that, no matter what, no woman would ever be worth him losing Arlene over, and it was settled. In his mind, he found his queen. He could only hope that she would be willing to accept him as her king.

"This is so amazing," Arlene said as the wind blew in her hair. Dorrian nodded in agreement. He borrowed a friend's yacht, and they were out in the sea. He was glad he'd thought of it. It was the perfect getaway for the both of them.

"Lunch is ready," the chef said, appearing before them.

"Thanks. We will be there in a few minutes," he said, dismissing him. He joined Arlene by the railing and wrapped his arms around her waist. He pulled her into him and sucked in her neck making her moan in pleasure, which caused him to brick up. Dorrian had it bad for Arlene. One touch from her had his pole standing at attention, and he was always ready to dive in and swim in her ocean of love.

"What are you doing to me, woman? I could spend the rest of my life with you," Dorrian confessed, surprising himself because he wasn't ready to toss out any clues or hints of him actually proposing.

"Dorrian, baby, I love you, and I couldn't imagine my life without you in it. I'm so glad that your ass is as stubborn as a bull and you insisted that we go out," she confessed with a smile.

"So, are we good? Things good with us? We're in a good place?"

"Of course, why would you ask something like that? If we're not good, he's certainly excited about something." Arlene sexily retorted while grabbing Dorrian's erection.

"You know my thoughts about that. Don't get him up, unless you ready to take him down. You know you not ready for your lover boy to hear you screaming and calling on Jesus," Dorrian teased.

"What lover boy?" she asked with confusion laced through her tone.

Dorrian smiled, then removed her hand from his dick because, with Arlene, it was more than just sex. She was the first woman to take up residency in his heart. He turned her around and had her facing the beautiful spread that the chef laid out for them. "Let's go and wash up and prepare to eat. I'm ready to eat, then work up an appetite, eat some more, and then finish this conversation with me finding my dessert," he commented while showing his gorgeous smile and adjusting his dick.

Dorrian wanted everything to be perfect. He didn't want to ruin any part of this day because he was certain that it would be one of the most memorable memories that they would be able to tell for generations to come.

He spanked her ass, and she squealed. "You better go cover up that big ol' thang. I have seen the way the chef looked at you. I ain't gonna allow him to do that again or Julius the chef will go missing."

Arlene laughed. "I guess I got to change so his death won't be on my conscience," she said, heading for the cabin.

He, as well, went to change into shorts and a shirt. He double-checked to make sure the little box was in his pocket. As he had told the chef to do, when they came back out to the top of the deck the beautiful spread was now covered with rose petals, and the soft tunes of Luther Vandross played in the background.

"Wow," Arlene said, joining him. He smiled and took her hand, leading her to the table. He pulled out a chair for her.

"My lady," he said, bowing, making her laugh. He chuckled as he wondered what his niggas would say if they saw him in such a lovey-dovey way. Damn, he had become a pussy, but he did not care as long as it was with Arlene.

"This is beautiful," she said both to him and the chef, whose eyes were fixed on Arlene's cleavage which popped out in the red-hot dress of hers.

The chef opened the first dish, and they dug in. Even though the guy was getting on Dorrian's nerves, he had to admit that he was a pretty good cook. When they were done, the next course followed and then the next.

"Oh my God, I have never been this full," Arlene said, rubbing her flat stomach.

"Really? What about this morning when I had you spread out on the bed? I'm sure I was filling you up, with all of the screaming and creaming you were doing," Dorrian said, and then he heard a gasp and he smiled when he saw the chef's red face. At least that would get him to keep his eyes off his woman.

Arlene swatted him. "You're such a bad boy. Stop it."

"Only bad when I'm inside you. A boy I am not, but a man, baby, I'm all yours. As bad as I wanna be."

Arlene smiled and had never felt so much love, and even more so, appreciated in all of her years of dating. She felt that things were perfect. She could only pray that this was real and not another attempt of being played by another playboy.

"Thanks for bringing me here. This is one of the best nights of my life." Arlene beamed as Dorrian got up and walked to her side of the table, and stood her up to face him. He planted soft, moist kisses on her lips, she moaned into his mouth, and he knew it was now or never.

He took her hand, and they went to the rail.

"Forgot the glasses. Let me go get them," he said, returning to the table. He took the wine bucket and was glad that her back was turned to him. He went down on one knee and pulled out the box, which he opened.

"Arlene," he said. She turned around and gasped at the sight of the ring in the box.

"Dorrian," she whispered, shocked.

"You were the first woman who tap-danced into my heart and allowed me to feel things that I never knew existed. You make me a better man, and in my heart, I know you are my queen, and if you'll have me, I wanna be your king. I don't want to imagine life without you in it. I don't want to walk in front of you or behind you, but I want to walk beside you, hand in hand, arm in arm, as my spouse, my lover, my confidant, and eventually, the mother to all ten of my kids. Arlene, you're it for me. Will you marry me, baby?" Dorrian asked.

Arlene was speechless. The last thing she had expected was for Dorrian to ask her to marry him. Did she love him? Yes, she did. But she felt it was too soon. Marriage was a serious commitment, the ultimate sacrifice from the single life they lived. It was going to require patience and understanding. There was so much about him she did not know, and likewise. But then, she thought of her parents' marriage. She knew many people were surprised it was still going strong. Dorrian was a good man, and she cared for him deeply. She couldn't imagine life without him either, but in the back of her mind, she was wondering if they were moving too fast, too soon. She wanted to tell him so much in this moment but now wasn't the time. The man she'd fallen hard for just asked for her hand in marriage.

Rather than saying yes, the first thing out of her mouth was, "Are you sure, Dorrian? Marriage is real. It shouldn't be taken lightly. I have to know, are you sure? Are you ready for this? Are we ready for this?" she asked, making sure that he understood.

"I know, Arlene. I know it takes trust, patience, and determination, and I am willing to give it my all, I promise you that. Baby, don't leave me on my knee. Give me an answer. Will you do me the honor of becoming my wife?" Dorrian asked again.

Arlene looked into his eyes and was delighted to only see pure love dancing around in them. In that moment, she didn't care what anyone thought. She didn't care if they'd only been together a few short months. She couldn't deny the feeling she had when she was with him. She couldn't deny how he made her body feel, and she knew that she would want that for forever and a day. Without any more hesitation, and with tears in her eyes, Arlene blurted out, "Yes, Dorrian, yes, baby, I will marry you!"

Dorrian breathed a sigh of relief and found his smile. He had to admit that, for a minute, he thought she was going to say no. He saw the bit of uncertainty and doubt in her eyes. Her refusal would have crushed his heart, but now he was elated. He slid the ring on her finger and stood up. He grabbed her ass and kissed the hell out of her as she clung tight to him. She was his fucking woman, and everyone was going to know it.

"This is beautiful," Arlene said, looking at the ring.

He kissed her. "I love you, babe, don't ever doubt that. I know you have your reservations, but I promise you, all I want is for you to continue to love me the way that you have, and I'll be the man you desire, need, and will forever want. You have my heart, and just like I treat yours as an egg, I want you to do the same to mine."

"I love you, too. And what's with this egg you keep referencing?" Arlene asked with a smile as Dorrian wiped tears from her eyes.

Dorrian smiled and said, "In due time, sweetheart, I'll tell you the story of the egg. Let's celebrate for now."

Los was sick and tired of Keera's attitude. He told himself he wasn't going to give a shit about her anymore. Why the hell couldn't she move on from William's death? Yeah, he understood that she had lost a son, but the shit was becoming boring as hell. Nothing he did could make her change. He had taken her out a couple of times to this ice cream shop he knew she loved, but she looked at the ice cream like it was shit. He had taken her shopping to get some clothes, but it was like he was talking with a zombie. He had no idea how to deal with her anymore, and it was pissing him off.

"Hey, Los, you okay?" Roshon asked.

"Yes, boss has been down for days now," Falicia, with her loud mouth, added.

"I'm cool. Just Keera, she ain't getting better, and it's frustrating me," Los said.

"You giving her all the shit women want?" some guy asked.

"Yeah, that and much more, but it's like she's not even there. I'm just sick and tired of it all. Getting fed up with it. Why the hell can't she get back to normal?"

"You need to be patient with her. On some real shit, she lost a child. I'm sure that's not the easiest thing to get over. Hell, you lost a child too. Even though you wasn't in li'l man's life like that, you should at least have a heart knowing that your li'l man was laid to rest. Seriously, Los, the way you going about this situation is fucked up. You keep hollering about her getting better and moving on, but you need to realize where she's coming from," Roshon said.

"Los, I come in here to shoot the shit with you all, and you fellas are like nephews to me. You have to understand that it's not easy on Keera. Even though Keera's fucking crazy, what I know is that she cared for her son. She fucking shot you in the leg because you cursed your son. Now everything she had is no more, and she has no idea what the hell her life will now become with William gone. I'm not coming at you sideways on this, young man, but you need to understand that the clouds are dark around her now and the loss of a child will, or should, bring any parent to their knees," James, one of Los's regulars said.

"Brother talking some sense," Dorrian said, joining them in the shop. "Bro, think about it. Everything she has ever loved has been taken away from her. That's why she fought so hard to have it. When she had William, she felt loved and needed, so whatever li'l man was going through wasn't a burden on her because all she wanted was to feel loved and needed. Keera is crazy as fuck, don't get me wrong, but William brought out the best in her, and truth be told, so did you. You don't have to front for us. Her crazy ass has your heart, and you need to figure out how to make it right. You can't make up for the time you weren't there, but you can be here now and make the future a whole lot brighter." Dorrian was spitting real knowledge, and the guys were looking at him like he was crazy.

Los knew perfectly well about Keera's background. Her mama was in jail, and her dad dumped her with his grandma who didn't give a shit about her. Just down the street, her dad lived comfortably with his new family with no one giving a shit about her. No one had loved her for real, and the only hope she had was gone.

"What are your plans for her?" Roshon asked. "You still want to be with her or move on?"

"I dunno," Los confessed. Yeah, he still loved her, but he was not a one-woman kind of guy. He preferred to have several women. What was the use of being tied down to one woman when there were several around? Los didn't want to look like a lovesick puppy like Dorrian's ass, so he did what dudes did when they were ashamed of being in love: he deflected the conversation by incorporating another woman in the mix.

"I don't know what I want to do about Keera, but all I know is I got a date with Latifah," he said, doing a dance.

"Ohhhhhhhhhh," everyone said in a whoop.

"Can't believe you got that bitch to go out with you. How did you do it?" Pablo asked.

Los smiled. "I'm a ladies' man, ya know. All the fucking bitches love me. They all want the D," he said, doing a little dance as if he were hitting a girl doggie style.

"Come on, bro. After all you just heard, you thinking about Latifah?" Dorrian asked. Dorrian huffed in frustration. He couldn't believe that Los was playing like he didn't give a damn about Keera, and it was pissing him off.

Los, being the man that he was, he spoke up. "Dorrian, just because yo' lovesick ass tied the hell down don't mean that I wanna be tied down. No ball and chain for my ass. You know I'm a player," Los said.

Los knew that in his heart he wanted to be with Keera, but he couldn't offer her anything except more heartache. When it came to Latifah, she was the one everyone wanted, but she never gave them any play.

When Latifah heard about Los losing his son, her heart went out to him, and of course, he capitalized on that.

"You got it, Los, do you, but make sure you're using the right head when you're around here making decisions," Dorrian added while sitting in the chair and waiting on Los to cut his hair.

The guys had a brief staring match through the mirror. Only speaking with their eyes, Los broke the stare and began cutting Dorrian's hair with Keera at the forefront of his mind.

"You okay, Ant?" Carly asked as she rode him, popping her pussy as hard as she could. Although she was pissed off with him, her body couldn't deny the pleasure from Ant's dick, and she couldn't help but coat his pole with her juices.

"Yeah, sure, why?" Ant asked as she began staring into his eyes while working her hips to put it on him and make him know that she was the only woman for him.

"Because you aren't telling me something. Don't I satisfy you? Isn't it my pussy you crave? That's what you said, right?" Carly commented, squeezing his dick with her pussy muscles.

"Fuck, Carly, what the fuck are you talking about?" Ant asked as he hissed, loving the feeling from Carly's pussy.

She slapped him hard on the chest, and he yelped.

"What the hell was that for?"

She got off him and threw him a nasty glare. "What the fuck are you still doing messing around my sister, huh?" Carly asked.

Ant sighed. *So it's about that shit, huh?* "I just wanted to talk with her."

"Talk with her? Fucking talk with her? You know what the hell that means? I am fucking the dog shit outta you, and you now wanna talk with my sister, huh?" she yelled at him.

"I was fucking your sister before I fucked you!" Ant yelled back.

Carly threw him a dirty look. "Let me tell you shit now, Ant: Janelle is dating some guy, and he's got it all. Don't think for a fucking minute that she will go back to you."

"Come on, bae," Ant said, taking her hand. "I'm just messing with her mind. You know I need some cash, just wanted to ask her. She the only one who can help me."

Carly rolled her eyes. *So that's it, huh?* She picked her purse up and handed him some bills. "I don't want you to go to Janelle for anything, nothing at all, understand?"

Ant took the money and set it on the nightstand. He flipped Carly over and rammed his thick dick back into her awaiting dripping wet hole.

"You wanna get an attitude and hit a nigga? I'm 'bout to fuck the shit outta this pussy."

"Yes, daddy, fuck me up. I've been bad."

Ant took his dick and slapped it on the slit of Carly's opening and enjoyed watching her juices coat his member. He wanted to teach her a lesson, so he went in slow and touched her soul. Her moans echoed off the walls, and that turned him on. He knew that Carly was a nasty freak, so he pushed her on the floor in front of Janelle's full-length mirror and turned her head to the mirror so she could watch what he was about to do. He tooted her ass in the air and held her face to the floor with his left hand as he hovered over her asshole and guided his dick inside her tight ass. Thrusting in and out and watching her squirm and beg for mercy was his pleasure.

Treating her like the ho that she was, he yelled, "You ready to catch this nut?"

"No, daddy, just cum in my ass."

"Fuck that shit, I'm running this shit. You do what the fuck I say, bitch," he spat, still ramming his dick in her ass. "I'm ready to bust. Catch this nut!" he ordered.

With her ass juice on his dick, Carly turned around and sucked Ant's dick clean as if it were her last supper. Pleased with her work, she rose and tried to kiss him on the mouth.

"You got shit on your breath. Don't fucking kiss me," he spat, picking up his boxers and grabbing his shit, headed into the master bathroom to clean up.

When he came out of the bathroom, Carly was lying in the center of the bed, playing with her pussy. Ant took the money she'd given him and placed it in his pocket.

"Janelle should be back with the girls soon. I'm still trying to find a place of my own since the landlord from the previous place turned me down. But what I'm not understanding is why can't I move in with you? If I moved in with you, we wouldn't have to keep sneaking around like some damn high school teenagers."

Ant smiled. That sounded good, but he was pretty sure Carly was a worse version of her sister. He lived with one sister once, and he was not going to do the same shit again. After a brief conversation, she showed him to the door, and he gave her a head nod before walking off.

"Damn!" Carly cursed. How good Janelle must be feeling because Ant was asking her for money. She knew Ant was just another nigga, but Janelle had really liked him. Besides, he was damn good in bed. There was just something about him that made her like him so much as well. It still didn't mean she wasn't going to have her fun with Kareem though.

She heard a knock on the door and went to it. Speak of the devil, it was Kareem. "Hey, handsome," Carly said, pushing her boobs forward. The man looked damn fine today.

"Hey, Carly," Kareem said. "Where Janelle at?"

"Not home yet," Carly said, pulling his arm farther into the house. "How was your day, huh?" she asked, leading him to a chair before sitting on his lap.

Kareem smiled and pushed her off his lap. "When will she be back?" he asked, looking at the time.

"Oh, you naughty boy. You know you wanna fuck me, don't you? I'm sure I'm way more fun than my boring-ass sister," Carly said, moving closer to him.

"No, Carly, I ain't fucking you. I ain't messing up with Janelle. Get that shit through your skull. I don't know what type of bullshit you on, but I'm not that nigga," Kareem said. The door opened and in walked Janelle and the children. She stopped when her eyes landed on them; then she forced a smile.

"Kareem, when did you get here? Sorry I didn't come sooner. I was stuck in traffic," Janelle said.

Carly got up with a smile, as if she had not been trying to seduce Kareem a few seconds ago. "Come on, girls, let's go get some lunch and leave Mommy and Kareem alone," Carly said, ushering the girls into the kitchen.

"What was she up to?" Janelle whispered as she saw Carly leave.

"Your sister is sick, I swear. She really wants to fuck me, which is fucking sick since I am dating her sister. I hate coming over here 'cause of her. You need to kick her ass out, for real," Kareem said with a frown.

"I'm so sorry," Janelle said, fighting the urge to go pounce on Carly. "Why don't we meet over at your place moving forward? Or before you come around, give me a call?"

Janelle was fucking pissed at Carly. What the hell was wrong with her ass? Every day that went by she was thinking of smothering her sister while she slept. She was not satisfied with having all the other men Janelle had dated. Now she wanted Kareem as well. She was such a shameless slut. No matter what she did this time around, she was not going to let Carly have Kareem. She had already done too much.

But she wasn't going to let her anger with her sister ruin her plans. She was going to be patient. After all, the patient dog ate the fattest bone. When hell was unleashed, Carly was going to hate her fucking self. Janelle didn't care what was going to happen to her. She deserved everything and much more. She trusted Ant would do a good job. The bastard didn't give a shit about any woman, and although she considered herself stupid for ever screwing him, at least she was done with him.

"Don't worry about her, Kareem," Janelle said with a confident smile. She knew that it would only be a matter of time before she brought her sister down a few notches.

Chapter 14

"How are you doing, Roshon?" Mrs. Covington asked as she held baby J.

"Fine," Roshon said. Looking at her, he was sad to see how stressed she was with her husband's illness. She looked really bad with her eyes getting more sunken every time he saw her.

"The children seem happy," she noticed.

Although it was still fucking hard, especially when the children were shouting, it was actually nice to have the kids around.

One of Natalie's girls ran down the stairs, followed by RJ; then they ran out the back. Mrs. Covington gave him a curious look. "Who's that?"

"My girlfriend's daughter," Roshon said. It actually felt nice to call Natalie his girlfriend although they had not had a serious talk about what they were doing. They were screwing around, having play dates with their kids, and most of all, being friends, which he liked. Were they in a relationship? He did not know. Right now, he just wanted to take things slow. They both wanted to. They had been hurt in the past by those they cared about, so they knew better to be careful next time.

"Oh, that's good," Mrs. Covington said. "You know I felt so bad when you and Brandi split. I knew it was the biggest mistake of her life, and I was right," she continued, trying hard not to cry. "You were and are still a gentleman. It's hard to find good men like you right now when you young boys are concerned about sleeping around and making money at all costs. But you put others before you. You're willing to sacrifice. Your mama sure raised you right. I'm sure she would be proud of you."

Roshon smiled. Mrs. Johnson had said the same thing, and he guessed in a way they were right. There was not a moment that went by that he didn't think about his mom, and he truly missed her. Growing up, he had faint memory of his dad, who had died when stationed abroad. His mom had been weakened by her husband's death, but she had made sure she cared for her son well. His mom had never failed to whoop his ass when the need arose, as well as praise him when he deserved it.

Seeing how determined she was to make a good future for him had pushed him harder. Although they had stayed in the hood, she didn't want him to be like the niggas around. As a matter of fact, he had to sneak out to hang out with his friends for some time until she allowed him to. She didn't want him to end up with baby mamas everywhere, depending on food stamps and the rest of the stuff from government assistance. She usually told him that he was capable of anything. Him being black was no barrier to him succeeding and surpassing anyone. All he had to do was be determined.

He was damn glad he had made her proud. He had done well in school and had even graduated at the top. Every award he gave to her had made him happy as the smile on her face overwhelmed his heart. Seeing his mama happy was the best gift ever. And when he had gotten accepted for admission to a top school, she cried hard as hell from joy. Damn, that woman had been strong. She had motivated him, spent late nights with him while they talked about his homework, and when she couldn't help, she had paid for a tutor. She didn't care if she didn't get all the clothes her friends had or wasn't driving a convertible. All that mattered was her son's success.

It was just sad that she had left the earth so soon, before Roshon could start making money to let her reap the fruit of her labor. She had fallen sick but had not told Roshon until it was too late. A few minutes after he got to her, she had given up and succumbed to death. He was completely broken. The woman who had been his pillar for as long as he could remember was gone. He had almost wanted to give up on everything. After all, she was the one he was doing everything for. But Mrs. Johnson talked to him and made him realize he had started something and needed to end it. He had to make her proud of him wherever she was.

As he looked at RJ, he wished he had got the chance to meet his mother. He knew she would be disappointed that he had gotten a woman knocked up before marriage, but he knew she would understand and love RJ regardless. He was grateful to her every day for the way she shaped his life. At times, some of the boys teased him, called him a mama's boy, but if he was going to have a mother in the next life, he would want her. He wasn't boasting when he said he was different from the niggas in the hood. When he saw the shit niggas did in the hood, and the records they ended up with, he was damn glad he had chosen another path. He was still on his way to success, but he was damn glad about the way his life was.

A few hours later, Mrs. Covington said goodbye to the kids, promising she was going to come around again. He knew if he directly provided financial support she was going to turn him down, so he was going to slip it to her through her husband. It was the best he could do with all that had happened.

He looked at the time. Natalie was supposed to have come over so they could take all the kids to an ice cream parlor. He called her, but she did not answer her phone. He wondered what was going on with her. It wasn't like her not to answer when he called. He was just about to call her back when the bell rang. He opened it to see Natalie with a puffy face and red eyes.

"What's wrong?" he asked.

"It's Chris. He made good on his threat," she said, waving a paper at him. He took it from her and his blood boiled. The guy was really an ass. He had filed to get full custody of the three kids because he believed his kids were in danger as their mom was not caring for them.

"This can't hold. He's just being spiteful," Roshon said.

"I don't know, but what if it does? What am I going to do? I don't know anymore, Roshon. I don't even know what is even going on between us. I just . . ." Natalie said, her eyes getting teary.

"Mom, are you okay?" Sonia asked from behind Roshon.

"Yes, dear. Get your brother and sister for me. We need to leave now," Natalie said with a smile.

"Come on, Nat, we need to discuss this," Roshon said. She had always been there for him. Now it was his turn.

"I know, but I just need to be home with the kids and think things over, you know," Natalie said.

"Natalie, don't do this," he said, but she shook her head. The three kids hugged their mom and waved good-bye to Roshon and the kids. As he watched them go, he had a bad feeling it could be the last time he saw her.

The loud music pounded in the club with sweaty bodies dancing together in the normal section. Strippers could be seen dancing from the poles while half-dressed waitresses went around serving drinks. The party, however, was at the VIP section, which overlooked the regular section. This was where the big rollers were sighted, and where the strippers made thousands of dollars stripping.

Ant sat in a corner sipping from the glass of champagne Los had gotten. He looked around at the strippers. He finally had money to pay for a lap dance, yet he chose to only look around and check them out. He looked around at the bills niggas wasted on the bitches. *Damn.* Even though he had an income, he couldn't see himself just wasting dollars like that on a dance. Now, if he was getting some pussy after that lap dance, that was a different story. Those two things were his driving forces in life: pussy and money. To hell with all that love shit his boys talked about.

The VIP section chanted Dorrian's name when he got into the club. He had in his arms Arlene, who looked hot in a white gown.

"Dorrian, what's up?" Hakim asked, giving him a side hug. "She the one?" he asked, referring to Arlene, who clung to his arm.

"Yes, bro. This is my fiancée, Arlene," Dorrian said in introduction.

Hakim took her hand and gave it a kiss. "Hey, Arlene, you look really hot. Now, if my man Dorrian hadn't taken you, you would be my girl."

"Hey, slow down, pal. She's mine," Dorrian said, making all of them laugh. They joined the rest of the party and Dorrian introduced her to the rest of the guys who were his friends. Although Fridays were usually a packed day for the club, the club, especially the VIP section, was filled to capacity tonight. Dorrian had some big-roller friends who were from Houston, Atlanta, and Cali who usually came around a couple of times a year. It was sort of a reunion, and this time around, everyone was around to celebrate the success of all of them over the years.

"Where's your sleek friend at?" one of his friends, Jim, asked, referring to Roshon.

"Long story. He's home with his kids," Dorrian said.

The party turned up after that with everyone having mad fun. The strippers went into full mode, getting much money out of their clients. Dorrian was happy to reunite with his niggas again, especially with his woman by his side. Today had been half reunion, half presentation of his fiancée to them all. The news had been going around that Dorrian was engaged, and people were still speculating. It was time to set everyone straight and show them the hot damsel who he was getting married to. He could see the looks in their eyes as they looked at his lady, and he felt truly blessed.

"Hope you having fun," he whispered to Arlene. She had been feeling the vibe, but for some time now she had kept quiet. He wondered what was wrong with her as she had been very excited to go to the club to hang out.

"Come give me a lap dance," he said to Arlene. She gave him a weak smile then sat on his lap as she danced. The more she ground on him, the more he wanted to fuck her there in the club. But as he had come to realize, he had become a jealous man. He refused to let another man see any part of her body, even if it was only a peek of skin.

After Arlene blessed him with the lap dance he requested, he went around the club a few times to make sure his niggas were okay. Once that was done, he came back over to where Arlene sat.

He looked to her, and she yawned. "You wanna go home?" he asked.

"Yes, if you don't mind. I had a crazy day at the clinic today," Arlene said.

He got up and went to excuse himself from his niggas. "I'll be back in a few. Getting ready to take my lady home."

"Bye," Arlene said, her eyes fixated on her phone. It was obvious she wanted to get out of there.

"You sure you're okay?" Dorrian asked as he drove to her place.

"I'm just tired," Arlene said.

When he got to her place, he parked his car and escorted her to her door, making sure she got inside safely. "See you tomorrow?" he asked.

"Sure. Good night, Dorrian," she said, giving him a kiss on the cheek.

Dorrian knew something was wrong, but he didn't want to push her to talk about it. After she closed and locked the door behind her, he turned around and went to the car then drove back to the club. Things were still lit, and he joined his niggas in celebrating until the sun damn near came up. The party had been a success. Now it was on to the next one. When he got home, he was dead tired and passed out immediately.

When he woke up the next morning, he saw several missed calls on his phone. One was from Hakim, and then most of his niggas from out of town. They must have called to give him a thumbs-up for the party. He called Hakim first.

"Hey, Hakim, what's up? You must don't have any bitches by your side since you blowing up my phone so early?" he teased.

"We need to talk, bro," Hakim said.

Dorrian tensed up, noticing the seriousness in Hakim's tone. "What's up? You guys didn't have fun last night?"

"We did, bro, but shit went down yesterday after the party. Niggas from out of town got news about Arlene: bad news, bro," Hakim went on.

Dorrian froze. What the hell was Hakim talking about? "What the hell are you talking about, Hakim? You know I don't play with my woman. Why the hell you niggas talking about my woman in the first place?"

"Calm down, bro, we mean you well. Niggas were worried when they saw her because she looked familiar, and when they did some digging, they found out she was exactly who they thought she was. She's got a past, bro, a bad one back in Atlanta, and it ain't good. We had to warn you. You always got our backs, so now we got you," Hakim said.

"What you got on her?" Dorrian asked in a gruff voice. He was afraid of what Hakim was going to say. He knew his niggas didn't like interfering in another nigga's business unless it was serious. His blood ran cold as Hakim updated him on Arlene's past.

"Did you handle what I needed?" Janelle asked the scantily dressed Romona, as she stood at her side on the corner of the street.

Romona popped her gum and nodded. "We some sick bitches, you know that? You don't do shit like this. Damn, you mad with that nigga, bitch. I don't wanna ever screw over you. You dangerous as fuck," she said, laughing.

"You don't," Janelle said with a smile. "And you already know to keep your mouth shut, bitch. We in this shit together, the three of us. Takin' it to the grave."

"Of course," she said, nodding.

Janelle handed her the envelope, and she looked through it. "Yeah, we cool. Nice doing business with you," she said, blowing another bubble.

Janelle nodded and walked away. She got in her car and drove off satisfied. This was the first move in several phases of things that had started a few weeks ago. She was going to make sure she had a lot of fun with this. And what was more amazing was that Ant was not in on this part, so she was indeed going to have fun watching how this would play out.

A few weeks after Janelle paid Romona, their plan had started to come together. Carly staggered out of the bathroom with a confused look on her face. "What the hell is wrong with you?" Janelle yelled at her.

"I fucking feel sick. My fucking head is pounding, and I feel feverish. On top of that, I got a discharge coming from my pussy, and I got some weird-looking bumps down there. The hell?" Carly yelled.

"The girls are here, sis. Mind your words," Janelle said.

"Arrghhhhh. Sorry, but I feel like shit. It itches so bad," Carly said.

"Go wash that shit. You might have a yeast infection," Janelle said. She smiled as she watched her sister go to the bathroom.

The genital warts had just gotten started with her. By the time it took its full course, she was not going to open her pussy for any guy again. The itching was going to increase, and the bumps were only gonna get worse.

By the end of the day, Carly was in fucking pain. Her vagina was swollen red and itching like crazy, and she had a fever. She was also vomiting frequently. Janelle went to her room to check up on her with a cold glass of water.

“What do you think is wrong with you?” Janelle asked.

“I don’t know. I feel so fucking weak, and my pussy is on fire. I had to remove my panties because they were causing hell for me,” Carly cried.

“Maybe you should drink a glass of water,” Janelle suggested.

Carly shook her head. “I can’t. Then I’ll have to use the bathroom and my pussy gonna hurt like shit.”

“Carly, who have you been fucking?” Janelle asked.

Carly froze then shook her head in denial. “I ain’t fuck anyone.”

“Really? What about the nigga you had over here when I came home for lunch that day way back? You sure he ain’t give you nothing?”

“No, of course not. My nigga’s faithful,” Carly defended.

"Really? Because what this seems like is an STD, bitch. You should know better than to do it raw with some nigga," Janelle scolded her.

"I was on the shot. I know him. He ain't gonna fuck around on me, so it got to be something else."

"Well, you need to go to the doctor and handle that. Your pussy is messed up. You got all the signs of being fucked up by that nigga. I guess he's not as faithful as you thought he was. Who knows how many females he's been fucking around with? For you to get this shit, he got to be screwing with every slut out there."

"Nah, he ain't doing that. He loves me," Carly stated, and Janelle almost burst into laughter.

"Shit, you scaring my ass. My pussy been having a weird discharge and itching a little bit. I'm about to make me a fucking appointment," Janelle lied making Carly think that Ant had fucked her too. Janelle was getting so much joy out of fucking with Carly's mental. Carly was gonna make Ant's life a living hell for giving her this shit, and there was no way he was going to be able to deny it because his ass was probably feeling like his dick was about to fall off right now.

"Who you been fucking with other than Kareem?" Carly asked with wide eyes.

"Shit, I hope not the same nigga you been fucking with." Janelle chuckled. "For real though, sis, you need to go to the doctor and get a test, just so you can know what's going on. There's some real shit out there that can fuck you up for life. Some shit you can't get rid of, and some that can destroy your whole reproductive system, make your pussy stink so bad that ain't no nigga gon' wanna slide up in you. Worse than that, you could even die. You need to get checked out, sis, for real."

"You serious or just kidding with me?" Carly asked.

"No, I ain't. I am damn serious. These STDs are damn mean. They can live in you for years, killing you from the inside," Janelle said.

"Damn, I got to go get tested then," Carly said, slowly getting off the bed in pain. Janelle watched, amused, as Carly staggered around the room trying to get dressed.

Damn, it is so easy to get the bitch all riled up, she thought as she smiled on the inside.

After Romona told her and Tasha that she had genital warts, Tasha came up with a plan for her to transfer that shit to Ant and Mike, and since Janelle knew that Carly was fucking Ant, she was getting a two-for-one special. Romona had educated them on the symptoms, and all the ways that it could be transferred, and they put the plan in motion. It took no time for Romona to gain the interest of Mike and Ant, and it was even easier to get them in bed. Janelle and Tasha decided to compensate her for helping them.

A few hours later, Carly came home with red, puffy eyes as if she'd been crying, and she looked pissed off.

"What happened? What's wrong?" Janelle asked, faking concern.

"I got genital warts, that fucking bastard!" she yelled.

"Calm down, Carly. See what I told you? Nigga has been fooling around, fucking other bitches. You know, he could be fucking some bitch now. So, what are you going to do now? The doctor told you what you needed to do?" Janelle asked.

"Yeah, he gave me medication and told me how to treat it. He said that this shit could last for years, shit, a lifetime even. He said that I'm gonna have outbreaks. This shit is so fucked up, man. This shit hurts like hell and damn, it is gonna cost a whole lot. I swear I am gonna kill A . . ."

"Who?" Janelle asked, hiding a smile.

"Kill Anthony," Carly said.

How convenient. "Well, you're gonna be okay. Just be careful. You can pass that shit around. I mean, it's okay if you fuck around, but not when it's gonna affect other people around you. This is serious shit. Maybe you should go over and stay with Mom."

"Come on, sis, I can't go stay with Mom. She's gonna make sure with her loud mouth that everyone knows I got this shit," Carly begged.

"Just be careful. We gonna make sure we don't eat from the same plates and shit. You're quarantined. It may sound harsh, but shit has to be done to keep us safe," Janelle said.

Carly screamed out of frustration, threw the papers on the floor, and ran out of the room. Janelle picked up the test results from the ground. She took a shot of it with her phone camera and sent it to someone. She knew in a few seconds the shit was going to be uploaded on Instagram and Facebook. She laughed. It felt so good to be on the winning end.

"Damn! Y'all see this shit? Janelle's sister got genital warts. You know, that bitch with the ass?" Falicia said, looking up from her phone.

"Carly?" Los asked, looking up from the head he was cutting.

"Yeah, Carly. This nigga uploaded her test results. Said she came into the lab scratching her pussy. Bitch got genital warts and shit," Falicia said, reading from her phone.

"You just hearing the shit? It went viral two days ago. Niggas who fucked her recently been going to do tests. What the hell was the bitch thinking doing it raw, huh?" Cole said.

"Wow! That's Dorrian's cousin, you know," Los said, shaking his head. "Bitches never learned to not fuck niggas raw. It's just plain stupid. Now her name is out there in the streets."

"Shit, nigga, you talking about bitches? Y'all niggas need to wrap that shit up too. Y'all don't know where these hoes been," Falicia said, placing her hand on her hip.

Los heard some shit about a bitch running around with that shit, but he never knew it was Carly.

"Damn, whoever posted that shit must hate her ass. That shit was mean as hell, and it's not gonna just go away. People gonna remember that shit and hold on to it forever. You know how it is: once it's on social media, it's out there," Rhonda said, shaking her head.

The door opened, and Ant walked in looking like he was sick. His skin was pale, and he had a disgusted look on his face.

"Ant, nigga, you look like shit. Fuck wrong with you?" Los asked with furrowed brows.

Ant nodded. "I'm good. I just feel fucked up right now," Ant replied, sitting down in one of the chairs by the windows.

"Shit, nigga, whatever you got, don't bring that shit in here. Muthafuckas already running around here with some shit I don't want or need," Los said with a slight chuckle.

"What you talking 'bout, Los?" Ant asked.

"You heard about Janelle's sister, Carly? The bitch got genital warts," Falicia said.

"Damn, are you serious? How you know?" he inquired, seeking answers. Ant already was wondering if he'd caught something from that bitch he left Dorrian's club with, but after hearing this shit, he thought maybe he had the same shit Carly had. His mind had been going a mile a minute trying to figure out what he might have. At first, he thought that it was gonorrhea, but this shit was far worse.

"Yeah, man. It's been going all around the hood, and some nigga uploaded her test results on social media. Niggas hauled ass to the clinic and shit." Los chuckled, shaking his head.

Ant sat in silence with his head down. Some nigga had uploaded her test results to social media, so the shit was all around the hood now. There was no way in hell he could fuck with her again. Not only her, but he had to chill out on fucking period until he was sure he was straight. Deep down, he wanted to kill Carly's ass, but he realized this was his karma.

Los picked up on the way Ant was acting, and he remembered their conversation from Cracker Barrel. *Well, I'll be damned,* Los thought, putting two and two together. He remembered that Ant told him he had been fucking both Carly and Janelle. What he couldn't figure out was why in the hell Ant would fuck his girl's sister raw. *This nigga gotta be a special kind of stupid,* Los thought, and slightly chuckled to himself. He wasn't going to call Ant out on it, but he definitely stored it in his mental Rolodex.

"Anyone seen Dorrian?" Ant asked, changing the topic.

"Nah," Los said. "Not since his nigga called him with some info on Arlene." Los was surprised by what Dorrian had told him that the nigga said about Arlene, but he wasn't telling a soul. That was Dorrian and Arlene's business to tell.

"And Roshon? Nigga ain't been here in a while," Cole asked.

"He busy with work and the kids. He got Brandi's other kids with him now. That shit ain't easy," Los said.

"Well, I hope all is well with them niggas. We miss them around here," Cole said.

"So, how far you got with Latifah? You fucked her yet?" Ant asked.

"Yeah, nigga, who am I?" Los boasted.

"Damn, you get all the pussy. You know how many niggas been trying to bust the pussy open?" Cole shook his head.

"You get the player of the year award for that one. Shit, it would've been a battle between you and Dorrian if his ass ain't get all locked down and shit," Falicia said.

"Man, bye, Falicia. I still would be player of the year. I bag the bitch every nigga in the hood been trying to hit. I knocked that pussy out the frame. Shit, she got some good shit. A nigga had to beat that shit up. Had that bitch screaming so loud I felt like Trey Songz 'cause her neighbors know my name. Them muthafuckas know my whole damn government."

"Damn, bro, I wanna be like you when I grow up," Cole teased, making them laugh.

"Keep fucking around and Keera gonna shoot you in the other leg," Rhonda joked.

"See, Rhonda, that shit ain't even funny." He chuckled. "Got my ass walking with a serious-ass limp, but I ain't mad no more. My limp makes me look cool as shit. It matches the playa in me," he added.

Los hated the fact that they brought up Keera's crazy ass all the time. After dealing with the aftermath of losing William, he decided that he needed to start distancing himself from her.

Nothing he was doing was helping her situation. She became severely depressed and just gave up on life. He refused to be around that. He had lost their son as well, so he felt she should get over it like he had. And now that he was with Latifah, he knew what the fuck he had been missing all this time. Latifah knew her place, and she knew how to act. She wasn't ratchet like Keera, and she wasn't trying to tie him down with a child.

"You sure you okay, Ant? You over there scratching your balls. You got that shit too?" Falicia asked, cackling.

The whole shop laughed. Ant was pissed that she said that shit, but he had to play it off. "It's called adjusting my balls. Them muthafuckas big as grapefruits. You wanna come hold these bitches?"

Los burst into laughter. "Pick up yo' face, Falicia."

Ant wondered for a brief moment if Janelle was behind the shit, but then he shook his head. The bitch wanted revenge, but she wouldn't go to that extent. The Janelle he knew could be grimy when she wanted to be, but she would never do no shit like that. He thought back to the conversation he had with Janelle earlier when she called and asked if he had bumps on his dick.

"What? Why you asking me that shit?

"Did you fuck Carly raw?" she'd asked, and he didn't respond.

"Damn, you stupid, Ant. Why the hell you fuck her raw, especially when you fucked me with a rubber? I guess pussy made you weak. You so damn dumb. What the fuck I ever see in yo' stupid ass?"

"Fuck you, Janelle. Shit, how the fuck I supposed to know your sister a ho? You asking me about bumps and shit, and I been scratching my balls all damn day. Did she give me something?" he had snapped.

"You're pathetic. I just asked because I wanted to find out was you stupid enough to fuck a ho raw, and yep, you are. Anyway, ain't shit gon' ever change with you. Just remember, we have a deal," Janelle said.

"Janelle, how can I fuck her again if my shit itching?" Ant complained.

"Raw, just like you been doing, or you can refund me my money, all of it!" Janelle yelled in his ear.

"Fuck you, Janelle. I already spent that shit." Ant chuckled.

"Then you and yo' itchy balls better find a way to get up in Carly. I ain't gonna repeat myself again, Ant. We had an agreement, and you gon' go through with it, whether you want to or not. Remember, I can make yo' live a living hell, or just send yo' ass back to the slammer. The choice is yours." Janelle ended the call before Ant could say anything.

He had no idea why she was hell-bent on revenge. Maybe she had some shit to settle with Carly, and now he was caught in the middle. He knew Janelle's ass could do some wild shit, but this shit right here was crazy as fuck. However, he wasn't fucking with her ass. She was on some other shit, and he wasn't trying to end up back in jail. Those five years for robbery had been hell for him, and he had no interest in ever going back. If it weren't for Dorrian, Roshon, and Los checking up on him and sending him shit, and constantly telling him to stay calm and lie low, his ass probably would have gotten himself in more trouble, and gotten some more time added to his sentence. He hated to be Janelle's puppet, but as of now, he had no other choice. That was the price he had to pay for fucking around with two crazy-ass sisters.

Chapter 15

Dorrian stared at his ringing phone pissed and not wanting to be disturbed. It was one of the niggas who supplied him with drinks for the club. He had enough drinks: wine in his hand and a bottle of Absolut on the desk. He didn't feel like talking or discussing anything with anyone, be it business or personal. His mind was in a haze as he tried to piece together the broken pieces of his heart.

A couple of weeks had passed since he heard the shit about Arlene. He'd been stunned and had gone over to her place to confront her. When Arlene opened the door in a robe and with puffy eyes, he knew she'd been crying, which indicated that his boys already got to her and exposed her ass for exactly what the fuck she was: a ho. With tears in his eyes and an unexplainable pain in his chest, Dorrian spoke in almost a whisper as they held each other's gaze.

"Is it fucking true? Don't lie to me, Arlene. Tell me they got it wrong. Is it true?" he asked, almost begging and praying that she would have a perfect explanation and things would go back to normal and he and his queen could pick up where they left off.

She nodded, and the small glimmer of hope he had was killed in that moment. In the back of his mind, he just knew his niggas had been talking about someone else, not his Arlene. When he left Arlene's house that day, he was at a loss for words. He didn't need to say what was already understood. He couldn't turn a ho into a housewife, and the shit she did in the few flicks he saw, there was no way he would ever live that shit down with his guys. Damn, he understood that everyone had a past, but him seeing that shit live, in living color, was something totally different.

Dorrian was sitting in his office thinking about how fucked up his situation really was. No matter how he looked at it, he was damn near ready to jump the broom with the ho of ATL. He couldn't believe that after all of the hesitation and saying how marriage was supposed to be built on trust, she would deceive him and not mention her past. He threw the glass of wine against the door. He had fucking given her a ring, something he had not given any woman before. He rested his head on the desk. He should have known all women were bitches. There was not one good, wholesome woman in America. They were all the fucking same: hoes, bitches, and pretenders, just waiting for a come up.

Since the revelation of Arlene's past, Dorrian hadn't been able to concentrate. Damn, he loved the shit out of her, and there was no denying that.

His phone buzzed. It was Roshon calling. He'd been calling him for days to check up on him, but Dorrian just wasn't interested in talking to anyone. Arlene continued to call his phone as well, leaving messages and begging for him to talk to her. He wasn't interested in speaking to her either. All he could think about was her playing him for a fool. He laughed at the thought of her being excited that she was able to get a six-carat pear-shaped Tiffany's special out of him. *Fuck it. She can fucking keep the ring*. What the hell was he going to do with it? Hang it on the wall so he could see how bitches were? No, she could keep it. She fucking deserved it. Hell, after seeing her in action, she worked for it.

Dorrian wanted to hide his feelings and mask how deeply hurt he really was. One of the girls from his club named Thunder had desperately been trying to fuck Dorrian, and to get Arlene out of his system, he was going to do it.

Wiping the tears from his face, he took the rest of the Absolut from the bottle straight to the head. He pressed the speaker on his intercom that spoke directly to the girl's locker room, and his voice boomed and slurred, "Thunder, get yo' ho ass up here."

It hadn't been a good two minutes that passed and Thunder was tapping on the door. She had on a diamond string bikini, and although she was sexy, Dorrian still only wanted Arlene. Snatching Thunder by her throat, he roughly pushed her to his couch. Unbuckling his pants, he growled, "You want this dick?"

With her head shaking yes rapidly and her juices prematurely flowing, Thunder couldn't wait for Dorrian to tap her ass so she could become the headliner of his club. She was ready to toss her ass in a circle and swallow his dick whole.

The anticipation was killing her, so when she looked back, the sight before her eyes was pitiful. Dorrian stood with a limp dick and in tears. "He won't get hard for anyone but her. She fucking ruined me."

Thunder tried to rush to her knees and was prepared to suck and stroke his dick back to life. He moved her and pulled up his pants.

"Get the fuck out!" he screamed, ashamed that Arlene had that type of a hold on him.

With his head resting on his desk, he heard his door open. His eyes were closed, and his tears were streaming down like a river.

"Get the fuck out!" he yelled.

"Dorrian, baby, we need to talk. You have to allow me to explain."

It was her: his kryptonite, his heart, his soul, and the love of his life. Arlene.

She is avoiding me again, Roshon thought as he saw Natalie walk the other way when he came out of his office. He understood where she was coming from. Her children came first. He had done the same as well, but he missed her like hell. He hated that she was hurt because of her asshole of an ex-husband. He wanted to fuck Chris up and make him pay for what was going on. The kids missed her as well. They were always asking about Natalie. Even Mrs. Johnson had asked about her. Every one of them fucking missed her. He had finally admitted something to himself that he had not realized before: he loved her. Yeah, he loved her. And it hurt him that they both were in a fix. But he needed to do something about it. He could not let an awesome woman like her slip away from his life.

He needed a way to get her back by overcoming all the problems that presented themselves.

He smiled when he thought of the plan he had in place. If things went well, he was going to have her by his side. He had not planned for all of this, for him to be at his age with three kids who were not his, or to be in love with a white woman who had three kids of her own; but things had panned out the way they were, and he had to accept them because he knew they were for the best.

A few days later, he stopped in front of Natalie's office. He knocked on the door then peeped his head in. She looked surprised to see him, and he closed and locked the door after they locked eyes. He noticed the stress that seemed to find its way to her face.

"Hey there," he said.

"Roshon," she said, averting her eyes from landing on him. She didn't want to face him. She didn't want to endure any more sorrow than what Chris was already putting on her.

"You have been avoiding me, and I need for you to help me understand why," he said.

Natalie laughed nervously. "I haven't. I told you I needed some space, didn't I?"

"And it has been weeks. You're not picking up my calls, and it is driving me crazy. The kids miss you, and I miss you."

"I miss them too," Natalie said with a smile.

"And me? Do you miss me too?" he asked.

"I do, Roshon, a whole lot, but we just can't do this. Someone's going to get hurt, and we will regret it in the end," Natalie said, shaking her head.

"And what if I tell you that I love you? That I don't give a shit about the drama that idiot is going to bring?" Roshon asked.

Natalie stared at him, surprised. "You love me?"

"Yeah, I do. Took me a while to accept the truth, and although it scares the shit out of me, I'm not going to let it go. You know about Brandi. I told you how she ruined me for good and how I never thought I was going to love another woman. But then you came around. You showed me that it was all right to love again. Shit, what other woman will accept me and all of this shit I have going on?" Roshon confessed.

Natalie was silent for a while, and when she looked up, there were tears in her eyes. "I love you too, Roshon, but we just can't."

He was elated at her words. "You love me? You really do?"

She nodded. "Yeah, you and that tight ass of yours, your kids, and even Mrs. Johnson, but this shit won't work. We got too much to lose, and I don't think I have any strength to fight anymore."

"And what if I told you we get to combine our strength and fight for what we want? Nat, you're in here: in my heart. My kids love the shit outta you, and so do I. You love me, and together there's nothing stopping us. I don't give a fuck about Chris, but I love and care for you. You, Nat. It's me and you. Don't give up on us without giving our love a full chance to thrive," Roshon said with so much passion.

"You sure you can withstand it? Chris can be an asshole, and I'm sure that he's not going to stop until he knows I am not happy with anyone," Natalie said.

"Chris won't be disturbing us again," Roshon said with a confident smile.

"What do you mean?" Natalie asked.

He handed her the folder he had in his hand, and she looked through it with her hands shaking. "That fucking douche bag!" she said angrily.

"I'm sorry it hurts, but with this information, we have enough to make him not disturb us anymore," Roshon said, referring to the custody battle Chris was having with one of his girlfriends who had enough proof that he molested her kid. "I went over to his place and showed it to him. No fucking judge would let him take the kids. I know it wasn't in my power, but I threatened him that if he tried to hurt you or the kids, you would get full custody," Roshon said as he watched Natalie's look of stress turn into a sigh of relief.

Natalie hugged him tight. "Thanks so much, Roshon. You didn't have to do that."

"Shhhh," he said, placing his hand over her lips. "You don't tell me what to do for you. I want us together, Nat. I know we got issues to deal with, niggas and white folks who don't wanna mind their business and are gonna say shit about us being together, but we gonna throw it in their faces. We gonna make sure we're happy. That's our priority: the kids and our happiness."

Natalie giggled for the first time in a while, with happiness. She swatted him playfully. "You're such a dork. I love you so much. We need to kill that 'n' word. I despise it. I don't want any of our kids seeing color. They will only see love."

He laughed. "For you, babe, anything. Anything for you."

Carly was so damn pissed with Ant. She knew the fucking bastard had given her genital warts, and although the bumps were gone, she could not forget the humiliation she had gone through.

She didn't know the fucking cunt at the clinic who had uploaded her test result and shamed her into not going back there. She had become a laughing stock in the hood, at work, and with her friends who, after weeks of the shit going down, could not stop talking.

The itching and the pain caused by the genital warts was almost unbearable for Carly. She hated drugs, and she had to continuously take them even after the pain was gone. Then there was the shit with Janelle, who made it clear to the kids that Aunt Carly had some deadly disease and they would die if they came close to her. She could not believe her sister would do shit like that to her.

Her mama was even worse. The old hag had called her laughing that everyone in the hood knew her daughter got infected. "Keep your pussy closed from now," she had warned.

But it had been the longest Carly had gone without fucking. And the problem was she couldn't even fuck any guy in the hood. No nigga wanted to roll with her, even the ones who had been trying hard to get with her. It was like she had a fucking plague. The other day, she had almost sat on Kareem's lap while Janelle was at their mother's house, and he had asked her if she was fucking ashamed that she had genital warts, and that he was never going to fuck her, not even if she was the last woman on earth. How the hell was she going to get fucked then?

Her phone buzzed. Why the hell was Ant calling her? The nigga had to know she was going to kill him. Imagine he had the nerve to say she had been the one to gave him the disease when they both knew it had to be some hooker he fucked. "What do you want, Ant?" she asked.

"I wanna fuck you, Carly. Look, I'm sorry, and I really do miss you, you know. Come on, I know that pussy ain't been fucked in a while now," Ant said.

The nerve of this bastard. "You think I am gonna fuck with yo' genital-warts-having ass? No way. I'd rather use my fingers."

"I told you I ain't do shit, and by the way, I'm clean. I took a test yesterday. Come on, don't tell me you ain't miss riding daddy," Ant said.

Carly paused. Yeah, she fucking missed him. At least the idiot still wanted her pussy. "Bring your ass over here then and fucking bring that report here. I ain't letting you touch even my boobs without it."

"And Janelle? I hope she ain't there," he asked.

"What you think I am? Stupid? She is gone with the girls and won't be back 'til tonight, so get your ass over here," Carly said. When she hung up, she went to take a bath then changed into some sexy underwear. At least if he was gonna fuck her, she needed to feel good.

A few minutes later, she heard some knocking at the door and found Ant there. Damn, he sure did look good, and without caring about the report, she kissed him. "You okay? You look nervous," she said, pulling him in.

"Naw, I'm good, just missed you," he replied, pulling her ass to him.

"We still got issues to talk about, but first,I wanna see that report so you can fuck the hell out of me," Carly said. He pushed the test result to her, and she glanced at it. "Good," she said then led him to the room.

"And yours?" he asked. She glared at him and pointed at a sheet by her bed, which he did not bother looking at. His dick got hard as she removed the robe, leaving on just the lace underwear. He pulled off his shirt and joined her on the bed, ready to fuck the shit out of her.

Carefully, Janelle tiptoed to the window and could hear them fucking like rabbits. Damn. The bitch called her sister was fucking stupid. Today, all hell was going to break loose. She tiptoed and crossed the street to the car where her girlfriends from work sat.

"They fucking, right?" Tasha asked.

"Yeah, they fucking," Janelle said, shaking her head.

"I got to say you definitely not that bitch's sister. Is she dumb or something?" Leona asked.

"Maybe. Y'all ready to do this?" Janelle asked.

"Been ready. We gon' show that ho you don't screw with someone else's boyfriend, especially when she's your friend or sister. We don't fucking break that code for anything," Ayesha said, getting out of the car. She was the crazy one among them, and she was ready to treat a ho to a much-needed lesson. They left Janelle behind in the car and went to the house. Carefully, they opened the door and went inside. In a few seconds, there was a rumble inside the house.

The three girlfriends of Janelle found them fucking in the room, and while they pounced on them, one of them took videos.

"Who the fuck are y'all?" Carly asked, her boobs stained with sweat as she looked at the three girls surprised.

"So, Ant, this is the bitch you fucking with, huh? You cheating on me with this ho, huh?" Ayesha asked.

"Who the fuck are you?" Ant asked, looking at the women also in surprise. *What the fuck has Janelle gotten me into?* he wondered. She had called him earlier to come to the house, and he had been too stupid to figure that shit was going to go down.

"You denying me now, huh?" Ayesha asked before giving Carly a slap, which made her fall off Ant with a scream.

"I swear I don't know who the fuck you are!" Ant yelled.

"Don't fucking play with my friend, you dirty-dick nigga. You been fucking her for weeks now, calling her your girl, and now you wanna act like you don't know what the fuck is going on. In here fucking this stankin'-pussy-ass ho," Leona said.

Carly got up and jumped at Ayesha who was ready for her. She gave her another slap, which sent her to the floor. Before she could get up, Ayesha and the other girls dragged her and Ant, who had managed to get into his boxers, out of the house.

The sound of the fight attracted bystanders, and niggas were already gathered around the house. They booed as they saw them bring Carly and Ant out. Ayesha yelled at Carly.

"You ho. Tell me, you fucking loose-pussy, disease-infected, dry-face-ass, stanking-ass bitch, how long you be fucking my man, huh? How long, bitch? Tell me so I can fuck you up! I've been waiting to catch his dog ass. Both of y'all getting fucked up today."

Carly was already embarrassed by the shit that was flying out of this crazy-ass girl's mouth, but with the crowd forming, she didn't want to be embarrassed even more by not sticking up for herself. Carly might have been outnumbered, but she was ready to take that ass beating and go out with one hell of a bang.

Carly was trying to think of a clever comeback, and the first thing that came to her head she blurted out. "He's my man, not yours, bitch. You coming over here to our shit embarrassing yourself. You can't fuck, bitch. That's why the fuck he with me. Maybe you should come on up and watch a real show. Fuck all you muthafuckas filming with your damn cameras. If you can't please yo' man, Carly got you, bitches. Fucking 101 is now in session. Ant is my nigga. We been fucking, and you and your ratchet-ass friends can leave or come back inside and take notes."

"Carly, chill with that shit yo," Ant whispered.

"Naw, ain't no chill, Ant. You know what it is. I'm sick of hiding this shit. Janelle couldn't keep you happy, so you came to me, just like everyone else who was sick of fucking her weak ass. Now these hoes mad 'cause you left her weak ass and she found you fucking me."

The camera was still rolling, and Leona wanted Carly to hang herself on the cross. "Who is Janelle?

Do I need to beat her ass, too?" Leona asked, still pretending as if she was mad.

"Janelle is my sister. So what? Judge all you want. Fuck you, hoes," Carly boasted.

"You one dirty-ass bitch. Whatever happens to you, yo' ass deserves it. Fucking yo' sister's nigga, you dumb bitch," Leona said before slapping the shit out of Carly.

It was in that moment that Carly realized how crazy she must have looked to the neighbors and the crowd. Carly had forgotten that she was asshole naked and out there acting a fool. The crowd started yelling obscenities, and Carly began to tremble.

Carly tried to cover her nakedness, but there was nothing that could be done. Niggas were taking their phones out to take pictures. Ant was mad as hell. He knew Janelle was responsible for this shit. That fucking bitch was crazy. He should have known never to trust her.

"Janelle—" he started before Ayesha punched him in the mouth.

Suddenly, Janelle's car pulled over, and she got out with groceries. "What the fuck going on here?" she asked.

"What you care?" Leona asked, still playing her role.

"This my fucking house. Why you got my sister naked? Ant, what the fuck you doing here?" Janelle asked, touching her chest.

"This ho your sister? She been fucking my man for weeks now. Bitch just claimed that he was your man too. Isn't she the bitch who got genital warts? You gave my man genital warts, huh?" Ayesha asked.

Janelle slapped Carly across the face, then gave her another slap and another until she was held back by some niggas. "You a fucking slut, Carly. You fucking slept with my man, huh? How many of my men you slept with, huh? I thought they were lying, but you fucking ho, you did that shit. I took yo' ass in when you didn't have shit, and this is the thanks I get? You out here naked and bragging on fucking a dick that should have been off-limits to you. You sat in my house with all types of shit jumping out yo' pussy, and this whole time you got it from fucking my man. I hope yo' run-down pussy fall off, bitch. Get the fuck outta my shit!" Janelle said, trying to hold back her tears.

Although she had planned for shit to go down, nothing had prepared her for this moment, to see how wicked and ungrateful her sister was. Carly stood there, took the slap, and had the nerve to have her arms folded as if she didn't do shit.

Janelle was pissed, and the guys who were holding her couldn't hold her much longer. She was fuming. The moment she was able to get away from them, she didn't hesitate to jump on Carly, making sure she threw a couple of punches to her face before she moved to Ant and gave him a few slaps.

Thankfully, Kareem had appeared. "Come on, Janelle, you got to stop," he said, pulling her away from the drama. He opened the house door and took her inside where she collapsed in his arms, crying.

Carly thought she was going to die as the crowd continued to take videos and pictures of her. Ant had gone into the crowd, and some niggas gave him clothes to leave. They were even hailing him for banging her. One of the bitches who dragged Carly out of the house slapped her. "You fucking nasty bitch," she said, and then hawked up a wad of spit and chucked it in her face.

"Come on, Ayesha, let's leave the fucking ho bitch alone," another one said.

"Yeah, Leona, she can have the nigga for all I care." The girls laughed and went on their way. They'd accomplished what they had set out to do.

The crowd soon dispensed, and some sisters gave her some clothes to wear, and she followed one inside her house to calm her nerves. She was going fucking kill Ant. Once again, because of him, she had been embarrassed: actually, humiliated in front of everyone. By evening, she was gonna be trending on social media because of the pictures and videos they had taken. Everyone in the hood was going to be talking about her.

When it was late in the night, she decided to head back to Janelle's. She was going to ask for forgiveness and talk about the devil using her. They were sisters after all. Bitch couldn't do anything but to forgive her. However, when she went to the house, she found her bags outside. She banged on the door. "What the hell you doing, Janelle? I am your fucking sister. You can't do this shit to me."

The door opened, and she stepped back when Janelle filled the space. "My sister, huh? Sisters don't go around fucking all the boyfriends of their sister. They don't fuck their sister's baby daddy, they don't fuck their boyfriends on their beds, nor do they try to seduce their new boyfriends. So cut that fucking shit."

Carly went pale. "How the hell you know?"

Janelle cackled. "You thought I was stupid? You thought I wasn't smart enough to see how much of a ho you are? How you think you got the fucking clap, huh? Me, you slut. And you think those bitches who beat you up really knew Ant? You dumb, big sister, you dumb. You think you can play the game, huh? But I am fucking ahead of you!" Janelle said with a satisfied smile.

Carly rushed to her, but Janelle pushed her back. "Get your shit off my porch before I call Ayesha and the gang back to finish beating yo' ass," she warned before shutting the door in her face.

Carly slid to the ground in shock. *Fuck Janelle. She is nothing but a fucking whore, and she has ruined my life,* she thought as she began to cry.

Dorrian replayed the video of his cousin Carly getting her ass whooped, and he shook his head. He knew Janelle well, and when he saw her slap Carly and talk shit to her knowing the camera was rolling, he knew Janelle had planned it. Carly deserved what went down. You don't fuck with family. And Ant? That nigga had to see him, sooner or later. He knew he was going to beat Ant's ass.

He decided to leave the club, and he went over to Los's. The niggas were surprised to see him after he'd been in hiding. He nodded at Los and Roshon, who seemed to be in a happy mood as he hummed.

"What the fuck wrong with him?" he asked Los.

"He doing good with that white bitch. He thinking of moving to a bigger house," Los said.

Dorrian shook his head. His friend was crazy. Yeah, he fucking was. That was seven kids in total. Roshon definitely needed some fucking kind of deliverance.

"Welcome back, bro," Roshon said then glared at Los. "And don't fucking call my woman a bitch, nigga."

"You fucking lost it, bro. You getting married to a white chick. Not that I got anything against them though, but after Brandi?" Dorrian asked.

"You gon' love Natalie when you see her, and I know I was hurt by Brandi, but I have moved on and found myself someone else to love. That's the thing about life. I made the decision and asked myself what kind of man I want to be. Do I wanna keep searching around for that perfect woman? I ain't perfect. I ain't shit. If I want that woman, I am gonna keep searching and searching and won't find her. I got to accept what I have. Yeah, she got kids and all that, but we good together. I'm happy, and that shit is what matters," Roshon said.

To Dorrian, it seemed like Roshon was doped up or high on crack. Whichever it was, that was some potent shit.

"Yo, you seen your cousin's video?" Falicia asked. "It's trending and shit on Instagram."

Dorrian shook his head. "They all crazy, I swear. Anyone seen Ant? That nigga need his ass beat."

"He came around and was proud of the shit he did. Said some acting company down in Atlanta wants him to come do a few auditions. Think he gon' be the next Morris Chestnut," Los said, and they all hollered.

"Yeah, well, I hope the nigga make it because after I beat his ass, he gon' need that job to pay me back every dime I gave him," Dorrian hissed.

"And Latifah? What's going on with you guys or whatever?" Roshon asked.

"We done. I'm back with Keera," Los said. The shop went silent, and everyone hollered in unison.

"You nuts, man, you are fucking nuts," Cole said.

Los shrugged. He surprised himself as well. Yeah, Latifah was a catch, but shit wasn't the same as with him and Keera. He had to admit that he and Keera had chemistry. They were like oil and water, but they matched like hell. As he drifted from her, he realized something: it wasn't about finding some classy woman or shit like that. Keera knew him fucking well, and he knew her as well. He fucking loved that crazy part of her. It was her identity.

He knew she was damn surprised when he returned. She was seeing a doctor and getting help. Right now, they were starting as friends, and he didn't care. She had always been around for him, so he wasn't going to leave now. They may not end up being together forever, but whatever happened, he was gonna take it. He hadn't owned up to his responsibility when William died, but it didn't mean that he wasn't going to be there for her now. "I just want to be there for her like I should have been. She's been through hell and back, and partly because of me. Now we gon' do this shit together and see what happens."

"You okay, Dorrian?" Falicia asked when he suddenly got up.

"Yeah, gotta handle some shit. I'll holla at y'all later," Dorrian said with a nod, as he headed out of the shop on a mission.

Spending time with his niggas helped him clear his head, and he knew what he needed to do. He got into his car and drove over to Arlene's. After the way he dismissed her that day in his office, he knew now was the time to make shit right. No matter what anyone thought or said, he knew Arlene had his heart. He was just hoping that it wasn't too late for him to express that to her.

Pulling up to Arlene's, it felt like the first time. His palms were sweaty, and his heart rate increased. He rang the bell and waited for her to come to the door. Arlene was damn surprised to see him. They stared into each other's eyes in silence, as if they were both afraid to speak the first word. Tossing caution to wind, Arlene took the lead.

"Hey," Arlene spoke as she offered a half smile.

Damn, she done lost some weight. "You lost some weight," he said, and she laughed sadly.

"Yeah, I was a little sick," Arlene retorted.

"We need to talk. May I come in?" Dorrian asked.

She nodded and moved to the side, allowing him access into her home. They were both nervous. Neither of them knew what the other was thinking, but Arlene was more than happy that he was at least willing to talk. All she wanted was closure, and with the fact that she hid her past, she was prepared to accept whatever judgment he came to render. Dorrian walked in and sat in a chair. "How you doing, Arlene?" he asked and then cleared his throat.

"I'm good, and you?" she asked.

He nodded and then confirmed that he wasn't doing too bad.

"So, let me guess, you're here because you want to know about my past, am I right?" Arlene asked.

"Arlene, sweetheart, I've never felt this way about any other woman in my life. I only came for the truth. Just tell me. Why didn't you tell me about your past? We could have been past this. Arlene, I love you. I carry you here," Dorrian said while pointing to his heart.

Arlene sighed. "Shit was in my past, and I never knew it would come back to surface. I moved and everything. I guess you can say that I was young and dumb. Back then, everything was about a dollar. My ex had my mind so warped that I did anything and everything he asked of me. If that was to have sex with another man, then so be it. I did it. As time progressed, I realized he never loved me and that I didn't love myself either.

"I never thought that I would find a love like yours that was so pure. I don't even understand how we even came to be, but, Dorrian, I fell hard for you, and when my past came up, I was sick. My worst fear came crashing down on me and ruined my entire world and took away my happiness. The day you kicked me out of your office and said that you never wanted to see me again, my world stopped."

Dorrian felt like shit seeing the pain that Arlene was in. If he was being honest with himself, he had to admit that the shit he did in his past would possibly bury him. After realizing that he overreacted to a past that was long before his time, he decided to take them both out of their misery. He stood and approached the sofa where Arlene was seated. Taking his thumb, he swiped away her tears and then spoke.

"I ain't gonna lie: that shit fucked me up. You were the only woman I've ever cared about and for my boys to see you like that did something to me. You're my queen, not some fucking slut niggas pass around like a fucking football. I can't fucking stop thinking about you. I can't fucking stop loving you, and it's driving me crazy. Arlene, baby, tell me what we can do to make this work. I can't live another day without you being in my life."

Arlene smiled sadly with tears in her eyes. "You're not the only one who's been messed up. You've always been in my thoughts, and it fucking killed me not to be able to call you or see you. I was dying without you. I couldn't breathe. You're my air, Dorrian, and I need you, baby."

He pulled her into him and embraced her. Damn, he missed his girl. "Where do we go from here, Arlene? I fucking need to know."

"We start over or pick up where we left off. I made some mistakes, but I'm not that person anymore. If you say that you can forgive my past, then you have to promise not to toss it in my face at the first sign of a fight."

"Look, I can honestly tell you that your past don't mean shit anymore. I think God told me that I have to marry you. My dick won't even get hard to fuck another bitch. You are it for me. I love you, Arlene."

"I love you too, Dorrian. Thank you for talking to me."

"You don't have to thank me. Nobody said this road would be easy, but at the end of the day, if we don't have communication, we don't have shit. Now is there anything else I need to know?"

Arlene sighed and felt that now was the perfect time to tell Dorrian everything. Arlene opened her heart and her mouth and began telling Dorrian the entire story about her ex, Tornado, who was a big-time drug dealer she used to deal with. Tornado and Arlene dated and lived in the fast lane for years as a happy couple in ATL. When Arlene ended up pregnant, it was Tornado who beat her ass and got her strung out on drugs. He forced her to have sex with multiple people at a time, and it was because of him that those videos were circulating. Arlene met a pastor one day when she was on a stroll. This pastor helped her clean herself up, put her through rehab, and she relocated in order to turn over a new leaf.

Dorrian was attentive while Arlene was speaking. He heard about the cat named Tornado from ATL who use to run the shit outta the A until he was gunned down by a nigga in his camp. Realizing that Arlene did some things in her past that wasn't completely her fault, Dorrian began to open up about his parents, and they both put all of their dirt on the table.

"Thank you for trusting me with the truth," Dorrian said to Arlene. He stood her up, placed his hands around her waist, and planted soft kisses on her neck until they found their tongues doing a very familiar dance.

Breaking away from their passionate kiss, Arlene spoke. "So does this mean that I'm still your fiancée?"

"This means that you're my queen, and I'm your king. Now put my ring back on your finger and come show your man how much you've been missing him."

A smile stretched across her face. Arlene ran in the back and grabbed the ring. Placing it in Dorrian's hand, she asked, "Can you do the honors please?"

Dorrian flashed his million-dollar smile and obliged her request.

The two lovebirds kissed with so much passion, and the heat radiating from their bodies caused them to want each other that much more.

In one quick motion, Dorrian scooped Arlene up, placing her legs around his waist, and backed her up against the wall.

"Tonight, all I want to hear is you continuing to tell me yes," Dorrian said, nibbling on her ear.

"Yes, Dorrian," Arlene breathlessly stated.

Dorrian put her down, freed his growing erection, and then stripped her of her clothing as they stared at each other with passion. Dorrian knew that he'd made the right decision. Arlene might not have been perfect, but she was damn sure perfect for him.

Dorrian scooped her back up, placed his dick into her welcoming, gushy center, and bounced her up and down on his rod as he banged her while standing up. After a few more deep, penetrating thrusts, Arlene found herself trembling at his touch.

"You know that this is only the beginning. The first one was a freebie. Next time, you cum when I tell you to."

"Yes, baby," was all that needed to be said as the two reunited as if it were the last time.

Chapter 16

Before Roshon could completely move on in life with Natalie, he still had to handle the situation with Joe. He felt he owed that much to Brandi, and also to his son. Word on the streets was that Joe had been going around telling people that he was the one who had killed Brandi. Roshon didn't put it past him considering he was a crackhead and would do anything for money. What disturbed Roshon deeply was what he'd heard about Olivia.

After having spoken with Samuel, and Samuel informing him that Joe had indeed been the one to hit RJ, Roshon began to look for mutual acquaintances of his and Brandi's. One night he was on his way to Natalie's house, he saw a guy who looked familiar, but he paid it no mind. The next day, he went back over there, and sure enough, it was Brandi's old classmate Jason. Brandi had introduced the two one night when they were out eating at a Pappadeaux, one of

Brandi's favorite restaurants. When he walked up on Jason, the guy immediately dapped up Roshon, remembering their brief encounter.

"So what's been going on wit' you, man? Yo, I'm sorry to hear about Brandi, brah. That shit was crazy," Jason said as they sat on the hood of Roshon's car.

"Yeah, man. I've been dealing with it the best I can. I got all of the kids with me now, and that shit hard as hell raising them without their moms, you know?"

"Shit, I can only imagine. And the sad part is, that fucked-up nigga Joe said fuck his own seed. Baby J ain't did a thing and didn't ask to be brought in this world. That's sad, for real," Jason said with his head down. He could only imagine what Roshon was going through.

"Speaking of Joe, have you seen dude anywhere around? That's actually who I'm trying to get up with," Roshon informed him.

"Oh, so you must have heard."

"Heard what? What's going on?"

"I hate to be the one to tell you this, but that nigga Joe is the one who killed Brandi. He wanted her to contact you to get some money, but evidently, that plan fell through. He got her high out of her mind, but when she came down off her high, she started flipping on him because he was pressuring her to let him stage a kidnapping with your son in order for you to pay a ransom. Shit didn't go well, and he ended up hitting her across the head with a crowbar. The only reason I know this is because the trap house they used to be at, one of the fiends up in there was my cousin. He told me about the shit, but I didn't know how true it was. You know heads will lie for less," Jason told him.

Roshon was seeing red. What the hell did Brandi ever see in this dude? And then to have him around her children, knowing the type of man—or lack thereof—he was. After he got that information from Jason, who also informed him that Joe had a crib off Carter Street, he set his plan in motion.

He refused to get the police involved knowing they weren't going to do anything. Hell, they weren't even interested in solving Brandi's murder. He had received more information from Jason than the police ever provided. Roshon decided to take matters into his own hands.

Having just gotten off the phone with Natalie, and making sure the kids were tucked in and Mrs. Johnson was straight, Roshon grabbed his Glock and headed out the door with the intention of killing Joe. Killing Brandi was one thing, but setting up a kidnapping of his son and putting hands on him was something totally different.

He jumped in his car and sped off, headed toward Carter Street. Sure enough, when he got on the street, he noticed Joe and a few of his friends sitting outside. Roshon made sure to stay a far enough distance away to not be seen. What he saw next really blew his mind. He knew that Ant had his own crib, but it didn't dawn on him that this was the same street he stayed on. Ant was still up to his old shit. He was walking some chick to her car, and from the way he was palming her ass, you could tell he had just finished hitting it.

"Ol' dumbass done lost his job and everything messing around with these broads," Roshon said aloud to himself as he chuckled. He sat in the car for an hour until Joe was the last person sitting on the porch. Roshon checked his surroundings before making his exit from the car. Ensuring that his Glock was in place, he briskly walked across the street over to where Joe sat.

When Joe looked up and realized it was Roshon, he laughed as if someone had told the funniest joke he'd ever heard. "To what do I owe the pleasure of this visit?" Joe asked, still laughing.

"I heard you like to hit on kids and shit. Hell, if I knew you liked throwing hands, we could have been had a one-on-one." It was now Roshon's turn to laugh. Evidently, Joe didn't find shit funny.

"What yo' pussy ass want? You missing Brandi? I mean, I know the feeling. Her pussy was worn out, but, whew, she had a helluva mouthpiece—" Before he could finish his sentence, Roshon slapped him across the head with the gun.

"I'ont give a fuck about what you talking. I wanna know what made you think it was okay to put your hands on my son, huh? An innocent-ass boy who ain't did shit to you. His only fault was loving his mother and siblings and standing up for them. But nah, you saw that as a sign of disrespect or something, right?" Roshon asked. He was fed up, and all he could see was the faded mark on his son's arm.

"Man, fuck yo' boy! You and that little nigga can suck my dick!"

Roshon had had enough. He began beating Joe across the head with the gun. All the pain and anger he felt was unleashed, as he repeatedly slammed the butt of the Glock into Joe's head. Every ounce of frustration he had from the day Brandi left this earth, he let it go on Joe.

Out of nowhere, Ant ran across the street and caught Roshon's arm midair.

"That's enough, bruh, he's gone. Let it go. He's gone," Ant said, still holding on to Roshon's arm. Ant felt every bit of his boy's pain at that moment.

As fucked up of an individual as Ant was, the one thing he valued in life was his friendship with his boys. They had been through thick and thin together, to hell and back. Roshon had his whole life ahead of him. He was engaged to Natalie, and they had seven children to raise together. Ant saw his life as one failure after another. It seemed as though every time he tried to take a step forward, he got knocked ten steps back. His own mother couldn't even show him love. He began to think about all the shit he'd done and all the pain he'd caused. He wished shit could have been different with him and Janelle. She seemed to have truly loved him. Ant started hearing sirens in the distance and knew the police would be there shortly.

"Yo, man, you gotta get up outta here," he pleaded with Roshon, who was still huffing and puffing as if he wanted to bring Joe back alive and kill him again.

"Damn, Roshon, do you fuckin' hear me? Better yet, do you hear them damn sirens in the distance? You gotta go, man. Let me handle this."

"What you mean, let you handle this? I'll face my shit like a man. This punk deserved exactly what I gave him."

Ant knew he didn't have time to go back and forth with Roshon. He quickly snatched the gun out of his hand, wiped his prints off, and replaced them with his own.

"Ant, man, you don't have to do—"

"I don't have to, but I'm going to. You, Doe, and Los have always been there for me. Y'all have come through each and every time I needed y'all. You have RJ and the rest of all them damn kids to look after," Ant said with a chuckle. "My life is fucked up enough as it is. I owe so many people, you being one of them. I got this, brah. Get me a good lawyer to fight this case, and I got this. I'll say it was self-defense or some shit. Everybody on this street knows Joe is a piece of shit, so ain't nobody even checking for ol' dude like that anyway. Let me do this one thing, brah."

Although Roshon really didn't agree with it, he understood what Ant was trying to do. Although he would never be able to right all of his wrongs, he was on a path to working on becoming a better him. Roshon couldn't do anything but respect it, and he definitely appreciated it.

"I got you, man. I'll call the lawyer ASAP. Yo, brah, thank you, and I mean that shit." They gave each other a brotherly hug before Roshon hopped up and began lightly jogging to his car.

"Roshon!" Ant called out.

Roshon turned around.

"Tell Janelle I really am sorry, for what it's worth. And tell Doe I never meant for none of this shit to happen," Ant said.

Roshon nodded his head to let him know he would. That night, Ant was on his way to redemption.

Epilogue

The yard was filled with laughter and the aroma of barbecue. The children laughed and played about with the women talking and exchanging gossip. Keera, Arlene, Natalie, and Mrs. Johnson sat in a corner talking and making wedding plans for Arlene and Dorrian.

In another corner sat Roshon, Los, and Dorrian. They all looked happy and relaxed. "You heard from Ant?" Dorrian asked.

"Yeah, went to see him last week. The dude still has the audacity to be talking about he a rapper. Even started rapping and shit on the visit," Roshon said.

"It's dope?" Los asked.

"Listen to this shit," Roshon said, shuffling through his phone. A loud rap filled the air. "Shit went down, and I fucked two bitches . . ."

"Now that's dope," Dorrian said with a whoop as the track went on. "He good, right?"

Roshon nodded. Although he had provided the best legal help for Ant, he was going away for four years. That was better than the eight they'd originally planned to give him. The truth of that night was a secret the four of them shared alone. He had not even told Natalie, and it was not because he didn't trust her. There was just some shit you had to keep with your brothers. Although Ant had told him to stop with the debt shit, he knew he fucking owed him. He would not have this life today if it had not been for him. He was a man indeed. The three of them made sure Ant was good on the inside.

Keera, though still not completely over the death of William, had completely done a 180, as well as Los. The man who once said he could never be a one-woman man had become just that. He realized all along that it was him provoking Keera to do some of the things she'd done. Los decided to push aside his childish ways for the sake of her sanity and to help her get well, and it matured him in the process. He even paid child support and spent time with his other children frequently. Keera, of course, was trying to make another baby, but Los didn't know if he was *that* committed.

Janelle and Carly still were not on speaking terms. Carly felt no remorse for sleeping with

Ant or any of Janelle's exes, and Janelle felt no remorse for allowing her to get genital warts and getting her ass beat. No dude in their right mind would fuck with Carly, and that's exactly what Janelle hoped for. Although she had not forgiven Carly, she did forgive Ant. After Roshon told her what Ant's last words were before he got locked up, she decided to visit him. During her visit, she learned about Ant's childhood and why he was the way he was toward women. She truly felt sorry for him. She couldn't imagine anyone going through life not having felt loved, especially in a relationship. She and Kareem were engaged to be married and also had a baby on the way. He moved her out of her government-assisted apartment and put her and the girls in a house.

Natalie and Roshon didn't waste any time tying the knot. After exposing Chris for the scum bag he was, Natalie gained full custody of the kids. Mrs. Johnson and the four in the home embraced them all with open arms. It was a relief for Mrs. Johnson to finally have another woman helping out in the house. Although she had joked with Roshon previously regarding his choice to date a white female, she loved Natalie and the kids as if they were her very own.

Unfortunately, Mr. Covington passed away shortly after the situation with Joe. Mrs. Covington was still active in the kids' lives, but her health had rapidly declined since the loss of her husband. And having not fully gotten over the death of Brandi had taken its toll on her. The doctors informed Roshon that there was nothing else they could do for her but to let her live her last days in peace. He and Natalie took the kids over there every chance they got. Even Natalie's kids enjoyed going to see "Mama C," as they called her.

Each of the guys sat back and reflected over the past year. Each of their lives had changed drastically, but they couldn't be happier with life than they were at the moment.

"Cheers to good life," Dorrian said, lifting his glass.

"Cheers to friendship," Roshon said.

"And cheers to being a man," Los added.